D0615954

Praise for Steve Rushin's

THE PINT MAN

"The hero of this hilarious debut novel . . . is one Rodney Poole, who never met a phrase he couldn't twist, tweak or trace to its obscure origins."
—*The Hartford Courant*

"Rushin emerges as one of the sharpest wits on the scene." —*Publishers Weekly*

"Clever, bracing, and full of laughs."
—Carl Hiaasen, author of *Star Island*

"An exceedingly enjoyable first novel. . . . It's Rushin's narrative voice, guileless, digressive, and ribald, riddled with wordplay and trivia, that makes this such a pleasure. . . . Great company for an evening, with or without a pint at your elbow." —*Booklist*

"A wisecracking, rib-shaking, beer-stained, warmhearted romp of a novel about a Midtown ne'er-do-well adrift in that elastic period between post-adolescence and manhood."
—Jonathan Miles, author of *Dear American Airlines*

Steve Rushin

THE
PINT MAN

Steve Rushin, the author of the nonfiction books *Road Swing* and *The Caddie Was a Reindeer*, wrote a beloved weekly column called "Air & Space" for *Sports Illustrated* from 1998–2007. He and his wife, Rebecca Lobo, live in Connecticut with their four children.

www.steverushin.com

THE
PINT MAN

A NOVEL

Steve Rushin

ANCHOR BOOKS
A Division of Random House, Inc.
New York

FIRST ANCHOR BOOKS EDITION, MARCH 2011

Copyright © 2010 by Steve Rushin

All rights reserved. Published in the United States by Anchor Books, a division of Random House, Inc., New York, and in Canada by Random House of Canada Limited, Toronto. Originally published in hardcover in the United States by Doubleday, a division of Random House, Inc., New York, in 2010.

Anchor Books and colophon are registered trademarks of Random House, Inc.

This is a work of fiction. Names, characters, places, and incidents either are the product of the author's imagination or are used fictitiously. Any resemblance to actual persons, living or dead, events, or locales is entirely coincidental.

Grateful acknowledgment is made to Time, Inc., for permission to adapt an excerpt from "Grave Concerns" by Steve Rushin (*Sports Illustrated*, October 25, 2004). Reprinted by permission of Time, Inc.

The Library of Congress has cataloged the Doubleday edition as follows:
Rushin, Steve.
The pint man : a novel / by Steve Rushin.—1st ed.
p. cm.
1. Single men—Fiction.
2. Bars (Drinking establishments)—Fiction. I. Title.
PS3618.U743P56 2009
813 .6—dc22
2009017599

Anchor ISBN: 978-0-7679-3183-0

Book design by Michael Collica

www.anchorbooks.com

Printed in the United States of America
10 9 8 7 6 5 4 3 2 1

For Rebecca, Siobhan, Maeve, and Thomas—
All the days and all the nights and all the years.

THE
PINT MAN

1

To say that Rodney went there religiously was not just a figure of speech, for Boyle's resembled a church even at noon, when no one was yet kneeling in the Gents, asking God for His mercy.

At that hour, a shaft of sunlight shone through stained glass. Which is to say, windows whose glass was comprehensively stained—by a double-glazing of nicotine and automotive exhaust, and the secondhand smoke of a half-century of bullshit.

There were just the two windows—flanking the punched nose of a red front door—so that Boyle's faced the world through befogged spectacles. Whether these were the befogged spectacles of a man who has just come into a warm place from a cold one or of a man wearing permanent, prescriptive beer goggles depended largely on what one wanted from Boyle's.

Suffice to say that over the decades the bar and its regulars had begun to resemble one another, in the way of pets and their owners or old married couples.

It was now impossible to tell whether its customers smelled of Boyle's or Boyle's smelled of its customers, only that both smelled, unmistakably, of corned beef and Lysol.

Rodney sat at the bar, his right hand slapped up against his brow, so that the ballpoint pen plugged between two fingers appeared to grow from his forehead, like a unicorn horn.

He looked up from his crossword, to the bottles of the back bar: there was something provocative about those jewel-toned vessels, their backs turned to a mirrored wall, as if trying on pants in a department store dressing room, as if checking out their own bottoms in a new pair of jeans.

More than a few of Boyle's regulars regarded the bottles that way—voyeuristically, with what amounted to lust.

A bottle of Cockburn's was shelved next to a bottle of Dry Sack. Given their proximity, Rodney thought of them not as port and sherry but as twinned male medical afflictions, the former leading inevitably to the latter.

In front of him, a pint of Guinness, with its clerical collar of foam. Behind him, four booths, snug as confessionals, their rosewood benches salvaged from St. Michael the Archangel's. Two million asses, squirming through Masses: they had burnished the pews, leaving a rich patina that looked to Rodney like Murphy's Irish Red.

He thought of how, when he farted in church as a kid, his mother whispered, "Now you're sitting in your own pew."

Boyle's church pews, like Boyle's dogs, had found a better home in Boyle's. A sign above the first booth quoted Mark 2:16:

WHEN THE SCRIBES AND PHARISEES SAW HIM, THEY SAID UNTO HIS DISCIPLES, "HOW IS IT THAT HE EATETH AND DRINKETH WITH PUBLICANS AND SINNERS?"

Armen set Rodney's lunch plate heavily on the bar. It settled like a spun coin. Armen's name was Gary Garabedian, but to anyone who'd been to Boyle's more than once, he was Armen. Armen the Barman.

Rodney and Armen once passed a summer's evening compiling a list of notable people, like Armen, of Armenian ancestry. The list consisted entirely of famous surnames that ended in -*ian*: Dr. Jack Kevorkian, Cherilyn (Cher) Sarkisian, basketball coach Jerry Tarkanian. "Yossarian," Rodney said. "From *Catch-22*."

"Raffi Cavoukian," Armen said, citing a multiplatinum children's troubadour whom Rodney had never heard of. Rodney was not merely childless but as bereft of children as a man can be—a kind of orphan in reverse.

Rodney played to his strength and countered with sports personalities of the 1970s: Notre Dame football coach Ara Parseghian, Miami Dolphins kicker Garo Yepremian, and NFL field judge Armen Terzian, who was knocked unconscious by a thrown whiskey bottle after costing the Minnesota Vikings a playoff game against the Dallas Cowboys.

At the end of the bar, another man being slowly knocked unconscious with a whiskey bottle said: "Conan the Barbarian."

Rodney turned to look at the guy. He had a face like a punched pillow. His jug-handle ears—and the emptiness echoing between them—called to mind golf's Wanamaker Trophy, given annually to the winner of the PGA Championship, whose highlights were just then playing on TV. In time, he would become known to everyone at Boyle's as Wanamaker—except on the back of his Boyle's softball jersey, where his name would be abbreviated in the way that old baseball box scores abbreviated Gionfriddo as "G'fr'do" or Vandermeer as "V'D'M'r."

On his softball jersey, "Wanamaker" was contracted to "Wan'ker."

During nights like that one, celebrating celebrated Armenians with a group of strangers, Rodney had all the companionship he needed inside Boyle's.

As new people entered through that swinging red door, they were challenged to name an Armenian celebrity whose name ended in -*ian*. When an old man said, "Ruffian," Rodney recalled how the great thoroughbred filly was buried where she had collapsed—at Belmont, her nose pointed for all eternity toward a finish line she'd never reach.

It was about as apt a metaphor as he could think of for the comic futility of life.

Rodney forked a piece of porterhouse into his mouth and chewed it like a cud. He fed a French fry to Edith, the bulldog who spent entire days asleep under the bar, a courtesy extended to only a few of Boyle's regulars.

He had no idea where or whether Edith went when Boyle's closed. But Rodney *had* seen Edith drink Bushmill's directly from a dog dish in a match race won by Wanamaker.

Until a year ago, the bar had two bulldogs. But Edith was widowed when Drinketh died of pneumonia, leaving Edith that most disappointing of all creations: a setup without a punch line.

Rodney had a blind date tonight, a setup that would almost certainly have no payoff.

He took a pull from his pint of Guinness and his brain began to run on its hamster wheel to nowhere: *Guinness is stout, stout is a kind of porter, porter was popular among porters in the street markets of London, who drank it in porter houses, which served steak, which is why they call the swatch of suede I am now masticating a "porterhouse steak."*

Rodney wondered if he should order a second porterhouse

tonight, on his date, so that he could regale her with this history.

He looked again at his crossword clue: "Spot remover." With the safecracker's disdain for the locksmith, he inked in DOGCATCHER. Then his right hand went back to his forehead, and the ballpoint again was unicorned to his brow.

Before the smoking ban, when that pen was a cigarette, it looked like a smokestack for his brain. That brain remained a bustling widget factory, three shifts working round the clock to make a product that nobody needed, at least not outside of Boyle's.

Some people have a mind like a steel trap. Rodney had a mind like a lint trap. It retained only useless fluff: batting averages, ancient jingles, a slogan glimpsed once, years ago, on the side of a panel van, for an exterminator ("We'll Make Your Ants Say Uncle") or a window-treatment supplier ("A Couple of Blind Guys") or a septic tank specialist ("Doody Calls").

High in a corner behind the bar, beneath a ceiling tiled to look like tin, hung an ancient TV, a Zenith at its nadir. Armen turned the sound up. *Family Feud*, with a new host, who said: "One hundred people surveyed, top five answers on the board, name a famous Rudolph."

Rodney clicked the ballpoint pen with his thumb as if it were the plunger on *Jeopardy* and said: "Red-Nosed Reindeer, Giuliani, Nureyev, Valentino . . ."

Armen said, "*Wilma* Rudolph."

Wanamaker said, "Wilma Flintstone."

"It's famous Rudolphs," Armen said. "Not famous Wilmas."

"There *are* no other famous Wilmas," Rodney said.

Armen said, "Not true: Wilma Mankiller. Chief of the Cherokee Nation."

On TV, the host said, "I need an answer."

A young woman in a lime-sherbet pantsuit held her palms upward as if waiting for rain. She cringed preemptively and said: "Hitler?"

Armen roared and shouted, *"Rudolph Hitler!"*

Rodney thought how "Rudolph" sounded benign, "Adolf" malevolent. He wondered aloud if names were destiny.

"You mean, would I be a barman if my name weren't Armen?" Armen asked. "It's like Alicia Keys. She plays the piano and her name is Keys."

"Her real name is Cook," Rodney said. "Her stage name is Keys. Just like your real name is Gary. Armen's your stage name. You're Armen *because* you're a barman, she's Keys *because* she plays piano."

If Cook's name was her destiny, Rodney reflected, she'd be making pot pies with Vance, the Boyle's cook who seemed to pop his head out the kitchen door once a day, like a cuckoo from a clock.

"I'm talking the other way around," he said. "Like the archbishop of Manila was Cardinal Sin. The team dentist for the San Francisco Giants, his name is Les Plack."

Armen said, "I read that an unusually high percentage of people named Dennis become dentists."

"What about Wilma Mankiller?" Wanamaker said. "How'd you like to go on a blind date, you ask her her name, she says, 'Mankiller.' Probably didn't have a lot of second dates."

"*Mankiller, party of one.*" Armen said jauntily. But the four booths of the Boyle's dining room were empty.

Rodney felt compelled to point out that Wilma Mankiller did not become a killer of men, but Armen had already moved on to Lorena Bobbitt, who famously hacked off her husband's wang with a kitchen knife and flung it out a car window. "Lorena, *bob it*," Armen said. "That's destiny."

Wanamaker said to Rodney, "What am I missing?"

Rodney thought of all the possible answers: hair, brains, job, class, deodorant. But all he said was "Look it up."

Armen turned to the back bar and examined Boyle's reference library of Quiz Night argument stoppers. His fingers passed over a 1986 paperback copy of *The Guinness Book of World Records*, its cover torn off, its corners rounded with wear, and plucked instead the paperback dictionary next to it. He cleared his throat theatrically and read:

"*Bob* noun, second definition: Something that has been cut short, for example, a horse's tail when docked, a dog's ears when clipped, your johnson when removed with a Ginsu knife . . ."

The men at the bar roared. And so the conversation stayed aloft on an undercurrent of fear. Fear of women. Armen had a twelve-year-old daughter whom he almost never saw. Rodney once asked him why and Armen forestalled further inquiry by saying, "She lives with her mother," in a tone that suggested, "She lives with a feral wolverine." And so women were literally castrating, metaphorically man-killing, at least until one of them walked into the bar, which didn't often happen until after five. Then, everyone sat a little straighter, began smoothing out imaginary neckties, a cupped hand in front of every mouth casually checking for halitosis.

At this hour of the afternoon, Boyle's was as male as a monastery.

As Rodney was well aware, monks have been synonymous with beer since at least 800 AD, when Gall began brewing at his monastery in Switzerland, a tradition that continues to this day in the alpine town of St. Gallen.

Saint Gallen. Rodney wondered if he too could be sainted for drinking beer in a holy place.

"You're not a monk," Armen reminded him. "Your celibacy is *in*voluntary."

High behind the bar, perched on the plinth of a stereo speaker, was a bottle of Frangelico—a bottle shaped like a Franciscan friar, in a brown habit with a white rope cincture around his waist. It bothered Rodney that this Italian hazelnut liqueur was named for a Piedmontese painter and Dominican—Fra Angelico—when Dominicans wore white habits that were never belted by a rope.

Involuntarily, he thought of the anagram: DESPERATION = A ROPE ENDS IT.

"Think there's beer in heaven?" Rodney asked Armen.

"*In heaven there is no beer,*" Armen said. "*That's why we drink it here.* Says so right in the polka."

Rodney wasn't sure. At home, he kept a laminated prayer card magnetized to the fridge:

I'd like to give a lake of beer to God
I'd love the Heavenly
Host to be tippling there
For all eternity . . .

The Meat Puppets said hell was a lake of fire. Could both be true? Heaven a lake of beer, hell a lake of fire? Rodney liked this notion—of the afterlife as a choice between beer or barbecue, a tailgate for all eternity.

. . . I'd sit with the men, the women of God
There by the lake of beer
We'd be drinking good health forever
And every drop would be a prayer.
—St. Brigid of Kildare (c. 451–525)

Rodney wasn't the first man who found drink to be a convivial companion in the absence of women. He thought of the thirteen men drinking wine at the Last Supper; of the lifers at Leavenworth making pruno in prison toilets.

His lunch went cold. Or rather, the warm bits went cold while the cold bits went warm. The beer was warming, the porterhouse cooling. That was the day's special, Guinness and steak, what the wipe board behind the bar called the "Murph & Turf."

Rodney let his hand fall idly on a stack of Harp coasters, so that he appeared to be taking an alcoholic oath of office.

His bladder twitched, and for the first time in two hours Rodney alit from his stool, with its view backstage into the kitchen. The thrum and slosh of the dishwasher reminded him of childhood, of sitting three feet in front of the TV after dinner, the green shag carpet serving as elephant grass for his army men, while his parents recapped their respective days over coffee in the kitchen.

When the cool darkness of the bar had given way to the fluorescent light of the Gents, with its bouquet of disinfectant urinal pucks, Rodney stepped onto the tiled platform in front of the toilets. The riser was only six inches high, but it gave the full-bladdered man the pleasant illusion that he wasn't so much taking a leak as delivering a keynote address. Indeed, over the years, many of Rodney's fellow urinators *had* turned orators, delivering incoherent valedictories from these very urinals, their eyes fixed on the white tiled wall a foot in front of them.

Giza had its pyramids. Boyle's had its urinals, three of them, each one nearly capacious enough to be a walk-in toilet, a stand-up sarcophagus, five feet tall and filled with ice cubes, so that steam rose primordially while Rodney took a whiz.

On the wall, a machine dispensed cologne and condoms, the alpha and omega of the one-night stand.

The condom machine bore a graffito: KATERINA KLESZCZ IS EASIER DONE THAN SAID. Rodney admired the wordplay while deploring the sentiment.

He shook, shivered, and zipped. He flushed with his elbow, turned the faucets on and off with his wrists, dried his hands on his pants, and then gently kicked open the swinging door of the Gents with the sole of his right running shoe.

Only when he was back in the bar proper did he reflexively begin to breathe through his nose again.

Boyle's was as narrow as a ship's galley and Rodney shuffled sideways between the bar and the four booths, headed for the front door, slapping two singles on the bar after swigging the last of his pint standing up.

Then he stepped out onto Columbus Avenue. When Columbus discovered America, he found natives drinking brewed maize resembling, in the words of his journal, "English beer."

Rodney blinked against the sunlight. He had forgotten it was day. He'd only had two beers, but his head was pleasantly a-tingle, as it always was when going from a dark place to a light one, when going into the real world from a slightly unreal one—as when emerging from a matinee movie or Christmas Mass, the theme from *Rocky* or "Joy to the World" still ringing in his ears.

When people claim to have died and come back to life, they always describe death this way, as the movement toward a bright light. So perhaps the next world is the real one, Rodney thought, and *this* is the slightly fantastical one. This world is a cathedral. This world is a cinema. This world is a pub.

———

Rodney inserted his mail key into box 4K, marked POOLE, and reached inside. Nothing. He reached in farther still, all the way up to his elbow, and felt around at the back, as if trying to conjure a rabbit from a hat.

It should have been a relief, having no Pottery Barn catalog, no dwindling bank statement, no blue Valpak of coupons addressed to "Occupant," which is precisely what he was in this apartment, nothing more. So why did it feel like a rebuke, like he was *unworthy* of junk mail?

He took two flights of stairs, two stairs at a time, then inserted a slightly larger key into the door of his apartment: POOLE again, written in the same hand, on the door to a box only slightly larger than the one for his mail, and just marginally better appointed. The slate gray wall-to-wall carpeting was a topographical map of other people's furniture: dimples and depressions where their beds, couches, and dining tables had been.

Rodney could trace the lives of previous tenants from bachelorhood (the faded spot on the wall once dominated by a fifty-inch TV) to cohabitation (the iron burn on the bedroom carpet) to marriage (the vacancy that allowed Rodney to move in here in the first place).

Marriage mandated moving out of this kind of apartment, and Rodney, at thirty-four, was upsetting the natural order by not moving on.

Keith was moving on, to Chicago, in the morning. And Rodney was helping him. And so his best friend wouldn't pass his thirty-fifth birthday at Boyle's—or his fortieth, fiftieth, or sixtieth, for that matter—a spectacle they had both witnessed others "celebrating" before: Armen dashing next door to the deli to buy an Entenmann's coffee cake, dousing the lights, and holding over the cake a lighter in lieu of candles as he hustled to bar or booth. In the dark, all anyone saw was a flame floating through Boyle's, like the Holy Spirit in search of a supplicant. And then the flame touched down, lighting a single jack-o-lantern face, which stared directly at the light source, as in that famous photograph of Casey Stengel gazing into a crystal ball.

Rodney was gazing into a crystal ball and seeing a future he felt powerless to avoid. He lay on the bed. It was just after three in the afternoon. The depressant effect of beer was now kicking in.

There wasn't a deli next door to Boyle's anymore. The deli had become a place to buy expensive French soaps, just as the newsagent on the other side of Boyle's had been eaten by a cell-phone store. Boyle's was being squeezed on both sides by retail chains. He thought of them as fingers trying to pop a zit. But Boyle's refused to burst.

He set the alarm for five. The clock radio was on his night-stand, on top of his laptop. Where the power cord connected to the computer there was a light that glowed red when the battery was depleted, green when it was fully charged, as it was now.

That light was another madeleine of Rodney's childhood, the same glowing green as the lighted numbers on the clock-radio in his boyhood bedroom. He kept the laptop next to his bed so he could check baseball scores and play Ms. Pac-Man late at night and to feel something warm on his lap in the morning. But it also served, in the hours in between, as a night-light, a beacon of comfort.

Rodney had long since abandoned any notion of being delivered from this life. It didn't help that he was meeting a strange woman for a drink at 6:30. A man with no work going for an "after-work drink."

Coming, as he just had, from Boyle's, he might have proposed instead some after-drink work. They could have met at an office and shuffled papers.

He extended his legs under the covers and heard a pair of pants fall to the floor from the foot of the bed. Rodney tried to keep his apartment clean, his twenty-by-thirty-two-foot box, subdivided into two smaller boxes. It was one of life's noble struggles, he thought: dusting, though dust thou art and to dust though shalt return; vacuuming, though we are each of us bound for yet another box, where the dirt will always win.

At 5:30, Rodney laid out his clothes as if for his own funeral and, with a contradictory surge of optimism that even he found heartbreaking, scrubbed himself meticulously in the shower.

Then he got dressed, and passed another heartbreaking interlude selecting his boxers, as if *those* stood any chance of being seen tonight by anyone but him: maybe if he was hit by a taxi, or an exploding steam pipe blew his pants to tatters, as in a cartoon.

But alas, neither of these things happened on his walk to Midtown—sixteen blocks with his gaze fixed in the distance like a car's headlamps.

On the street, Rodney only ogled women for as long as it took them to pass from his path. He never turned his head, seldom shifted his eyes, merely looked straight ahead with an expression of pained preoccupation. He feared women noticing him noticing *them*.

Five years ago, as he sat on the 1 train at a stop that wasn't his, he stared absentmindedly at a girl on the platform whose eyes seemed to be elsewhere. After a long delay, the train pulled away with a heavy sigh, at which time the girl looked up, made eye contact, and flipped Rodney the bird.

So not for him the swiveling head, the sprung eyeballs, the wolf-whistling of those construction-crew-on-lunch-break birds of prey. Rodney respected the honesty, if not the indiscretion, of the Latin dude who—in response to a passing female—was now shaking a hand in front of him as if it had just been burned on a stovetop.

And yet these women, they were everywhere—the tourists, baristas, waitresses, hostesses, actresses, artists, cleaning ladies, clubbers, and college chicks—each in a state of August underdress.

It was somehow worse when they were fully dressed for business. Arriving early at Rococo, Rodney resolved to walk around the big block between Seventh and Sixth, and was halfway around when he became hypnotized by a besuited executrix walking toward him. He allowed himself an incautious searchlight-sweep of the eyes. She returned a weary expression that seemed to say, "Did you get a good look?"

And so it was that Rodney felt his ears combust and his bowels seize as he arrived at an enormous glass door on which "Rococo" was etched in script.

He passed the maître d', whose expression of ennui was somehow consistent with the enormous limp pocket hankie that flopped from his breast pocket like a dog's tongue—or a driver's-side airbag, deployed then deflated.

If she liked this place—and she must; she picked it—what chance did she have of liking Rodney, or vice versa?

The bar was blue-lit, in the manner of a prime-time television game show. Men waved crisp twenties above their heads, trying to attract the attention of a bartender who pretended not to see them. They might have been waving sell orders on the floor of the stock exchange. Indeed, hours earlier, many were doing just that.

In front of nearly every seated man and woman was a cell phone or Treo or BlackBerry, placed on the bar as a pistol might have been in an Old West saloon.

After five minutes, the barman deigned to uncap an Amstel Light for Rodney and decant it into a pilsner glass, tall and fluted, more tulip vase than beer glass.

Rodney was seated at a bar table, nursing the beer and trying not to look at the door when a woman's voice said: "You wouldn't happen to be Rodney?"

He managed not to blowhole his beer in a single, Vesuvian spit take when he looked—chastely now—on the woman he had just ogled on Sixth Avenue.

She wore a business suit and carried a briefcase and smelled of oatmeal-scented soap. Rodney thought of her, not unpleasantly, as the attorney for the guy on the Quaker Oats box.

"Yes. I'm afraid so."

"Mairead," she said, extending her hand. "Like *parade*."

It was a note, she said, that her mother had her carry to teachers every fall on the first day of school: "Her name is Mairead, it rhymes with 'parade.' "

Rodney took Mairead's right hand and pumped her arm as if she were a slot machine full of quarters. *His* quarters. Was she ever going to pay out, or should he cut his losses instantly and move on to another machine?

It was a question that occupied him on most first dates.

"Rodney," Rodney said, though she already knew that. "As in . . ." He could think of nothing that rhymes with "Rodney," nor of anything clever to say, and so he just left the sentence to sit there on the table, unfinished. God willing, a busboy would hustle by and whisk it from their sight.

Mairead finally said, "Keith was right—you *are* tall."

"Am I?" Rodney said. "I was worried I'd look like a Smurf in this light."

She laughed and Rodney felt himself relax. She said: "How tall are you?"

"Six-five," Rodney said. "You?"

"Six feet. When I was a kid they called me Olive Oyl."

Rodney was reminded of a joke he'd heard at Boyle's that involved Olive Oyl and the punch line "Extra Virgin." But all he said was, "Would you like a drink?"

They both looked in vain for a server. "Where'd she go?" Rodney said.

"Disappeared," said Mairead. "She's in the Federal Waitress Protection Program."

Rodney laughed.

"It's not mine," Mairead said. "I heard someone else say it once."

"Whatever we drink, it'll look like antifreeze," Rodney said.

"Or Ty-D-Bol," said Mairead.

Rodney tried to think of another blue liquid and said, one beat too late: "The blue stuff the combs float in at the barber shop."

The silence that ensued sat on the table between them like an entrée that serves six.

A waitress, dressed like a ninja and every bit as silent, suddenly materialized at their table. She introduced herself as Celeste. Mairead ordered a pinot grigio. Rodney said, "I'll have the blue-plate special."

"Excuse me?" Celeste said.

Rodney said, "I'd just like a light beer and some water."

"Pellegrino?" Celeste asked.

"Tap," Mairead said.

"I'll bring a carafe," said Celeste. She pronounced it the French way: ca-RAHF. Rodney was pretty sure she'd pronounce charade as "sha-ROD" and the capital of Iowa as "Day Mwan."

"I thought carafe rhymed with giraffe," Mairead said when the blue-faced ninja Celeste had vanished.

"I'm just happy to see Violet working again," Rodney said. "After becoming a blueberry at the Wonka factory."

When Celeste returned with the drinks, Rodney sucked the foam from his fluted beer and said, "Pinot grigio. It sounds like a boxer. From the fifties. Lost on points to Carmen Basilio."

"I'm not much of a beer drinker," Mairead said. "Or a boxing fan."

Rodney reacted with mock horror. "Not much of a beer drinker?" he said.

"Sorry."

"This country was *founded* on beer," Rodney said. "The pilgrims, they landed at Plymouth Rock because they ran out of beer. True story."

"Then they should have called it *Rolling* Rock," Mairead said.

"They found a journal kept by one of the passengers," Rodney said. "He wrote, 'We could not take time for further search, our victuals being much spent, especially our beer.' "

"You memorized that?"

"It's only one sentence," Rodney said.

"*Vittles* is not a word you hear a lot these days," Mairead said. She leaned into the table, almost imperceptibly, and said:

"So tell me, Rodney"—and here she inclined her head ever so slightly to the left—"do you read a *lot* of pilgrim journals?"

"I do," said Rodney, inclining his head to mirror hers. "I have a thing for pilgrims. Just today I bought one of those big hats with a buckle on it."

"I never understood the point of those," Mairead said. "A belt around a hat? What was that all about?" Rodney was relieved. She was getting into the spirit. It's a conversation he might have had at Boyle's.

"You know how some people unbuckle their belts after Thanksgiving dinner?" Rodney said. His last relationship, his *only* relationship, ended on Thanksgiving weekend.

"Please tell me you don't do that," Mairead said.

"Okay," Rodney said. "I don't do that."

"Oh God," Mairead said, shaking her head. "You *do*."

Rodney continued: "I wonder if the pilgrims, at that first Thanksgiving, leaned back in their chairs after dinner and unbuckled their *hats*."

Mairead was smiling when she said, "You have a lot of free time, don't you Rodney?"

"I do, actually." He wasn't kidding.

A comfortable silence settled over the table, like a muffling snowfall. Rodney seized the chance, said, "Excuse me," and went in search of the men's room. What he found instead were two doors, one marked "Ragazzo," one marked "Ragazza," and Rodney thought: *Oh for fuck sake*. He wanted to take a leak, not play The Lady or the Tiger. But now he was forced to choose, without so much as the kind of hint you get in bad seafood joints that call their cans "Buoys" and "Gulls."

He grabbed the handle of the door marked "Ragazzo" and pulled. It was like *Let's Make a Deal*. What was behind door number two: the Pontiac Bonneville or the donkey eating hay?

Rodney guessed right. He knew this was the Gents because

it looked like a German disco. Stepping up to a black marble wall, Rodney peed into a perpetual waterfall as smooth and thin and clear as Saran Wrap. He knew this was going to cost him. And sure enough, as he turned toward the wall of sinks, he reflexively cupped his palms together, as if preparing to collect rainwater, so that the middle-aged Hispanic men's room attendant could dispense a sad ejaculate of liquid soap into them.

The man wore a white jacket, and Rodney resented whoever had made him do so, as if it were somehow more dignified to listen to the percussive farts of bond traders while dressed *as* Bond.

Worse, the attendant's presence foreclosed a second visit to the john. It was too awkward to see this guy repeatedly, even though he's pretending not to see *you*: he just stands there like a cigar-store Indian until you've shaken and zipped. But all the while he's thinking you must have a bladder the size of a walnut.

And what Rodney was always thinking on his fourth visit to the bog after breaking his seal was: Christ, I've already taken half a pack of Big Red from this guy's gum basket and I'm down to my last single and I'm sure as hell not asking him to make change, so after this one I won't be able to take another leak. I won't be able to *afford* to take another leak. And I don't have many rules in life but one of them is: Don't borrow money to take a whiz. Or as Armen once told him, "Don't pee on credit."

It was in the bathroom that Rodney missed Boyle's the most.

He hated these bars, where even the commode was com-moditized.

Was that the root of *commodity—commode*? Rodney resolved to look it up later.

When he returned to the table, Mairead was putting her cell phone into her briefcase. They were, respectively, a BlackBerry and a Burberry, an observation Rodney kept to himself.

"Sorry," she said. "Work."

"Keith says you're in . . . marketing?"

"Right," Mairead said.

"I was in a bar once," Rodney said, neglecting to mention it was Boyle's, and he'd been there more than once, "and we were trying to come up with the most unmarketable product imaginable. I won with E-Cola, a soft drink that combined the negative associations of E. coli and Ebola."

"They tried that," Mairead said. "Only it was called New Coke."

Rodney laughed and Mairead did too, revealing a slight overbite that gave Rodney a spreading warmth in his chest, like a sip of Jameson's going down.

"And you're in . . ."

He knew it was coming. "Debt," Rodney said. "Not really. Not *yet*. But I did lose my job six weeks ago. Keith didn't tell you?" Rodney couldn't believe Keith hadn't warned her, or at least warned *him* that he hadn't warned her.

"I'm sorry," said Mairead.

"Don't be," Rodney said. "I got downsized. Or rightsized. 'Smartsized,' I think they called it."

Whatever it was, I've capsized, Rodney wanted to add. But instead he said, "I worked at Talbott. In corporate communications."

He left it at that. He always did. Perhaps he'd been fooling himself, but Rodney thought *corporate communications* had a nice, alliterative lilt—implying a poetry that was absent from the actual job. Rodney had edited annual reports, written speeches for corporate officers, concocted epic obfuscations for the company website, and endlessly vetted bullshit memoranda written by superiors who thought his attention to misplaced commas was quaint, as if he were a bootblack or a candlemaker or some other faintly ridiculous anachronism.

When a VP at the Talbott Corporation was named by a female employee in a lurid sexual harassment suit, Rodney wrote a speech, approved by Legal, for CEO Thomas Girard to read at the next shareholder meeting. It was a righteous manifesto about caring and corporate responsibility. "I make it a point, once a month, to dip my hand into every complaint box in our headquarters," Girard said. "And more often than not I come away with compliments."

Only he didn't say that. Not exactly. Rodney missed the typo, and so did Girard, who stepped before one thousand shareholders in the Grand Ballroom of the Phoenician Resort in Scottsdale, Arizona, just after breakfast, and said: "I make it a point, once a month, to dip my hand into every *compliant* box in our headquarters. And more often than not I come away with compliments."

Rodney was smartsized before lunch, long before it hit YouTube.

"Fortunately, I still have the first nickel I ever made," Rodney said. He didn't want Mairead to think he was broke, so he allowed her instead to think he was cheap. But it was literally true, about Rodney's first nickel, as he didn't spend or ever carry change, and despised those fastidious counters-out of coins who were always ahead of him at checkout counters. *Three-ninety-seven? Hang on, I've got ninety-seven cents right here*, before they pucker their coin purses and begin counting out pennies. His ex-girlfriend did that.

Every night, Rodney put all his change in the plastic souvenir Shea Stadium beer cup on his dresser, and when that was full, he emptied it into sixty-four-ounce energy-drink bottle in the closet, and when *that* was full he decanted it into the

Coinstar machine at Food Emporium, where he got ninety-three cents on the dollar, and a grateful world economy got a hundred bucks in nickels and dimes that smelled powerfully of Fierce Grape Gatorade.

Rodney was explaining all of this to Mairead when she said, "So you don't wash your clothes?"

"Is it that obvious?" Rodney asked, and made a show of sniffing both armpits. To his horror, there *was* a pong coming off his shirt.

"I wasn't going to say anything," Mairead said, wincing. "But since we're on the subject . . ."

Rodney remained silent, mortified.

Mortify: To kill.

A smile fissured across her face and Mairead said, "How do you do laundry if you never carry change? That's what I'm asking."

"Oh," Rodney said. "Right." He felt his face flush. "The machines in my building, they take those debit-card readers. I add twenty bucks at a time to my laundry card. Eliminates the need for quarters."

After a short silence Mairead let out an involuntary burst of laughter and looked at Rodney, to Rodney's mind, the way one might look at a puppy in traction.

Even lit blue, she was magnificently brown-eyed. Rodney found himself avoiding direct eye contact with Mairead, treating her eyes as twin solar eclipses. He was tempted to make a pinhole projector with two paper plates before looking directly at her, this brown-eyed girl. But it was another Van Morrison song, "On Hyndford Street," that he couldn't get out of his head.

When Mairead announced after a second round of drinks that she'd best be getting home, Rodney said, "Yeah, we could talk till we're blue in the face, but . . ."

She smiled again.

Rodney realized, with some relief, that she wasn't going to bring it up, his ogling her on Sixth Avenue five minutes before they met. What was the etymology of that pleasing verb, Rodney wondered. He made a mental note to Google *ogle*, a phrase—*Google ogle*—he now found pleasing in its own right.

"But what?" Mairead said.

"But I have to get up in the morning, too," Rodney said, and for the first time in a long time it was actually true. "I'm helping Keith move. He's too cheap to pay movers."

Rodney saw her into a cab, said, "I'll call you," and stepped out of earshot before she could protest. Then he waved goodbye to Mairead-Rhymes-With-Parade, to Carafe-Sounds-Like-Giraffe.

And then Rodney walked home, "On Hyndford Street" playing in his head, "feeling wondrous and lit up inside, with a sense of everlasting life."

2

Keith's apartment lay dormant beneath a drop cloth of dust. In his own apartment, Rodney could feel himself being pulled ever deeper into the metaphysical quicksand of bachelorhood, but Keith's place was filled with the *physical* quicksand of bachelorhood, a dust that doesn't just bury ambition, but actually eats the remote.

On the sibilant radiator were stacks of newspapers—yellowed and curling, like the toenail clippings that had turned the floor of Keith's bathroom into a constellation of crescent moons.

Despite sixteen years of friendship, Rodney had never set foot in this dump, and now he knew why. Walking through the door, he wore a face that was the photographic negative of someone who's been tipped off to a surprise party and is obliged to feign shock: Rodney *was* shocked, but had to feign normalcy.

"Nice pad," he said.

"You've been here," Keith said. "Haven't you?"

"I don't think so," Rodney said, failing to add, "if I had, I'd be wearing a hazmat suit and turning the doorknobs with salad tongs."

"Well," Keith said, "it's available."

"Imagine that," said Rodney.

That the tenant of this apartment had a surplus of women in his life—his fiancée, Caroline; *her* friend, Mairead—was a perversion, as was the fact that Keith had kept the boxes that all his filthy possessions had come in, and wanted everything packed neatly back into each of them. And so, into its box, like a casket into a grave, they lowered Keith's thirty-two-inch TV, its glass face unshaven behind a gray beard of dust.

Rodney felt like a pallbearer at a funeral for their friendship. Keith was moving to Chicago to get married and start a new job.

The two had been best friends since day one of college, though now that Rodney thought about it, they'd been best friends since the day *before* day one, the day Rodney was unloading his parents' chestnut Astrovan and moving into his freshman dorm.

Rodney was carrying a plastic milk crate he had stolen from his high school employer, the Jolly Elf convenience store. The crate was full of sneakers. On top were a pair of black-and-gray Nike Terminator high tops and Keith, walking out as Rodney was walking in, said: "You're not a freaking *Georgetown* fan?"

Rodney recognized the comment not as an insult or a threat but as a secret handshake—an introduction of sorts. From it, Rodney was invited to deduce that Keith was a basketball fan who knew the Hoyas had worn those shoes and who expressed affection in the same way that Rodney did: by ball-busting.

"I just like the shoes," Rodney told Keith on the front walk of McDonough Hall, and there followed a disquisition on their favorite sneakers and ballers.

That Keith was the first person on campus who spoke to Rodney went a long way to explaining the intensity of their bond. Rodney was passive in that way. He still ordered Chinese food from the first takeout joint that slid a menu under his door. He was the stray in the park who went home with the first stranger who patted his head.

So their friendship began when Keith helped Rodney move in. And Rodney couldn't help but wonder if the reverse was now happening: if their friendship was ending on the day Rodney was helping Keith to move out.

Looking around the apartment, Rodney could see that Keith's sleeping arrangements had not improved since college. His bed was in a loft, with four feet of clearance between mattress and ceiling. "Christ, Keith," Rodney said, climbing the ladder to the loft. "There's barely room to get a boner up here."

"Then don't," Keith called from the kitchen.

"You should have had one of those cardboard clowns at the top of the ladder," Rodney said. "Like at an amusement park: 'You Must Be Shorter Than Forty-eight Inches to Sleep with Keith.'"

"Believe me," Keith said. "It wasn't easy to get a woman up there."

Rodney didn't doubt it, and wondered if Keith slid them into bed on a long-handled platter, like a pizza into a stone oven.

This much was certain: Whoever *had* slept with Keith—a female firefighter? a housepainter? an Olympic diver?—had to have been adept at climbing a ladder, especially if they'd had a few drinks. And to judge by the state of this place, they *had* had a few drinks, or much worse, by the time they'd agreed to sleep here.

Perhaps Keith had been slipping roofies to roofers? Rodney liked the euphony of the phrase.

He remembered the slogan he'd once seen on a roof repairman's panel van: "Your Gutter Is Our Bread and Butter."

Rodney heaved Keith's mattress over the low railing of the loft and watched it land on the fake parquet floor. The impact sent up a mushroom cloud of dust and dandruff, and when it cleared, Keith began sheathing the mattress in some kind of KingKoil condom—an enormous plastic bag to preserve a mattress that already wore its fitted bedsheet like a butcher's coat: Stain-spattered. Crap-dappled. Sperm-spangled. Snot-mottled.

Keith didn't want it to get dirty.

Rodney threw two putrid pillows down, saving them the trouble of jumping to their deaths, and Keith promptly put them in protective garbage bags, when he should have done the opposite: put his garbage in the pillowcases.

"So how'd it go last night?" Keith said.

"Fine."

"Yeah?" Keith said.

"Yeah," Rodney said, somewhat defensively, as if Keith didn't believe him. "She was . . . nice."

"Think you'll see her again?" Keith asked. He was bubble-wrapping a bobblehead doll like an eighteenth-century Egyptologist transporting treasures from pharaonic tombs.

"I don't know," said Rodney, a hostile witness under cross exam. "I guess." He knew that second dates were seldom up to him, but he had to act as though they were. "I think so."

With curatorial care, Keith returned his crumb-filled toaster to its Styrofoam brackets and eased it into its original box. And so Rodney, too, began treating the filthy flotsam of Keith's bachelorhood as if it were priceless. He rolled beer posters as if they were Persian rugs. He tissue-wrapped Keith's

chipped china as if it were a set of antique heirlooms, not surplus plates from Waffle House, bought two for a dollar at Fishs
Eddy.

In a closet, Rodney discovered that Keith was something
of a bibliomane, with a passion for soft-cover—for soft-*core*—
publications. Scanning their titles, he couldn't help but think
of a billboard he had seen near Philadelphia, for a home
hardware showroom. It was called Knobs 'N Knockers.

"I'll get those," Keith said, without a scintilla of self-
consciousness. He began to handle the pages of *Celebrity Skin*
as if they were the leaves of a medieval manuscript, illuminated by monks. And as Rodney watched him do so, he
realized that Keith wasn't holding on to these things so much
as he was holding on to what they *represented*. It was his freedom, not his fetid futon, that Keith was consigning to that
U-Haul double-parked with its hazards flashing on West
84th Street.

But that was a guess. It wasn't just Keith's apartment that
Rodney had never seen, it was the entirety of Keith's interior
life.

When that U-Haul was loaded and legally parked two
miles away, in the first place they could find a space, they
walked through Central Park and Keith said, "It just hit me.
Everything I own is sitting overnight on a street in East
Harlem."

Everything Keith owned wasn't even enough to fill a
U-Haul. Rodney thought they should have left the back door
of the panel van open and let the homeless have at the accu-
mulated assets of Keith's lifetime. His guess was the truck
would have been mistaken for a garbage skip and been filled
with still more refuse when Keith went to retrieve it in the
morning.

"If some joy riders stole that van," Rodney said, "and the

cops found it on Monday in the South Bronx, smoldering like a charcoal briquette, which of your worldly possessions would you miss the most?"

"I'm hoping this is a hypothetical question?" Keith said.

"We'll know tomorrow morning."

"Let me think," Keith said, and there followed a rarity for him—a pregnant pause, one that passed full term and required Rodney, after a full minute, to deliver a conversational C-section.

"Come on," Rodney said. "You're not under oath. It's a simple question."

"Everyone says pictures, don't they?" Keith finally said. "When their house is on fire, and they're running out the door, they always grab the photos."

"Or the cat," Rodney said. "But you don't have a cat."

"Then I guess the pictures," said Keith.

But Keith didn't have any pictures. At least none had been on display. Which isn't to say Keith hadn't mounted any photos in his apartment. Rodney was betting he had. Or perhaps the photos had mounted Keith. Either way, Rodney could see news footage of an apartment building ablaze and Keith suddenly emerging from the flames, back issues of *Spank* and *Spunk* in either hand.

They were walking to Boyle's so Rodney could send his best friend off with a valedictory piss-up before delivering Keith to his beer-quashing fiancée.

Rodney realized "beer quashing" was a spoonerism of "queer bashing," in the way that "shining wits" were sometimes spoonerized into "whining shits."

The Reverend William Archibald Spooner was an albino Oxford divinity lecturer who once said from the pulpit, "The Lord is a shoving leopard."

When Rodney read in the *Post* that Brad Pitt and Angelina

Jolie had named their daughter Shiloh, he instantly wondered how they could have done such a thing, how they could have failed to anticipate the spooneristic possibilities of the school playground, how they could send the girl into a world in which classmates would so easily—so inevitably—spoonerize the name . . . *Shiloh Pitt*.

The thought occupied Rodney's mind for five full blocks, until he and Keith had washed ashore at the red door of Boyle's, where so many times before they had—a half-remembered phrase—"come optimistically, and left misty-optically."

As a boy, when Rodney asked his dad the meaning of a word he'd heard on the radio, his dad always said, "Look it up," and angled his head toward the red dictionary he kept beside his Archie Bunker armchair.

When Rodney was eight he discovered, in the musty stacks of the Our Lady of Sorrows library, a book of palindromes: *A man, a plan, a canal—Panama!*

And: *Go hang a salami, I'm a lasagna hog.*

He told his dad and his dad said, "What's a palindrome?" Rodney said, "Look it up," but his dad didn't. He just looked at Rodney, Kilroy-like, from atop the sports section, as if to say, Don't be a wiseass.

Two weeks later, they were watching an NFL Films highlight reel and his father looked at the Oakland Raiders center on TV, at the name on the back of his jersey—OTTO—and stage-whispered over the newspaper: "Palindrome."

His brothers, oblivious, kept watching the TV, but Rodney got goosebumps at this shared secret. In time the boy became a doer of crosswords, a lover of puns, of palindromes and anagrams and acrostics. And so did his father, who—in response to a joke they had both enjoyed on Johnny Carson—returned with all the Chins he'd torn from a Chinese phone book on a business trip to Hong Kong.

Wordplay was swordplay, at the Poole dinner table and years later, at the bar of Boyle's, which is how Rodney came to sit there with a pen apparently stuck to his forehead—as if the victim of a javelin accident—engaging in all manner of word-nerdery.

His last third date was irretrievably damaged when he took a painful stab at flirtation and told her, "Please me by standing by me, please," which was a palindrome he'd read somewhere, the sentence reading, word for word, the same backwards as forwards.

But she thought it was some kind of a weird come-on, that Rodney was the kind of guy who gets off by standing close to strangers on the subway. *Please me by standing by me, please?*

Until last night, Rodney hadn't had a date since, and now his best friend was moving, and he was beginning to fear he might become desperately lonely, the kind of solitary figure he had seen at Boyle's.

The kind of guy, come to think of it, who gets off standing close to strangers on the subway.

Boyle's was a different place after five, when the red door swung open and never really swung closed, blowing in couples dressed for the theater and men in Con Ed monkey suits and young women in severe eyeglasses meeting other young women after work. With every swing of that door came a cleansing breeze that made Wanamaker's comb-over briefly stand at attention, like the lid of an opened soup can.

Keith handed Rodney a Bass and said, "Get it down your neck."

An old man in a hound's-tooth jacket sat under the Zenith,

head on hand, like a Rodin sculpture: the Drinker. On the next stool, Wanamaker tongued the dregs from his empty crock of soup, as if the first word in the day's special—"French Onion Soup"—was a verb, and the whole phrase an item on his to-do list.

"Cheers." Rodney sucked an inch off the top and tried, without success, to remember the first bar in New York he ever set foot in.

Boyle's wasn't his first local. Before Boyle's there was the Emerald Inn, with its photographs of dead regulars framed on the wall, and before *that* there was the Dublin House, whose neon harp flashed pink and green like a lighthouse.

But he and Keith had also drunk at McAleer's and Malachy's, Black Finn and Baggott Inn, at Desmond's and Dunleavy's, O'Hanlon's and O'Flanagan's, McDooley's and McCarthy's (and the legendary McSorley's); at the Blarney Inn and Blarney Rock and Blarney Star and even, when ridiculously late or ridiculously early, the Blarney *Stone*; at Mullen's on seventh and Mulligan's on Madison; at P.J. Clarke's and Paddy Maguire's, at O'Neal's and O'Neill's, the Irish Pub and the Irish Punt and—blessedly—at the Old Town Bar, whose urinals rivaled Boyle's as the greatest achievement in porcelain since Belleek produced its first tea set.

"Look. At. *That*," Keith sighed as three young ladies walked through the swinging door. Wanamaker's comb-over briefly stood and then prostrated itself, salaaming them, bowing to their beauty.

Rodney was an uncomfortable rubbernecker at this intersection, where college-aged women, with unchecked IDs, crossed paths with middle-aged men, with unchecked ids.

Wanamaker's comb-over was a Boyle's bellwether. A bellwether, Rodney remembered reading, was a castrated sheep that wore a bell around its neck. The leader of the flock. But Wanamaker's 'do wasn't the only bellwether at Boyle's. The bar hosted a twelve-team darts league every twelfth Saturday, one in a rotation of sites, like the courses that host golf's British Open. On darts nights, Armen put a bell above the door, so that when it swung open, the throwers could step aside. The line, the *oche*, was just inside the door, seven feet, nine and three-quarters inches from the dart board on the wall. Thanks largely to a cop called Five-Oh, the last six league titles belonged to Boyle's, whose team called itself the Tossers.

Keith remembered his first bar in New York as if it were his first kiss: "Pig 'N Whistle, by the Garden. Before a Knicks game. I ever tell you that? Ewing had twenty-six rebounds on my first night in New York."

"Pig 'N Whistle," Rodney knew, was a corruption of "peg o' wassail," a bowl (peg) in which carolers (wassailers) collected beer after singing a song.

Rodney remembered singing as a kid in church at Christmas:

Here we come a-wassailing among the leaves so green
Here we come a wand 'ring so fair to be seen . . .

In fourth grade, Rodney didn't know what that meant and he damn sure didn't get a bucket of beer after singing it.

Love and joy come to you
And to you glad tidings too . . .

Rodney had his first taste of beer at age five, swigging from the near-empties after one of his parents' parties—cans of Hamm's, some with lipsticked cigarettes stubbed out inside, even though the living room was littered with the ashtrays he and his brothers had made in art class.

And God bless you and seh-hend you a
Ha-appy New Year . . .

He'd lift the couch cushions after those parties and collect the change. If they'd had Coinstar back then, he'd have cashed in.

Kids couldn't possibly make ashtrays in art class anymore. You could no longer smoke in Irish pubs or English pubs or French cafés, never mind New York bars like Boyle's, whose walls—and etiolated patrons—nevertheless smelled like cured hams.

And God seh-hend you a Ha-appy New Year.

The nuns never told them it was a drinking song. The kids at Our Lady of Sorrows never got to sing the second verse:

Our wassail cup is made
Of the rosem'ry tree
And so is our beer
Of the best barley . . .

"C'mon, Poole," Keith said. "You're falling behind." Rodney had an inch of Bass left, and another full pint in front of him, sweating in the on-deck circle of a cardboard coaster.

They were standing, sandwiched between the booths and the back of the occupied barstools, human slalom poles for everyone trying to get to the Ladies or the Gents.

"I just wanna find a bar in Chicago with ample bathrooms," Keith said.

"Ample Bathrooms," Rodney said, savoring every syllable. "Wasn't he a Negro League legend? A guy who went yard off Satchel Paige?"

"Ample Bathrooms," Keith said, "was a Delta bluesman."

"Southern senator," said Rodney. "With a voice like Foghorn Leghorn's: *I'm Senator Ample Bathrooms, and I approved this message.*"

"That fucker just stepped on my foot," Keith said.

Keith's right sneaker was a blinding white, like bleached teeth. But his left sneaker was newly besmirched by everything—spilled beer, sidewalk funk, the phlegmatic sneezes of Edith and Wanamaker—that another man's shoe could collect from the thriving petri dish of Boyle's floor.

A kid on his way to the Gents stopped abruptly and said, "Talking to *me*?"

Keith said: "No, De Niro, I'm talking *about* you. You stepped on my foot."

He was maybe twenty-five, in a white V-neck T-shirt that was pit-stained from the August heat.

De Niro crossed his arms in a gesture of forced nonchalance and said, as if speaking to a baby, "Did I hurt your foot?"

Keith crossed *his* arms, to make his guns look bigger, and said with what was meant to come off as quiet menace: "No, you hurt my *feelings*. You didn't say 'Sorry.' Or even 'Excuse me.'"

"What's the problem?" Armen asked, with the equanimity of a man who had long doubled as his own bouncer.

"No problem," Rodney told Armen before turning to De Niro. "Nobody has a problem. You stepped on his foot, he got pissed, that's all." Though Rodney was lean, his height made him a scarecrow, frightening off predators preemptively, before they figured out he couldn't fight, that he had no aptitude—and less appetite—for confrontation of any kind.

It was a trait that hadn't served him well at work, where he had difficulty telling superiors that their memoranda were inane, that a "magnetic-tape salesman" is a guy who sells videocassettes, but a "magnetic tape salesman" is a charismatic dude who sells anything adhesive. The hyphen mattered, but only to him, and he feared, in his final days on the job, that he was beginning to come off as a crank.

Three minutes later De Niro came out of the Gents and passed Keith without comment. Rodney pretended not to watch as he returned to his booth, sat down long enough to look like he was taking his time, then rose with his buddy, who looked like a longneck bottle of Budweiser, if a beer bottle were capable of bad skin and a bobbing Adam's apple.

Then, to Rodney's relief, De Niro and Longneck left through the swinging door.

"You know that prick?" Rodney said to Armen.

Armen said, "Never seen him in here before." And if Armen had never seen the guy in Boyle's before, the guy had never been in Boyle's before, because Armen—near as Rodney could tell—had never been *out* of Boyle's before, except to run out for the occasional birthday cake or going-away card, like the one that had accompanied Keith's first round, in which a cartoon secretary cupped the nuts of her boss, who said: "*Calls*, Mrs. Pennybaker. I said hold my *calls*."

Keith didn't start his new job for six more weeks, but he still had to leave for Chicago in the morning, driving straight through, because he and Caroline were meeting with their priest on Monday morning. It was all that Caroline required of him before their wedding. Rodney didn't envy Keith his Sunday, hung over in a U-Haul.

Rodney had rented a van once from a place whose name

and slogan, emblazoned on the side of every vehicle in their fleet, were: "U-Pull-It—Or Let Us Pull It For You!" He felt like he was driving a mobile massage parlor, especially when a car full of high school kids pulled alongside him and one of them yelled, "Hey, why don't you pull it for me?"

Keith called for two shots of Three Wise Men.

As Armen mixed the Johnnie, Jack, and Jim, Rodney asked Keith if he had ever seen Armen in real life, in the real world.

Keith hadn't. Armen didn't play on Boyle's softball team, hadn't run in Boyle's "5K, 10-Keg, You-Fly-We-Buy Fun Run." He sometimes mentioned his buddy, Cliff, which suggested he had a life on the outside. But Armen seemed always to be behind the bar, wearing its rosewood veneer like a figleaf, which he shed only for infrequent trips to the can. He was in Boyle's before Boyle's opened and there after Boyle's closed. Most Boyle's patrons would have no way of knowing if Armen wore pants, or indeed if he had any legs at all.

Rodney knew he wasn't legless because he'd once seen him vault the bar to break up a fight. Afterward, Armen paraphrased the basketball coach Al McGuire and said, "The key is, you gotta go feet first. Go head first and you're dead."

Rodney had also passed Armen once, two or three years ago, walking into a Subway sandwich shop, where they exchanged embarrassed, nearly inaudible greetings. It reminded Rodney of the night in junior high when he saw his social studies teacher, Mr. Anderton, working in the sporting goods aisle at Target, in a red vest and name tag stamped WARREN. The sight was unnatural and upsetting, like seeing an elephant ride a bicycle in the circus. And Rodney knew Armen found it every bit as awkward to see *him*, bereft of his Bass and his barstool.

The door opened. Wanamaker's combover clapped twice in rapid succession, an imperious hotel desk clerk calling for a bellhop. In walked Longneck, followed, five seconds later, by De Niro. They'd been sharing a smoke on the sidewalk. Rodney felt his stomach tighten.

Keith had his back to the door and didn't see them. Rodney raised his shot glass and said, "To Chicago. You'll be bigger than Oprah and Ebert combined." They sank the shots and Keith asked Armen for two more pints.

"I mean that literally," Rodney said. "You will *literally* be bigger than Oprah and Ebert combined if you continue drinking at this pace."

From the stereo came a violent volley of chords, then the Clash banging on about shit jobs and working for the Man on "Career Opportunities."

"I love this," Keith said.

"Me too," Rodney replied. "The thought of going back to work for some smug clown makes me sick."

"No," Keith said. "What I love are rock stars telling people 'Fuck work' and 'Quit your job.' Easy to say when you're a billionaire."

"Joe Strummer wasn't a billionaire," Rodney said, but Keith was on a roll.

"Lou Reed sang 'Don't Talk to Me About Work' like he spent the day in a cubicle instead of snorting coke off a supermodel's bum-crack," he said. "The guy who sang 'Take This Job and Shove It,' his name was Johnny *Paycheck*."

"There was a boxer called Johnny Paycheck," Rodney said. "Joe Louis knocked him out in the forties. That's where the singer got the name. Not because he was rich."

But Keith would not be stopped. "The point is, rich pricks telling working stiffs to stick it to the Man. It's bullshit."

"In fact, Johnny Paycheck went to prison and declared bankruptcy," Rodney said. "He had *no* money."

"Beck's got money," Keith said. "*And* he's got a song called 'Soul Sucking Jerk.' About his *boss*."

"So what?" Rodney said. "It's supposed to be cathartic. I can listen to 'Taxman' knowing the Beatles were tax exiles."

"I can't," Keith said. "Beck doesn't have a boss. I do, and he's a decent guy. My *dad* is somebody's boss. He's been at the same company for twenty-eight years, and I thank Christ he didn't quit *his* job because Dolly Parton said nine to five was no way to make a living. He worked nine to five so his kids could go to college, and *I* work nine to five—eight to six most days—so *my* kids can go to college. And to pay the taxman."

"Jesus," Rodney said. "I'm gonna start calling *you* Johnny Paycheck."

It annoyed him that Keith was right, so Rodney kept on disputing a point that he'd privately conceded: that rock stars singing about real jobs really *was* a load of shite.

"UB40 named themselves for the Unemployment Benefits form in the UK," Rodney said. "Because they were on the dole when the band formed."

"On the dole?" Keith said. "What the fuck is 'on the dole'?"

"On welfare," Rodney said. "Or sitting on a frozen Dole banana, in your case."

Keith turned a beer coaster on its edge, flicked it with his forefinger, and watched it spin.

"A lotta bands met in the dole queue," Rodney said. "Oasis, Pulp—those guys were all on the dole."

"You're American," Keith said. "You know that, right? You're not on the dole, you're unemployed. You don't queue up, you wait in line." Keith held the coaster like a ninja throwing star and pantomimed embedding it in Rodney's forehead.

Rodney could only think of that word: *unemployed*. Boyle's was full of them, the unemployed and the unemployable, and

Rodney was just now having the epiphany that Mairead would have had on their date: that he was an unemployed barfly.

Keith and Armen weren't his fellow idlers. Keith, in the week's nondrinking hours, worked his ass off. And Armen was paid to spend his nights in Boyle's, his bald head going red like a squeezed thumb, his sweat now falling into some schmuck's 7&7.

Rodney envied Keith his belief in the ennobling power of wage slavery, and privately resolved to get a job—aware, even as he was doing so, that he'd made manifold resolutions at Boyle's that hadn't survived the evening. Among these were the promise to compose a crossword that the *Times* would publish, to read every Penguin Classic from Austen to Zola, and to drink a beer in every bar in Manhattan. For this last, he went so far as to buy a Sharpie and a Streetwise map of the borough, vowing to black out every block as he made his way from Washington Heights to the Bowery.

"The only blacking out you'll do is on a barstool," said Armen, who was eventually proven right.

And so the sum of Rodney's ambition was little more than a series of bar bets. Mairead, he knew, would figure that out soon enough, if she hadn't already. Any woman would. Ambition was the cardinal virtue in America. It was especially true in New York, where Mairead was climbing a corporate ladder while Rodney plunged down a professional elevator shaft.

He *had* socked some money away. And that verb—*socked*—was devastatingly apt, Rodney knew. His money was more or less in a sock drawer, stashed in a savings account earning 4 percent interest. He couldn't help but see, in every drained beer glass, the hourglass of those savings running out.

In a small burst of enterprise after leaving his job, Rodney secured a single interview—an over-the-phone "pre-interview

interview"—to join the New York office of a Madrid-based bank called Banco Marinero.

Rodney couldn't fathom working in corporate communications for a "communicator" who used the word "pre-interview," which chafed him in the way that "prepackaged foods" did, or "pretaped programs." But the job paid well, more than his previous salary, and he found himself silently wanting it. Rodney didn't see himself as a banker, but he took comfort in the knowledge that T. S. Eliot worked in a bank.

"T. S. Eliot," Rodney just realized, was an anagram of "Toilets." For reasons he could not explain and did not care to have explained to him, Rodney thought about bathrooms more than most men.

He made a silent promise to keep the appointment with Banco Marinero, Monday at four. It would give him a job prospect to offer up in conversation the next time he saw Mairead.

"Career Opportunities" ended and Rodney recognized the opening bars of "Come On, Eileen" played at twice their usual speed.

"This isn't Dexys Midnight Runners," Rodney said. "Who is it?"

"Save Ferris," Armen said. "Ska-punk band from the nineties."

Rodney hated that kind of hyphenated bullshit, like the pan-Asian-fusion restaurants he assiduously avoided. The hyphen giveth and the hyphen taketh away. But he liked this cover. He liked it a lot.

Armen said, "The 'Dexy' in Dexys Midnight Runners was short for Dexedrine. Did you know that?"

"Dexedrine?" Rodney said.

"It's an amphetamine," Armen said. "Used to treat narcolepsy."

"Give him some," Rodney said, nodding in the direction of the Drinker, who had his head on the bar in a way that reminded Rodney of first grade, of resting his head on his desk at naptime. "Or at least give him a graham cracker."

Keith said there was a porno called *Come On Eileen*.

Rodney knew nothing about drugs, beyond a single joint he had smoked in college.

Keith said that most pornos were named for successful movies: "*On Golden Blonde, Saving Ryan's Privates*, that sort of thing. But I—"

"*Sorest Rump*," Armen interjected.

"Right," Keith said. "Exactly. But I can't think of another *song* that's inspired one."

Armen paused thoughtfully and said, "*Summer of '69*?"

There followed a chorus of contributions from the bar—"*Norwegian Wood*" "*Roll Over, Beethoven*"—each of which was thoughtfully chewed on by Keith, who often moderated these conversations, which were conducted with earnest gravitas, as if it were all being taped for *The Charlie Rose Show*. Rodney was going to miss him.

Over Keith's left shoulder, Rodney could see Longneck remove his gold chain and stick it in his jeans pocket.

Keith and two women seated at the far end of the bar were singing along to Save Ferris: "Too-RAH-loo-RAH, Too-RAH-loo-RYE-AYYY . . ."

It occurred to Rodney that what they were doing was the opposite of a wassail—he would happily give them a bucketful of beer if it would make them *stop* singing.

Longneck was rolling his head around like a linebacker doing calisthenics as he approached the Gents.

Al McGuire said when a guy takes off his coat he's not going to fight but when he takes off his wristwatch, look out.

Rodney could see that Longneck wasn't wearing a wrist-watch, that he didn't *need* a wristwatch: there were no pressing business or dental appointments in this guy's world, to judge by his eyes and his breath as Longneck drew near.

But he *was* wearing steel-toed Timberlands when he stomped hard on Keith's other shoe, Keith's right shoe, Keith's *clean* shoe.

Even over the ska-punk, Rodney could hear Keith's first, second, and third metatarsals crunch underfoot like a wine glass in a Jewish wedding. Only what Keith shouted wasn't "Mazel tov" but "Fuuuck," which he stretched into a gorgeous aria of obscenity, holding the note for at least ten seconds.

As he disappeared through the door of the Gents, Long-neck said over his shoulder, *"Excuse me."*

What happened next would be embroidered in Boyle's leg-end in years to come, imbued with bravado, enlarged by imag-ination, exaggerated by eyewitnesses who weren't actually there.

But in fact everything that happened next was purely reflexive. Not premeditated, but *post*-meditated, infused with purpose and courage only after the fact.

Keith pogoed on his left foot while trying to remove his right shoe and fell over onto the careworn Boyle's linoleum, which was laid in 1957 and neglected ever since. "Same as Wanamaker," as Rodney liked to say.

Rodney helped Keith to his feet—to his foot—and then strode purposefully toward the Gents, wondering what kind of dumbshit assaults someone on his way *into* the can.

Armen didn't go feet first over the bar, as so many would remember it. He threw open the hinged bartop and walked through the opening, cutting off De Niro before he could jump Rodney in the Gents.

When Rodney walked in there, Longneck was stepping up to the presidential podium of a Boyle's urinal, still rolling his neck.

Rodney gave Longneck a full five seconds to get a good ropy stream going before he applied the headlock from behind, pulling Longneck off the platform, pushing him through the bathroom door, then frog-marching him through the bar, still holding his junk in his hand.

He was powerless to resist Rodney. Indeed, Longneck didn't want to. He couldn't get to the front door fast enough. With his right hand, Longneck painfully pinched off his flow. With his left, he demurely tried to cover himself, his sphincter seizing all the while from its prolonged clench.

Armen, with the advantages of weight and sobriety, shoved De Niro into the night. Then Rodney did the same to Longneck. And then it was done, just like that.

The door swung open and the door swung shut.

The wave of Wanamaker's comb-over crested, then crashed, in a celebratory sea-spray of dandruff.

3

Under the best of circumstances, Rodney became—in the back of a New York taxi—both claustrophobe and agoraphobe, feeling at once confined and on display, his knees near his chin in that *Judgment at Nuremberg* booth of bulletproof Plexiglas.

He felt helpless, as if the bench seat beneath him might give way inside this rolling carnival dunk tank.

And these, to say the least, were not the best of circumstances. Drunk and lame, Keith was draped over Rodney when the cab pulled up to the curb. To get him in, Rodney had to hold Keith horizontally in his arms in a sacrilegious parody of the *Pietà*.

By the time he slid his friend heavily across the seat, Rodney was panting and Keith was moaning. As Rodney raised Keith's shattered bare foot and placed it gently in his own lap to keep it elevated, Keith exhaled, "Oh God oh God oh God!," exciting the attention of the driver, who existed exclusively as a pair of brooding eyeballs in the rearview mirror, overscored by a single continuous eyebrow that called to mind Bert from *Sesame Street*.

With Keith's exclamation, the unibrow became an angry V, a chevron of geese flying south, and the voice that belonged to it shouted through the Plexiglas in an Indian accent: "No hanky panky! No hanky panky!"

Rodney realized how it must have looked from the front seat, as though Keith were giving him a foot job, and he quickly scanned the cab for the hidden lipstick cameras of that HBO series in which drunks in New York and L.A. and Las Vegas get it on in the backseats of cabs.

"Take us to the nearest emergency room," Rodney shouted over the Bollywood pop. "My friend broke his foot."

What the hell was he doing here? If anyone should be giving him a foot job in the back of a taxi for possible broadcast on a premium cable channel, it should be Mairead. The last time he saw her, she was in the back of a taxi, probably texting a friend about the jobless, pit-sniffing pilgrim fetishist who told Ebola jokes on their blind date.

The cab washed ashore outside the strip-lit lobby of the ER. Through the window, Rodney could see the tired and the poor, huddled masses and wretched refuse. The unholy offspring of Lazarus and Emma Lazarus.

He thought of the Statue of Liberty: first, the lady in the harbor, then the flaming drink of the same name. In one of those first sleepless nights after 9/11, Armen filled a shooter glass with Sambuca and stuck his index finger in. Then he removed his finger, held it aloft and set it alight, letting it burn while he shot the Sambuca. Instantly, half the people in Boyle's were doing Statues of Liberty, their flaming fingers held high, beacon hands glowing a worldwide welcome—a haunting, alcoholic, fingerlight vigil.

When video of bin Laden appeared on CNN that same night, Keith ordered another Sambuca and submerged his middle finger. Then he held it high and Rodney lit it up and Keith flipped Al Qaeda a flaming bird. A "Freebird," Rodney called it, and Armen fired up some Skynyrd.

Keith let his middle finger burn for several seconds—*I lift my lamp beside the golden door*—then extinguished his flaming digit in Wanamaker's just-pulled pint of Harp.

The prodigious hiss that followed sounded like the air brakes decompressing on a city bus.

Having carried him across the threshold of the ER, Rodney signed Keith into the registry at the front desk, completing their awkward pantomime of a wedding night. To judge by the state of Keith, it had been one hell of a reception. Definitely open bar. But then, when Rodney turned to see the waiting room—ice packs on eyebrows, tourniquets tied to fingers, all those plastic seats in primary colors—he realized *everyone* was drunk. Or had been very recently.

The lobby's molded chairs faced a circular analog clock, still the preferred timepiece of schoolrooms and hospitals. It read 2:17 a.m., and its hands moved every bit as slowly as Rodney remembered from the second grade.

They waited, and Keith wondered aloud where he would rank in the triage Top 40. He would chart well below the car wrecks and knifings, he conceded, but surely deserved to crack the Top 20, above the presumed pill poppers (anyone who was lying down, Rodney and Keith had decided) and solitary sexual misadventures (anyone who was standing up, they were certain).

To pass the time, Rodney did what he had done in school and focused on the clock's sweeping second hand: a third-base coach windmilling a runner home from first.

It was 4:45 a.m. before a female doctor who looked nothing like the ladies on *ER* saw Keith in a curtained examination room, set his foot in a cast, and prepared a sling for his left shoulder, separated when Keith fell while pulling off his shoe.

Rodney sat on a pumpkin-colored chair in Reception and listened to the man next to him. His lungs were wheezing musically, as if he'd swallowed an accordion. Rodney was trying to decide if the man had a lung ailment or was busking for change when Keith emerged from the emergency room.

Emerged, Rodney thought. From the French *émerger*—"rise up." Which is what an emergency does, unexpectedly.

An aluminum crutch was propped under Keith's good armpit. "Thank God it's not your wanking arm," Rodney said.

By the time the newlyweds found a taxi and headed uptown, it was 5:30 on Sunday morning. Dogs were heading out and drunks were heading in, both to pee. In half an hour, the sun would be shimmering off the Hudson, which had brought the first white man to Manhattan five hundred years earlier.

Manhattan's first residents, Rodney knew from researching his own condition, were the Lenape Indians. They told a missionary years after the fact that the first white man had arrived by canoe, dressed entirely in red. They thought he might be the Supreme Being, "The Great Manitto." And so the Lenape toasted him, and he toasted them, and everyone got happily shitfaced or shithoused or Chi-towned—whatever people called it back then. And thereafter this island was called Mannahattanink, "The Island or Place of General Intoxication." Rodney wanted to believe it, even though he knew the story was bullshit.

General Intoxication: that was someone Rodney could go to war behind. Or Major Hangover.

Rodney thought of all this as he closed his blinds and

inflated an AeroBed in the living room, and fitted it with sheets for Keith, whose head throbbed in harmony with his immobilized foot.

"What the fuck happened tonight?" Keith said as Rodney helped him onto the floor.

The question was rhetorical, but Rodney answered anyway: "Your foot got plastered. And so did you."

"It better heal fast," Keith said, pulling the blanket up under his chin. Rodney resisted an impulse to tuck him in.

" 'Cause this is my ass-kicking foot. And if I ever see the motherfucker who did this, I'm gonna break his fucking neck."

"You might wanna pack a lunch," Rodney said. "Because his neck was three feet long."

Keith looked up at Rodney, helpless and grateful, like he was waiting for a bedtime story. Rodney was happy to have another person in his apartment. He always hated to see guests go, and take with them the comforting sound effects of family: a tap running in the middle of the night, spoons clinking in cereal bowls on Saturday morning.

Rodney put two bottles of water, a bottle of Advil, and the TV remote on the floor next to Keith. "I could suspend the mattress six inches from the ceiling," Rodney said. "If that'll make you feel at home."

Keith closed his eyes and said, "I'm gonna miss that apartment."

"You only slept with trapeze artists," Rodney said. "You had to climb a ladder to get into bed."

"So did Peter Brady," said Keith.

"True, but he was nine."

Rodney eased a pillow under Keith's right foot. And only then did it occur to him: This wasn't just Keith's ass-kicking foot. It was his *driving* foot—his accelerating and braking foot. Keith wouldn't be driving to Chicago today, or tomorrow, or anytime soon. And he no longer had an apartment to return to, only a U-Haul, parked across town on 117th Street, that would have to be *re*-parked every night or be towed. And in that instant Rodney saw his immediate future—endlessly circling Manhattan in Keith's foul-cargoed U-Haul, the automotive equivalent of that limboed garbage barge that no state would accept.

Keith farted mournfully and said, "What's wrong with being nine?"

In less than a minute he was snoring.

Rodney stood at his bedroom window at daybreak. Across the street, a shade went up, revealing a woman in a wife-beater and emerald panties. Seeing Rodney, she dropped the shade, as if her building had opened one eye, shut it, and returned to sleep. Rodney remained at his window. He watched the city segue from electric light to natural light and the very thought of that phrase—natural light—induced in him something close to panic.

Dawn wasn't the only thing dawning on him. To most people, "natural light" meant *sun*. To Rodney, it meant *beer*: Anheuser-Busch Natural Light. Beer had replaced the sun as the thing around which his world turned, and that epiphany filled Rodney with an existential despair—not a physical hangover (he didn't suffer those) but something far worse, what Kingsley Amis called a *meta*physical hangover: "That ineffable compound of depression, sadness (these two are not the same), anxiety, self-hatred, sense of failure and fear for the future."

Rodney felt all of those things as he watched a dog take a leak on a garbage bag.

Overnight, Rodney had crossed a Rubicon—into a world of dive-bar toilet fights and predawn ER visits to go along with his crippling unemployment anxiety. He pulled the shade, climbed into bed, thought of the Replacements, a band from his hometown, singing about needing a job and needing a girl. Rodney needed both. But he needed the job to get the girl. And he needed ambition to get either.

On other nights, Rodney would have lain awake thinking of crossing a Rubicon, then of Caesar crossing the Rubicon River into Italy, then of the Caesar salad, invented by Caesar Cardini in 1924 at his restaurant, Caesar's, in Tijuana, Mexico—a bit of trivia Rodney learned on Quiz Night at Boyle's, when Boyle's still *had* Quiz Nights. Armen ended them when two teammates fistfought over the question "Who said, 'Nonviolence is a weapon of the strong'?"

On other nights, Rodney's thoughts would have flitted from the Caesar salad to Caesar Geronimo—the former Cincinnati Reds centerfielder named for two giants of world history—and then on to that ancient conundrum, "What did Geronimo say when jumping out of an airplane?" And from there, he'd be thinking of all the hours spent at Boyle's playing Conundrums, asking, "Why do they sterilize the lethal-injection needles?" or "How does a blind man know when to stop wiping?"

But this night was different. On this night, Rodney's train of thought made only two stops—first at Julius Caesar, and then at *Julius Caesar*, in which Mark Antony lamented the title character's ambition: ambition, he said, "was a grievous fault."

Most Sundays, Rodney went to Boyle's for brunch, though seldom before 2 p.m., so technically it wasn't brunch so much as linner. Then he went to six o'clock Mass with a little bit of a buzz on. This Sunday, he skipped Boyle's and left Keith in his apartment just before Mass, with a pizza and the flipper, secure in the knowledge that his Sunday *Times* would still be untouched when he got home.

Other Sundays, Keith joined him at Mass, where he often engaged Rodney in a whispered catechism of questions. Staring at the crucifix behind the altar, Keith once asked Rodney: "How come every Jesus—every Jesus in every church in the world—has ripped abs?"

Rodney stared straight ahead.

"All that fish?" Keith said.

Rodney stared.

"That it?"

Stared.

"All those omega-3 acids?"

Keith did this at the movies, too, starting with the trailers, and Rodney never responded, and it never occurred to Keith to stop talking. Some friendships are comfortable enough to endure long silences. Rodney and Keith's friendship endured long absences of silence—not dead air, but its antithesis: air that refused to die, air that Keith kept on life support, its brain dead but its heart still beating.

Rodney was that way on first dates. He always felt like a SWAT commander trying to talk a jumper away from the ledge, afraid that if he ever stopped talking, it was all over. And so he babbled.

He wondered what Mairead was doing right now.

Rodney knelt for the Eucharist, looked up at Christ on the cross, admired his six-pack. A doctor in Florida had published a diet book called *What Would Jesus Eat?* and Rodney knew the answer: wine with every meal.

He liked St. Brendan's for the same reasons he liked Boyle's: the singing, the alcohol, the frequent invocations of the Lord's name. Conversation, comfort in ritual, and a sense of sanctuary. Neither Boyle's nor Brendan's threw bums out for sleeping inside. Both places were overseen by men behind waist-high counters. Holy men who heard confessions.

Mass let out. Rodney bounded down the steps of St. Brendan's feeling clean and responsible and filled with silent vows of self-improvement, like he had just been to the dentist and was promising to floss from now on.

A homeless man at the bottom of the steps said, "Excuse me . . ."

Rodney smiled at him, because he'd just come from Mass, but kept walking. The guy said: "Can you help me out?"

Still walking, Rodney returned his gaze to a point on the horizon and the guy called after him: "Can you help me out, young man?"

Rodney kept walking.

"Can you help me get my Grand Dad out of the liquor store?"

Rodney smiled, stopped, fished a dollar from his pocket, and put it in the guy's hand with a flourish, as if he were stuffing a fifty into a maître d's breast pocket.

He was going to call Mairead tonight. He walked home rehearsing the call, honing it like a telemarketer's pitch. Which is what it was, when he thought about it—trying to sell someone something they didn't know they wanted, didn't know they *needed*.

It had been forty-eight hours since they met for drinks at Rococo. For all Rodney knew, he was already on her Do Not Call list.

When Rodney walked in, Keith was where he'd left him, impervious to time inside a Bermuda triangle—the remote at one point, a ravaged pizza box yawning at another, the cordless phone at the third. Keith was watching *Sunday Night Baseball*, Cardinals at Cubs, and talking before Rodney could get the key out of the lock.

"First beer I ever had was right there," Keith said. "In the leftfield bleachers at Wrigley. Old Style from a waxed cup. I was fifteen. Some guy sitting behind me bought it."

"If you stomped on one of those cups just right, it sounded like a gunshot," Rodney said.

"To this day I won't drink Bud because of the Cardinals," Keith said. Rodney knew this was bullshit, had seen Keith drink Bud when it was all that was available, but he went along with this fiction, about his boycotting the family that owned the St. Louis ball club and brewery, because Keith seemed so convinced of its veracity.

"The Cardinals used to be sponsored by Griesedieck," Rodney said.

"Greasy Dick?" Keith said. "They were sponsored by a disease?"

Rodney thought Greasy Dick sounded less like a disease than a remedy—the curative, perhaps, for Cockburn and Dry Sack.

"Griesedieck," Rodney said. "It was a beer, out of St. Louis."

"A *beer*?" said Keith, never taking his eyes off the TV. "Can you see yourself ordering one of those at Boyle's? *Armen, get over here, I'm gagging for a Greasy Dick.*"

"If Greasy Dick were a disease," Rodney said, joining Keith on the floor, "the drug companies would euphemize it as GD. We'd be seeing commercials all over this game for the remedy. 'Ask your doctor if it's right for you.'"

Their backs were propped against the front of the couch. They basked in the glow of the TV and for a second it felt like a family room, like they were sitting down to watch *The Wonderful World of Disney* on a Sunday night after dinner, stealing precious minutes before they were ordered upstairs to do homework.

As college freshmen, Keith and Rodney lived on the same floor. Then as now, Keith was entirely free from stress. Many people said, "I could care less" when they meant "I *couldn't* care less." Not Keith. Keith really did have an endless reserve of indifference, to almost everything. And Rodney envied that. Rodney was a worrywart, Keith was Compound W.

Then, as now, beer and TV were central to the relationship. Sometimes beer was primary and TV secondary, as at Boyle's, where they strained to see the Zenith; and sometimes vice versa, as when, say, the Cubs and Cardinals were on.

Keith fished the last piece of pizza from the box, tilted his head back, and dropped it in like a sword swallower.

"Talk to Caroline today?" Rodney said.

"Yeah."

"And?"

Keith laughed. "She's pissed."

"What did she say?"

"Not much," Keith said.

"What did *you* say?"

"I told her the truth," Keith said. "I told her we were carrying my TV down the stairs to the van when you dropped it on my foot. I was in front, walking backwards, and fell down the stairs. The TV explains my foot, the stairs explain my shoulder."

"So it's my fault?" Rodney said. "She's pissed at *me*?"

"No," Keith said. "A little. *SIT DOWN!*" This last comment was directed to Albert Pujols, who had just taken a called third strike to end the Cardinals' first.

"Thanks," Rodney said.

"What do you care?" Keith said. "You don't have to be married to her. It's no biggie."

"Why didn't you tell her the truth? You didn't do anything wrong."

"Why didn't I tell her I got my ass kicked in a bar fight?" Keith said.

Rodney resented having to be complicit in this lie, even passively. It reminded him of the time he sat idly in the back of a taxi as the driver went on a racist rant in response to some news on 1010 WINS about a mother in the Bronx whose toddler fell down an open elevator shaft. Rocketing up Broadway, his life in the hands of another man, Rodney looked on impassively, allowing the driver to assume from his silence that they were on the same page.

He wondered if Caroline had already told Mairead about Keith's injuries, and who had caused them, and how. Rodney figured Caroline would assume he dropped the TV on purpose, to sabotage Keith's move, to keep his drinking buddy in town for another week. As if Rodney were the bad influence.

If Caroline *had* told Mairead, the best Rodney could hope for was to come off as a weak-tit who couldn't hold up his half of a TV. At worst—well, Rodney didn't want to think about this portrait: a jobless, friendless, alcoholic prick—*and* a weak-tit who couldn't hold up his half of a TV.

Of course Caroline would have told her. Women told each other everything, didn't they, and Caroline and Mairead were best friends. Not the kind of best friends who grew up braiding each other's hair at slumber parties and having pillow fights in their college dorm. Though once conjured, Rodney could not easily chase that image from his head, of the two of them in pajamas in a snow globe of down feathers.

Rather, Caroline and Mairead met on their first jobs out of college, at an ad agency in Chicago, where they shared a "work space" and a telephone extension and—after work, over Chardonnay, in some overpriced place near the office—their career ambitions and thoughts on men and devastating impersonations of coworkers. And that kind of friendship, Rodney knew, was every bit as strong as any from childhood—perhaps stronger, a friendship forged in the crucible of the cubicle.

Rodney remembered Caroline talking about all this—about her first job, and the friend there who helped keep her sane—on a long drive to a rented house on the Jersey Shore. It was six months since he'd broken up with the only girlfriend he'd ever had and only two weeks since he'd lost his Aunt Laura, the only person he'd ever been close to who had died.

So Keith and Caroline were dragging him down to Sea Girt to spend that weekend as a third wheel. Caroline was working in New York at the time. She rode up front in the two-door Chevy Cobalt while Rodney sat in the back with his ankles around his ears like a baked chicken.

But Caroline otherwise put him at ease. She was socially gifted, a child of Chicago's North Shore, those tony suburbs Rodney only knew from *Risky Business* and the John Hughes movies.

Tony suburbs. Whenever Rodney saw that cliché in a newspaper story about a place like the North Shore, he imagined a barbecue-aproned mafioso with that name: Tony Suburbs. They could have called Tony Soprano that.

But Caroline was not stuck up, like other girls he'd met from Tony Suburbs. She loved *Keith* for Christ sake, absolving her of any possibility of pretension.

She was as well informed as one could be without being

well read. "Well watched," Rodney called her, when she said she watched CNN on the treadmill. But she didn't get what he was talking about. Caroline liked Rodney, though she was uninterested in words and lacked a humor gene. Which wasn't to say she was humorless. She found Rodney's jokes funny— not their substance, but the fact that he persisted in making them.

It was that weekend in Sea Girt two years ago that Caroline first told Rodney he should meet Mairead. But he was wary of being set up. *Set up*, like he was walking into a trap. The phrase made him think of Marion Barry, the Washington mayor busted while smoking crack with an ex-girlfriend turned FBI informant, of whom Barry kept saying: *Bitch set me up*.

And so he politely put off the blind date. Mairead had declined it as well, for all Rodney knew.

That weekend in Sea Girt he slept in a child's bedroom. There were baseballs on the wallpaper, a collection of scallop shells in the otherwise empty chest of drawers, sailboats on the thin comforter. But then the whole room gave Rodney comfort.

He spent his days on the porch reading *The Seven Storey Mountain*, by Thomas Merton, a Trappist monk, Catholic mystic, and solitary writer. His father had given the book to Rodney when Laura died. Laura was a part-time English literature professor. Her brother—Rodney's father—thought she lacked ambition. He privately referred to the community college where she taught as "UCLA," for "University Closest to Laura's Apartment."

But Rodney's aunt, like Rodney's dad, revered language. She once fished out of Rodney's bedroom wastebasket a wadded piece of paper on which he'd typed an account of a baseball game he'd watched on TV. She wanted to jot a note to herself and needed something to write on. When Rodney saw that it was his story he tried to snatch it out of her hands. But he didn't try hard enough to take it from her, and he was secretly pleased that someone wanted to read it. His dream job, he told her years later, in the hospital, was to write things and have nobody else read them. "You should have gone into academe," she replied. "That's what *I* do."

And so Aunt Laura, with no children of her own, encouraged Rodney to write, right down to the end, when she was dying of chronic bronchitis but still hastily put on lipstick and arranged her hair whenever Rodney came to visit in the hospital.

She told him that all of English literature begins in a pub: the Tabard, from which the pilgrims in *The Canterbury Tales* set out on their journey. In the years since, Rodney found himself dog-earing his favorite pubs in fiction: He loved "the solid, comfortable ugliness" of the Moon Under Water, Orwell's dream joint. The "bar-parlour" of the Angler's Rest in Wodehouse. At the Sailors Arms, in the Dylan Thomas play *Under Milk Wood*, the clock hands were stuck at half past eleven: "It is always opening time in the Sailors Arms."

Laura taught him to abhor cliché and to recognize those prefabricated phrases—"Panamanian strongman," "fugitive financier," "Mafia kingpin"—that newspapers pinned to their subjects. Finding these two-word descriptives became a game between Rodney and Laura. When his aunt came over for dinner, as she did maybe twice a month, Rodney showed her the phrases he'd torn out of the *Star*: "storm-ravaged" coasts and "bullet-riddled" corpses. "Just once I'd like to see a storm-riddled coast and a bullet-ravaged corpse," Laura said.

Even now, when he saw the phrase "Shi'ite cleric" he thought of her.

And yet Laura's love of language had an unintended effect on Rodney. The more he read, the more he feared that just *wanting* to write would make him exactly what he and his aunt despised: a cliché—"aspiring writer," like "Cuban dictator" or "Libyan madman."

After the funeral, his father gave him Merton, who wrote two things that struck Rodney as contradictory: "When ambition ends, happiness begins" and "The biggest human temptation is to settle for too little."

Now, two years later, they meant the same thing to Rodney. Ambition—aspiring up the ladder in his previous line of work—*was* settling for less than he wanted.

Merton's solitary life in a Trappist monastery made Rodney feel less monastic by comparison. When Merton described the Abbey of Gethsemani as his *four walls of freedom*, Rodney recognized Boyle's in that phrase.

Rodney's favorite fictional pub by far was the Six Jolly Fellowship Porters, the ramshackle Victorian pile in *Our Mutual Friend* that impended over the Thames in "the condition of a faint-hearted diver who has paused so long on the brink that he will never go in at all."

These thoughts cheered him that weekend at the shore. After decades of being cloistered, Merton went to Bangkok in 1968 and electrocuted himself on the pull chain of a hotel ceiling fan while getting out of the tub, which gave Rodney an appreciation ever after for ironic ways of dying.

A roar brought Rodney back into the present: Keith cheering a Soriano double to right.

"Do me a favor," Keith said a minute later. "Drop the TV when you move the van tonight." Without looking up from the game, he added: "Enough to do cosmetic damage, but not enough to screw up the picture."

—————

After four rings, as Rodney was about to recite the extemporaneous message he had written out on the back of his electric-bill envelope, Mairead picked up: "Hello?"

"Hey, it's Rodney . . ."

"Hi."

"Keith and Caroline's friend."

"I know," Mairead said. "You're the only Rodney I've ever met."

Rodney was sitting on his bed, with the door closed. "Is this a bad time?"

"No."

"I thought I was going to get your machine." He was buying time, thinking of something to say.

"I could hang up, if you'd rather talk to my voice mail," Mairead said.

"Well, I *did* have a spontaneous message I rehearsed," said Rodney, as if it were a joke. And then, to keep the jumper from leaping off the bridge: *"Rehearsed*—what does a casket get when it falls out of a hearse."

Silence.

"Re-hearsed," Rodney said. And then, after the smallest of pauses. "Hello?"

"I got it," Mairead said. She was laughing, but not at the joke. "Thanks for explaining, though."

"When I was a kid," Rodney said, "my dad would let me stay up late to see Johnny Carson do Carnac the Magnificent on *The Tonight Show*. You know—*Sis-boom-bah*."

"Sis-boom-bah?" Mairead said.

"Sis-boom-bah," Rodney repeated. "Describe the sound of a sheep exploding."

Mairead laughed.

"My favorite was *Buckeyes*," Rodney said.

"Buckeyes," Mairead said. "I give up."

Rodney said, "What are even worse than buckteeth?"

Mairead's laughter was genuine and it emboldened Rodney. "I have a million more of these," he said. "And if you have dinner with me this week, I promise not to tell them."

There was a pause, after which Mairead said, "This week might be tough."

Rodney said, "Okay."

"Things are kind of crazy at work."

"Yeah," said Rodney. "Me too." And then, when Mairead didn't say anything, he added: "Wait a minute. I don't have a job."

"It's not that," Mairead said.

Rodney felt his scalp bead with sweat. "It's not that" meant "It's *precisely* that," in the same way that "Your call is important to us" meant "Go fuck yourself." He despised this corruption of English, even in the name of spared feelings. "The great enemy of clear language is insincerity," said George Orwell. But insincerity had grown since Orwell's day, expanding from the merely Orwellian to the magnificently *Spre*wellian: Rodney recalled the basketball star Latrell Sprewell, who demanded a raise on his $14 million salary by saying, with epic insincerity, "I've got my family to feed."

After three full seconds of silence, Rodney said to Mairead, "What's not that?"

"Nothing," Mairead sighed. "It's more—I just don't know if I want to date anyone right now."

It sounded like bullshit to Rodney. But what did he expect? She was in advertising. Orwell again: "Advertising is the rattling of a stick inside a swill bucket." But Rodney, too, had committed manifold crimes against language, crafting the kind of corporate euphemisms that eventually got him right-sized. "Words fail me," a lady he worked with had e-mailed him when she heard of his dismissal, and Rodney's first thought was: *No. I failed words*.

Rodney's boss once complimented him on his "verbal ambidexterity." Rodney knew he meant verbal *dexterity*, but later realized the former was more accurate: he was, in his job, verbally ambidextrous—speaking with a forked tongue or out of both sides of his mouth.

"Who said anything about a date?" Rodney said to Mairead. "I thought maybe we could, I dunno, go deer hunting or something."

Mairead said, "It's just—"

There followed a long sigh, after which Mairead said: "I haven't met a lot of stable guys in New York."

Rodney said, "I'm a stable guy."

"I didn't mean it like that," Mairead said. "I wasn't saying you're not. What I'm trying to say is . . ."

Rodney said: "No, I really *am* a stable guy. At Belmont. I'm mucking out stalls 'til I can find another job."

Mairead's laughter sounded like a symphony to Rodney.

"They liked my résumé," he said. "In my previous job I shoveled a lot of shit."

"I'm sure you did," Mairead said. "Me too."

"Plus, my boss was a horse's ass, so I'm used to working with those."

"Sounds like my boss," Mairead said.

Rodney said, "You think *you* work with a bunch of neigh-sayers . . ."

"I do," Mairead said.

"N-E-I-G-H," Rodney said.

"*I got it!*" Mairead said. "I'm not an idiot." And then, with a smile in her voice, "Relax. You don't have to try so hard all the time."

Rodney said, "Let's get a drink this week."

When she didn't immediately reply, Rodney said, "Someplace where I don't have to grease the bathroom attendant."

Rodney wondered if *that's* what Greasy Dick was: one of those unguents in the arsenal of a men's room attendant—some bottled balm kept next to the Brut and the Bay Rum.

Mairead sighed and said, "I could do Tuesday night."

Rodney sat stock still on the edge of his bed while his heart galloped inside his ribcage.

4

Keith was still asleep when Rodney slipped silent as a butler through his own living room. It was 10:45 a.m. The shades were drawn but that familiar sound—taxi tires on slick streets—told him it was raining.

Outside, Rodney bought a *Times* on the corner and sheltered it inside his raincoat. Then he dashed across the street to the diner, wondering which Greek hostess he'd get: the chipper daughter or the brooding mother. Each had a face fallen off a frieze at the Parthenon—a comment on beauty for the daughter, age for the mother.

Would Rodney get the concerned greeting from Mom— "Just the one?"—or the festive greeting from Daughter: *"Party of one?"*

To his delight, Rodney was welcomed as a solitary celebration, a one-man Mardi Gras. Which is exactly how he felt, at least until the stolid waiter denuded his table of its superfluous place setting. It reminded Rodney, always, of some ancient ritual of reprimand—a slap in the face with a white glove.

No matter. Rodney was a man comfortable in his own solitude. He wasn't self-conscious reading in restaurants or sitting alone in a darkened theater, which is where he found himself after breakfast. It was one of life's pleasures, the weekday-morning movie—in an empty old palace like the Ziegfeld or in this, his neighborhood googolplex. Rodney read the paper in his seat until the trailers came on, then sat rapt in the darkness, his face lit up as if by a birthday cake at Boyle's.

His spackler's bucket of popcorn would be empty before the feature started. Then he'd eat whatever kernels he could find in the folds of his T-shirt. After that, he would suck the husks off the unpopped kernels and spit out the old maids. They made a satisfying *click* when they hit the floor.

Old maids: Never been popped. Society made the single person feel less than whole. Or at least the single *woman*, with her biological clock and collection of cats.

A guy told Rodney a joke at Boyle's: A woman is checking out at the grocery store. The man behind her in line—the *drunk* behind her in line—is watching her groceries get scanned: half a gallon of milk, two Stouffer's microwave meals, a ten-pound sack of kitty litter . . .

"Excuse me," the drunk says, "but you must be single."

The lady looks down at her groceries, impressed. "I *am* single," she says. "But tell me—what gave it away?"

And the drunk says, "You're ugly."

Rodney couldn't help but notice: the guy who told the joke was all by himself and one ugly bastard.

Rodney was not unhappy being single, especially not here, in the shared solitude of a movie theater, sucking on sixty-four ounces of soda. That's what Boyle's provided. That's what all of New York provided: not companionship so much as shared solitude.

He had only wanted the twelve-ounce soda, but for a quarter more he could get the thirty-two and—as a combo with the large popcorn he had already ordered—it was *less* expensive to get the bladder-busting sixty-four, the near-equivalent of a six-pack.

"For another nickel," Rodney wanted to tell the lady behind the counter, "have the boys from Ladder Company Number Seven snake a fire hose down my throat and let fifty thousand gallons of Diet Coke cascade into my kidneys."

But instead he said, "Thank you" and retreated to the theater, his popcorn bucket in one hand, his soda bucket in the other—Lady Justice with her scales. He chose an empty row in the rear and recalled a church marquee he had once seen while driving through Georgia in a rental car: COME EARLY, GET THE GOOD SEATS IN BACK.

Rodney read the *Times* until the lights dimmed, then experienced what Wordsworth called "the bliss of solitude." The soundtrack swelled and the first trailer appeared on the screen, for a frat-house comedy. Only then did Rodney realize that he was alone in a dark theater, at 11:30 on a Monday morning, wearing an open raincoat with a newspaper on his lap as some chick half his age danced in a dorm room in her underwear. And his solitude, for the first time in a long time, made him self-conscious.

Two hours later, Rodney left the theater as he often did Boyle's, bloated and blinking against the daylight. The rain had stopped. His tongue worried a popcorn husk stuck between his front teeth. He gave his face a rub and bits of popcorn fell from his three-day beard like spring snow from a Fraser fir.

He headed home to floss.

When Rodney arrived Keith was on the floor, at the foot of the AeroBed, his left arm held tight against his torso, his right foot elevated on the air mattress. He looked like a stuntman who had fallen from a great height and just missed his mark.

"I don't know if I should help you up or outline your body in chalk," Rodney said.

Keith was watching TV upside down. "You want to help me out," he said, "outline my body in aerosol cheese."

Rodney didn't say anything. He was thinking of the verb *crash*, how Keith looked to have crashed at his place in every sense of the word.

"I can't eat anything I can't reach," Keith said. "So when you're not here, I go hungry."

"You want breakfast in bed?"

"Not in *this* bed," Keith said. "I don't want *anything* in this bed. I don't want to eat bacon and eggs off Halle Berry in this bed. I slept like this most of the night. On the floor. This fucking air mattress—I kept dreaming I was at sea in a life raft."

"I sleep on it when my parents are in town," Rodney said. "It's not bad." But he knew it was. He'd had the same dreams as Keith. Rodney would hear the hydraulics hissing on a garbage truck and think his life raft had sprung a leak.

It would go like that all night—every five minutes Rodney popping up from his pillow, like a police academy firing-range target, his heart hammering out a John Bonham drum solo.

"I could get you an inflatable woman for your inflatable bed," Rodney said. "If that would help you sleep."

Rodney knew he should have offered Keith his own bed, but he also thought Keith was being a pussy.

"I already got a woman," Keith said. "She's meeting with our priest as we speak." Still flipping channels he said: "You think *he* likes our chances, when only one of us shows up for the marriage class?"

Marriage class. Rodney conjured an image of a college lecture hall full of gowned brides and tuxedoed grooms taking notes. "Marriage," he said. "That's a class you take pass–fail."

"I'm already failing," Keith said. And then, after a short silence, "Do you think we're right for each other?"

"Honestly?" Rodney said. "I like my women with less stubble."

"Caroline and me," Keith said. "I'm serious: what do you think?"

"I think of Ogden Nash," said Rodney, who could still recite from memory from a book of poems he pored over in his grade-school library. "He thought it was a good thing if a couple was incompatible, especially if he has income and she is pattable."

Keith didn't react. He hadn't moved since Rodney came in. He was still lying on his back with his feet on the foot of the AeroBed, his head straining toward the TV, like a sunflower to light. He had stopped surfing, settled on the Game Show Network and was now looking up at a vividly colored rerun.

"You're going to watch this upside down?" Rodney said.

"It's *Hollywood Squares*," Keith said. "The X's and O's are the same upside down."

Listening to the rhythms of a seventies game show—with its sponsored plugs for Rice-A-Roni and Broyhill furniture and "the Spiegel catalog, Chicago, Illinois, 60609"—Rodney was reminded of sick days as a kid. When you're out of work, every day reminds you of sick days as a kid.

On TV, host Peter Marshall said: "In Texas, they call this river the Rio Grande. What do they call it in Mexico?"

Paul Lynde pretended to think before he answered, "Washing machine?"

The studio audience roared.

"You can't say that," Keith said to the set. "You couldn't even say that in 1974. Could you?"

Rodney thought of a Kansas City Royals first baseman of that era. "The back of Pete LaCock's baseball card always said: 'Pete is the nephew of game-show host Peter Marshall.'"

"Pete *LaCock*?" Keith said. "That was the guy's real name? It sounds like Pepe LePew's porn name."

"Pete LaCock," Rodney said. "Real name."

Keith said, "Carnac *that*." He and Rodney often used *Carnac* as a verb.

"LaCock," Rodney said, playing a role his heart wasn't really in today. "What does a Frenchman wash once a week?"

"We're going to Paris on our honeymoon," Keith said. "I tell you that? Unless Father Dave already talked her out of it."

Something in his friend's laugh made Rodney wonder if *this* was Keith's honeymoon—his interlude of bliss before grim reality was rolled out before him like that white runner down the aisle to the altar.

Rodney walked over to Keith and stood above him, like Ali over the vanquished Liston.

"Listen," Rodney said. "I don't have a job. Or a girlfriend. I'm the last person to give anyone advice. But you haven't bathed in two days. You haven't *moved* in two days. Not five minutes ago you asked me to outline you in spray-on cheese so you could eat your way out of your own silhouette . . ."

"And?" Keith said.

"*And*," Rodney said, "you no longer have an apartment. All evidence of your earthly existence is in a U-Haul that has almost certainly been ticketed by now. Soon it will be towed. And soon after *that* the city will be entitled to auction it all off. Though I doubt Sotheby's will be clamoring to catalog your collection of souvenir stadium cups."

"Your point?" Keith said.

"My *point*," Rodney said, "is you have a wonderful fiancée. One who will be massively underachieving when she marries you. You'd be crazy—*crazy*, Keith—to screw this up."

There was a short silence, after which Keith said: "As much as I enjoy this view"—and here Rodney realized he was straddling Keith, who was afforded a mechanic's-eye vista of his undercarriage—"and as much as I appreciate your concern, everything's fine. I talked to Caroline this morning. She's flying out after work on Friday. We're driving to Chicago on Saturday."

"Good," was all Rodney could think to say.

"But thanks," Keith said. "Two days in your apartment, and I already feel like a henpecked husband."

Rodney felt a little embarrassed. It really was none of his business. But still. "You *asked* for my opinion," he told Keith. "Now you're complaining?"

Keith laughed. "I'm sorry," he said. "I must be stealing Caroline's moves. She's always, like, *How's my chicken? What do you think of these wedding invitations? Does this dress flatter me?* Just because someone asks doesn't mean they want the truth."

"So don't tell her."

"I don't," Keith said.

"If the dress doesn't flatter her, *you* do."

"Exactly," Keith said, hoisting himself into a seated position by the elbow of his good arm. "And let me tell you something else about women."

"This'll be good," Rodney said.

"Women are like golf grips," Keith said. "The temptation is to hold 'em too tight. You gotta hold 'em like you're holding a bird. Firm enough that it doesn't slip out of your hand, gentle enough not to crush it. Delicate-like. Let the club do the work."

Keith looked down at the cast on his foot, stuck the antennae of Rodney's cordless phone in through the opening at the toes and began moving it gently back and forth, like the bow of a violin. It produced the elegiac moans of a violin, too.

"Sweet Jesus," Keith said.

But Rodney was thinking about Keith's philosophy of women. As with most of Keith's advice, it worked better as golf tip than romantic counsel. But Rodney took it to heart, made it his new swing thought. He decided to take Mairead somewhere other than Boyle's tomorrow night. He would loosen his grip. It was too soon to introduce her to the family.

From the bedroom, Rodney called Mairead's home number, the only one he had, and felt a small stab in his sternum on hearing her voice, even if it *was* the standard New York paranoiac's outgoing voice mail greeting, stripped of name or any other identifying information, devoid even of intonation—just Mairead saying flatly: "Hi, leave a message."

Rodney had decided to freeball it. But he wasn't prepared for the abrupt beep after the abbreviated greeting. It reminded him of being out to eat, when the waiter asks, "Are you ready to order?" Rodney always said, "Sure," but liked to tell the other person to go first, buying himself time to decide. That other person almost always said something impossibly brief, like "the soup," after which Rodney panicked and ordered something he didn't really want. Which is more or less what happened when Mairead's voice mail beeped.

"Hey, it's Rodney," Rodney said, projecting like a TV anchorman. "Poole." (That was stupid.) "I forgot—you don't know any other Rodneys. But just in case Rodney—I don't know—*Dangerfield* is calling you, you won't mix up the messages." (Good

God. Rodney Dangerfield is dead.) "Of course, Rodney Danger-field is dead, so he'd have to be calling from beyond the grave." (*What?*) "Anyhow. Just checking that we're still on for tomor-row." (Why wouldn't we be? Why am I giving her an out?) "Lis-ten." (*Listen?* She's not a child.) "I thought we might"—and with that Rodney was cut off by another beep.

This beep had only signaled that his time was up. But it sounded to Rodney like the endless beep on an EKG machine, the one that signals that a patient has flatlined.

It hadn't helped that Keith allowed his cell phone to ring in the other room all the while Rodney was trying to leave a message for Mairead. Or not *ring*, exactly. Keith's phone played the guitar riff from "Back in Black," which was appro-priate for a closer sprinting in from the bullpen or a profes-sional wrestler, spandexed and slapping his pecs before vaulting the ropes into the ring. But Keith worked for an insurance company—he entered meetings and departed cubi-cles to AC/DC. Rodney could see Keith, in his oblivious way, raising an index finger to shush his boss in mid-sentence whenever Angus Young played those famous three chords.

And those three chords were playing all the time, at all hours. Rodney wondered if Keith was holding a telethon in the other room, raising money to fight some terrible affliction that was close to his heart. Greasy Dick, perhaps. Or Dry Sack.

"Could you keep the TV down in here?" Rodney asked Keith at five minutes to four. "I have to make a phone call about a possible job."

"Awesome," Keith said. "With who?"

"A bank," Rodney said.

"Which one?"

"Banco Marinero?" Rodney said.

"What's that mean?" Keith said. "Bank with red sauce?"

"Seamen's bank," Rodney said. "I think."

"You're interviewing for a job in a sperm bank?"

"Yes," Rodney said.

"You're in wanking, not banking."

"Good one," Rodney said.

"I'm just giving you a hard time," Keith said.

"It's a real job in the real New York office of a real bank based in Spain," Rodney said. "In other words, it's a *job*. You're the onè who believes so strongly in the edifying qualities of employment."

"I'm happy for you," Keith said. "If that's what you want to do."

"That's what I want to do," Rodney said, by which he meant: Fly to Spain on business. See Real Madrid play Barcelona at the Bernabeu. Have money, have business cards, have an answer for the question: "And what do *you* do for a living?"

"Then I'll keep my fingers crossed," Keith said. "For Banco Primavera."

Giving someone shit, Rodney knew, was a sign of love in Catholic families. And the same held true among Rodney and his friends. But he wished it weren't Keith's default setting, his auto-reply to everything.

Rodney retrieved the cordless phone and said, "Just keep it down in here. I've got to call."

He called from his bedroom. Guy's name was Curt Mayhew. Rodney had been surprised, on receiving the first e-mail from Mayhew to set up this pre-interview interview, that he was American. Rodney was expecting a Javi or a Xabi or a Raul. Every third player in La Liga, the top flight of Spanish soccer, was named Raul.

"Now then," Curt Mayhew said, when his secretary put Rodney through. "How are you, Mr. . . ."

There was a pause, and Rodney thought he heard papers shuffle before Mayhew came up with his name.

". . . Poole?"

"Yes sir."

"Now then," Mayhew repeated, buying himself time. "Before we begin, I want to have an open kimono here."

Rodney tried without success to stifle the visual before Mayhew went on: "As you know, our industry has undergone—is still undergoing—comprehensive consolidation. We could be acquired tomorrow, we could be acquired next year. Right now we're kissing frogs, but so far no princes."

Rodney wondered what the penalty was for kissing frogs with an open kimono, but Mayhew was still talking: "If we *do* find a prince going forward, then whoever fills this position could get RIFed by our new parent company. Just so we're open kimono."

"Okay," Rodney replied, wondering if O.K. was an acronym for Open Kimono.

"We don't expect that to happen, mind you," Mayhew said. "We wouldn't be doing this pre-interview if we weren't serious about hiring someone who can grow along with BM."

Rodney winced at the abbreviation.

Mayhew abruptly asked Rodney to hold, and when he came back a minute later he apologized. "It's crazy around here," he said. "I'm drinking out of a fire hose." Mayhew sighed. "Now then," he said, "where did we leave off?"

Rodney didn't answer. He was silently devising a Curt Mayhew drinking game, mentally shotgunning a beer every time the interviewer uttered his favorite oxymoron: "Now then . . ."

"Any experience over and above what you listed in your

profile?" Mayhew asked. "Anything above and beyond what I have on your résumé?"

To Rodney, each new redundancy was like a plucked hair. And Mayhew would be working above him—in Mayhew-speak, *over* and above him, above and *beyond* him—until Rodney was RIFed in the next round of layoffs, the next *reduction in force*, six months or six years or sixteen years down the line.

No matter. Rodney felt a sudden stab of longing for the position, wanted that business card with its gilded *BM*. It had been months since Rodney's ears had been violated by these business banalities. And yet as Mayhew yammered on, his manner of speaking became oddly musical to Rodney's ears, a jazz solo of cubicle slang, an extended riff on RIFs.

"Right," Mayhew said after five minutes during which Rodney scarcely spoke. "The folks in Human Capital will want to three-sixty your résumé, and if we decide to take a deeper dive and have you come in for an on-site—well, then . . . we'll give you a call."

Lord how Rodney wanted that on-site. He needed the job. That much Rodney knew. And not only because his savings were getting sucked up the Smoke-Eater at Boyle's. Mayhew had said to Rodney, just a minute ago, "What are your career goals going forward?" And Rodney, even while bristling at the buzz phrase, thought, that *was* his goal: going forward.

Boyle's was dead on Monday nights and Edith had the run of the place. She was under the bar. The only one there, so far. But it was early. Rodney thought a booth would be better for Keith's foot, but Keith was headed for two open stools. The stools, as it happened, were next to two young women wearing the kind of eyeglasses a librarian removes in old movies, along with her hair clip, to reveal herself as a sexpot. Except that all these young New York businesswomen—they *were* sexpots, dressed as librarians.

He couldn't deny it. They turned Rodney on, those young-professional-chick glasses that always called attention to themselves. Spectacles: that was the perfect word for them.

Before Rodney could help Keith onto his stool, Armen said, "There they are! Tango and Cash!" Rodney had no idea what this was supposed to mean, beyond the undeniable declarative fact of their presence.

"Here we are," Rodney replied.

"Can I be Tango?" Keith said.

Rodney helped Keith onto a stool, then took his own adjacent to a Sexy Librarian, whose body language shifted subtly, a ten-degree turn away that Rodney only picked up on from hard-won experience.

Keith had the Triple Crown of attraction going for him. He had the crutches, the cast, *and* the sling. Throw in the fiancée and he had hit for the cycle. Rodney *knew* Keith would be hitting it off with one or both of the Sexy Librarians. All he was missing, Rodney thought, was a dog, an oversight easily corrected when Edith toddled over, her tag jingling like the bells on a Budweiser Clydesdale in a Christmas commercial.

"What's up with Edith?" Rodney asked Armen. "She looks like Keith after his office Christmas party."

"She just had surgery," Armen said.

Edith was wearing an Elizabethan collar to prevent her from biting her stitches. It looked like an upside-down lampshade.

"*Awwwwww*," moaned a Librarian, her lower lip curling in a pout, when Edith made her way to Keith's stool. "You poor thing."

Keith fairly blushed and said, "It's no biggie." There was a big intake of breath, drawing him a little straighter on the stool, and he added: "Just a separated shoulder."

Rodney turned to the pouting Librarian and said, "Please tell me you were talking about the dog."

"I was," she said.

She had a terrifying pterodactyl-wing collar over her lapels and something about it called to mind the Flying Nun, which only made her more alluring to Rodney. The Nun Librarian.

Rodney had a nun librarian in grade school. Sister Roseanne. They called her Sister Roseanne Roseannadanna, a nickname passed down over the years and still active long after her inspiration on *Saturday Night Live* left the airwaves and nobody knew what it meant anymore.

This chick looked nothing like Sister Roseanne Roseannadanna.

"But your friend," she said. "He *does* look pretty pathetic." Seeing Keith's reaction, she said, "No offense." And then: "What happened?"

"Skiing accident," Keith said. "In Gstaad."

"In August?" asked the Librarian.

"No, in Gstaad," Keith said. He pronounced it as pretentiously as possible. *Shtod*.

"He fell off a barstool," Rodney said. "He just likes saying, 'Gstaad.'"

"Shhhhtaaaaahhhhd," Keith said imbecilically.

"It's impossible to say the name of a ski resort without sounding ridiculous," Rodney told the Librarian, by way of apology. "Notice that? Gstaad. *Banff*."

"I've been to Banff," she said.

"Why does it have so many *f*s?" Rodney said.

"I don't know," said the Librarian.

"Nothing rhymes with Banff," Rodney said, talking the jumper away from the ledge. "It's like orange. Or pilgrim. Or silver. That's why there are so few good songs about Banff."

The Librarian didn't say anything, so Rodney said, "Or oranges or pilgrims or silver."

She smiled at Rodney, but it was a smile of incomprehension. Mairead, Rodney thought, would be returning all his serves, hitting winners down the lines, running him ragged on the baseline. But Rodney was enjoying this practice session: hitting a ball against a wall.

Keith, who had procured two pints from Armen, set one in front of Rodney and, seizing his opening, said to the Librarians, "Can I get you ladies anything?"

There was, at that moment, not a man in New York less threatening than Keith, and still Rodney was surprised when the Sexy Nun Librarian said, "I'll take a Tanqueray and tonic."

The other Librarian hadn't spoken yet. They were like Penn and Teller, these two. Rodney usually attracted the mute Tellers, but here he was staring at a chatty Penn. And she was staring back.

Rodney wanted to keep the conversation going. He was, in Keith's vernacular, working on his grip. He was on the driving range, preparing for Mairead tomorrow night. Or so he told himself.

But Rodney couldn't ignore the filament of necklace this woman wore, from which a small pendant hung, dotting the *i* of her cleavage.

"I'm Rodney," Rodney said.

"Karen," said the Librarian. "And this is my friend Ann."

"Keith," said Keith. "And that's Edith."

"Doesn't she look like the dog in those old RCA ads?"

Rodney asked. "Like she just got her head stuck inside the Victrola?"

Karen gave another smile of incomprehension. Her eyes were slick, like freshly Zambonied ice, and gin and tonic was beaded on her downy upper lip.

Rodney looked at that beaded lip and thought of the word *dewy*, somehow charged with eroticism, and from there he was thinking—he simply couldn't help it—of the Dewey Decimal System. Of erotically charged library science.

"I like your glasses," Rodney said.

"These?" said Karen.

Dorothy Parker was full of shit.

"Those."

Men made passes at girls who wore glasses. Men made passes at girls who wore neck braces, cockeyed wigs, prescription psoriasis creams—sometimes all of those things at once. Rodney had witnessed it in Boyle's.

Keith was talking to the other one—Teller—and ordered another round for all of them.

Armen set down a third round of drinks. By the fourth round, he seemed pleased to see Rodney still talking to the same woman. Either that, or he had something stuck in his eye. Rodney couldn't really tell. He was making hand signals that meant nothing to Rodney. For a moment, Rodney felt a panic familiar from childhood, when he would look at his Little League third-base coach tugging his cap and brushing his chest and wonder if that meant steal or stay.

By the time Armen brought the fifth round, he was clearly eager to help Rodney's cause.

Armen said: "This guy tell you what he did Saturday night?"

Karen said no.

"Some guy ambushes *him*"—Armen hooked a thumb at

Keith—"and Rodney here pulls the clown out of the men's room, *carries* him through the bar, and tosses him out on the curb like a bag of garbage. Which is what he was."

Karen swiveled her stool to look Rodney in the eyes. Their knees touched accidentally.

"You did that?" she said.

Armen answered for him. "Like Fred Flintstone puttin' out the cat. Place went apeshit."

Rodney returned Karen's gaze and wondered if the glasses were even prescription.

Their knees were still touching.

"Problem is, the cat comes back later and puts *Fred* out," Keith said.

"The cat on *The Flintstones*," said Armen. "But that other pussy, he's not coming back."

Karen's body was still turned toward Rodney's and she swiveled idly on her stool. Back and forth, ever so slightly, just enough to set her pendant in motion, a pachinko ball that flitted, then settled above the center channel of her cleavage. The swinging pendant put Rodney in a trance, like a hypnotist's charm or the gong in a grandfather clock.

"I like your glasses," Rodney said, forcing himself to make eye contact.

"You said that already. Guys in bars usually say they like my eyes."

"I like your eyes," Rodney said.

"Thank you," she said, as if the compliment had come unbidden.

Rodney said: "Ever heard of Ogden Nash?"

Keith, eavesdropping, sighed and said: "For the love of Christ."

Karen shook her head no. "Does that make me stupid or something?"

"Course not," said Rodney, who was having to remind himself that she was not an actual librarian. "He was a poet. He wrote, 'A girl who is bespectacled, she may not get her nectacled.'"

"Her what?"

"Her nectacled."

"What does that mean?" said Karen.

"Nectacled," Rodney said. "A girl who is bespectacled, she may not get her neck tickled."

"Oh," Karen said.

Rodney polished off his pint. Foam rings inside the Guinness glass marked his progress, like water marks left when a flood recedes.

Karen looked down at her glass, rearranged her ice cubes with a swizzle straw, looked Rodney in the eye, smiled. Then she leaned forward, put her mouth to Rodney's ear and whispered: "So I'm not going to get my neck tickled?"

"I didn't say that," said Rodney, who wanted to paraphrase another Nash poem to her: *She who attempts to tease the cobra / Is soon a sadder she, and sobra.*

Her shampoo smelled of peaches, her breath of distilled spirits. Rodney imagined making out with a bottle of schnapps, something he'd seen Wanamaker do on more than one occasion.

The bottle of Frangelico stared down in judgment from the stereo speaker.

Distilled spirits. That's what he had felt on his date with Mairead—her spirit, boiled to its essence and ingested in a single shot. The effect was instant and intoxicating. Tomorrow, he knew, that same spirit might make him feel like shit. But only metaphorically. For here was the thing about Rodney: He didn't get hung over. The lines marking the outgoing tides on his pint glass were not, for him, descending circles of

Dante's Hell, but their opposite. The more he drank, the more lucid he became. The more enlightened.

He felt pleasantly drunk, in the way that drunkenness was described by his friends and in novels. And his liver could not possibly be impervious to the physical ravages of alcohol. That much he knew. Beer rounded off and sanded down the corners of his mind—it took the edge off, as they say. But it also *sharpened* his mind, a paradox he didn't fully understand.

It was something he wouldn't have thought possible if he hadn't read about similar people in a scholarly book he'd found at the Strand. It now sat on his bookshelf, dog-eared and yellow-highlightered. The first time Rodney read *Dublin Pub Life & Lore: An Oral History*, he experienced a shock of recognition. The author, a social historian named Kevin C. Kearns, quoted an article by John D. Sheridan—they all had middle initials, so it all had to be legit—from a 1952 issue of something called *Irish Licensing World*:

> The man behind the bar knows the pintman when he sees one. It is not a matter of dress, or age, or social status; it is a sort of spiritual look. The pintman takes up the tumbler with ritualistic care. Nothing can touch him then. The clock ticks for you and me, but the pintman is on an island in time. He is no longer old or young, rich or poor, married or single. He is beyond the numbing grip of circumstance—a devotee at a solemn rite, a poet with an unfrenzied eye, a man with a pint. There is a restful, mesmeric quality about the whole business.

Rodney gulped down the last of his Guinness, leaving just two rings, and settled the check with Armen.

He wasn't cheating on Mairead. You couldn't cheat on

someone you'd sat at a table with one time. If anything, Rodney was cheating on *Keith*, unfaithful to a friend who'd have trouble getting a cab, much less hobbling home, without him.

He didn't mind cheating on Keith.

Rodney left while Keith was in the can. Armen would fill him in.

A moment later, Karen told Teller she was going home. Teller looked back in silent reproach, like the bottle of Frangelico.

Rodney hailed a cab and pushed Karen into it like a perp into a cop car.

In the backseat, there was a brief silence—a game of your-place-or-my-place chicken—before Karen caved and said, "Eighty-fourth and Amsterdam."

They rode uptown with their inside ankles crossed over one another's, both pretending not to notice. They said nothing, and when the cab disgorged them at the corner, Karen pulled out her keys, pointed them at the nearest apartment building, and walked straight toward the lock, as if taking a field sobriety test.

She put the key in and turned. Nothing. She jiggled it, as if trying to get a recalcitrant toilet to stop running. Still nothing. Rodney was reminded of *The New Hollywood Squares*, which gave contestants a car key that would start only one of the three vehicles on the set. Karen, evidently, had chosen the wrong car. Or the wrong building. "Oh my God," she said, looking up and laughing. "This isn't me." They were on Eighty-*fifth* at Amsterdam, which is why Rodney always made a point of enunciating like Sidney Poitier when giving his destination in a taxi.

They walked around the block to 84th. This time Karen's key worked. A piece of paper taped to the elevator said TEM-

PORARILY OUT OF ORDER. "Sorry," she said, "I'm on six." Rodney followed her up the stairs, his eyes level with the double vent of her suit jacket. It covered her rear end like a stage curtain waiting to be raised.

Rodney vaguely remembered a Monty Python sketch in which a milkman follows a seductress up the stairs to her room. She opens the door, lets him go in first, then locks the door behind him, while she remains in the hall. The milkman looks around the room to see a dozen dead milkmen in various stages of decomposition.

They continued to climb. Christ. Rodney never thought of sex as a conquest until now. This was a conquest, all right. The conquest of Everest.

"Karen," he said, pausing on a landing. It took a conscious effort to call her Karen, not Hillary: Sir Edmund Hillary. "I need to be short-roped by Sherpas the rest of the way."

"Almost there," Karen said, parceling the phrase out in two separate exhalations.

Rodney didn't realize he was going home with Rapunzel. Rapunzel on Rumplemintz, to judge by the way she was clutching the handrail, as if on a lurching ship at sea.

When they reached her door, Karen and Rodney were both flushed from the climb, and panting. "Was it good for you?" Rodney wanted to say as Karen put the key in the lock. There was a bead of sweat on her face, just the one, rappelling down from her forehead. Like when the beer breaches the brim of the glass. The perfectly poured pint in a commercial.

Her apartment had everything that Rodney's did not: plants and lilac-scented candles and a tragic spice rack, aspiring to domesticity, that tried very hard to pretend this was a real kitchen, and not something closer to an airplane galley, a place to tray the meals.

That spice rack—with its heartbreaking hopes and dreams—reminded Rodney of the water-skiing squirrels at the end of the local news.

Rodney picked up a throw pillow and sat on the couch, then put the pillow on his lap like a trumpet mute. Or a figleaf. It was funny how modest people became in these circumstances. How polite.

"Care for some water?" Karen said from the kitchen.

"Yes," Rodney said. "Please." His mouth was sub-Saharan.

She set a bottle of Poland Spring on the coffee table and curled up next to Rodney like a cat. Even in the lurid light of the stairwell she had looked hot. But she didn't *feel* hot. That's what she told Rodney on the couch, as if responding to his thoughts: "I don't feel so hot." Disingenuous supermodels often said the same thing on TV: "I don't *feel* pretty."

"Rapunzel, Rapunzel, let down your hair," Rodney said. She had one of those shark-toothed clips, like a bear trap, holding it back. That was part of the sexy librarian thing. They were always removing the chopstick that held the 'do in a bun.

But she didn't let her hair down. She just put her head on the pillow that was on Rodney's lap and moaned: "Can I get a backrub?"

"Can I get a frontrub?"

He didn't say that. He didn't say anything. Karen reached for an oversized purse on the coffee table and took out her eyeglass case. She removed her glasses and folded their arms, one over the other, the way Jeannie folded her arms before granting a wish on *I Dream of Jeannie*. Rodney was thinking of wish fulfillment when Karen repeated her inner self-loathing—"I don't feel so hot"—and comprehensively puked in her handbag.

Rodney shot off the couch, as if he'd spilled a drink. She

must have thought he was bolting for the door because she said, "I should give you my number." Her face was still buried in the handbag, as if searching for something on *Let's Make a Deal*.

Rodney made a gallant show of frisking himself for a pen before Karen, jackknifed on the couch, roaring again like the MGM lion, said maybe it was best if he just left.

5

Shame woke Rodney at 4:30, wanting company. Shame had been up all night, working late, multitasking. Shame—a noun, a verb, an admonition—made the most of its meager gifts. Rodney respected it but he also resented it. Shame had no right to wake him at this ungodly hour. And the hour *was* ungodly. Out his window, Rodney heard a bottle break, a woman's aria of Spanish cursing, the distant *whoop-whoop-whoop* of sirens.

He had cheated on a wife he didn't have with a mistress he never touched. Where was the shame in that? But that was the genius of shame. It crashed the gate, greased the bouncer, always got in, even where it didn't belong.

A few years ago, Rodney was watching TV with Rachel, his girlfriend at the time—the only serious girlfriend he'd ever had—when the cable news resumed its relentless reportage about a California fertilizer salesman who had murdered his wife. The guy, it turned out, had been cheating on her, inventing elaborate lies to tell both wife and mistress while shuttling back and forth between the two, neither of whom knew of the other's existence.

"I'm incapable of cheating," Rodney told Rachel, "if for no other reason than it looks exhausting."

Rachel turned to look Rodney in the eye and said, "So the only thing that's keeping us together is the one thing that could tear us apart: *Your laziness*?"

In the dark now, Rodney had to concede that he was *capable* of cheating. And the thought brought him more shame.

He lay awake until the hours turned godly. Just before eight, he sneaked past Keith's recumbent form and went to weekday Mass at St. Brendan's, just to top up the tank.

In kneeling, he lowered the age of the congregation by two decades.

The first reading was from Corinthians. Rodney had begun to doze and dream of the rich Corinthian leather that Mr. Rourke from *Fantasy Island* pushed in the old Chrysler Cordoba commercials when something the priest said nearly stopped his heart: "Wake from this drunken fit."

Rodney opened his eyes, expecting to see Father Maniago standing over him. But he was still in the pulpit, still reading from Corinthians: "Wake from this drunken fit. Live righteous lives, and cease to sin; for some have no knowledge of God: I speak thus in order to move you to shame."

Shame again. Shame had followed him here, had bum-rushed the octogenarians rubbing their rosary beads. You had to hand it to shame. It knew no shame.

Rodney was dozing again by the time the offertory rolled around. An elderly, blue-blazered usher extended the long-handled collection basket toward Rodney and nudged him in the ribs like a beat cop rousting a drunk with his night-stick.

Rodney woke with a judder, pulled a wadded bill from the

kangaroo pocket of his hoodie—a five; he didn't have anything smaller—and dropped it into the felt-lined basket.

Then he reached in and removed four singles.

The usher shook his head in dismay and Rodney felt himself flush. He had just dragged himself from bed and put a dollar in the coffers at St. Brendan's and somehow *that* brought a visit from shame? Shame, he thought, you are shameless.

On the bright side, for the first time in years, there were now people willing to touch Rodney with a ten-foot pole. The usher—literally and undeniably—had done just that. Rapunzel, too. And maybe even Mairead.

Mairead, Mairead. From a park bench, paper on his lap, Rodney called the work number he had for Mairead, prepared to leave a voice mail, when an unfamiliar voice picked up: "Mairead Quinn's line."

"Is Ms. Quinn in?"

"Who may I say is calling?"

"Rodney Poole."

"May I tell her what this is regarding, Mr. Toole?"

Rodney thought for a beat and said, "E-Cola."

"One moment, Mr. Toole."

After a short interval of silence, he heard her voice: "This is Mairead Quinn."

"Hi, it's Rodney. *Poole.*"

She started laughing and Rodney came to life.

"Or as your assistant calls me, Mr. Toole."

Mairead laughed. "I'm sorry. I had no idea what she was talking about. She said Mr. Toole was calling from Ricola."

"Rod Toole," Rodney said in a TV voice-over voice. "Adult

film star. For Ricola herbal candies." Then he yodeled the theme: "*REEEEE*-ko-laaaaah."

Mairead laughed. Rodney was about to begin babbling again, but forced himself to hold for the laughter, like a comedian or stage actor.

"I like Rod Toole," Mairead said. "It's a little redundant. But I had a date once with a guy named Logan Kennedy."

"Let me guess," Rodney said. "The relationship didn't take off."

Silence.

"I went to the prom with a girl named Heathrow LaGuardia," Rodney said. "Did I tell you that?" When Mairead didn't respond, he said: "Hello?"

"Are you finished?" she said.

"Yes."

"Can I tell *my* airport joke now?" Mairead said. "Only it's not a joke. This really happened to me. I was snowed in at O'Hare last year, and I'm standing in front of a sign that says, 'Welcome to Chicago, Richard M. Daley, Mayor.' And this guy from India looks at me looking at the sign and he says: 'It should say, 'Richard M. *Delay*.'"

Rodney laughed.

"Totally deadpan," Mairead said. "With an Indian accent. Then he walked away. It was perfect. A perfect moment between strangers."

I should walk away now, Rodney thought, while the moment is perfect. And we're still strangers.

They met at an upscale brick-oven pizza joint, a suitable halfway house between the blue-lit clientele of Rococo and the blue, lit clientele of Boyle's.

Rodney arrived first and took a seat at the bar. When Mairead walked in, wearing jeans and a stretchy black shirt with spaghetti straps, he stood and wiped his palms on his pants. Then he leaned in to kiss her cheek while she extended her hand for a shake. The result was a ridiculous hybrid of handshake and hug: the shug. They looked like once-warring rappers declaring a ceasefire.

"Wow," Mairead said. "If only we could bottle that awkwardness." But she was smiling.

Rodney knew he was screwed when he committed to the kiss after disembarking the stool. And he told her so.

"Do you *dis*embark something or *de*bark it?" Mairead said. "I've never figured that out."

"You debark a tree," Rodney said. "You can debark Lassie with a muzzle."

"Flight attendants say, 'Deplane,'" Mairead said. "But that makes you sound like Tattoo from *Fantasy Island*."

Their small talk was all about language because it was the one interest they knew they shared. It's why they'd been set up in the first place. "She likes the same things you do," Caroline had said, in a slightly patronizing way, by which she must have meant words. And so Rodney resolved to beat that particular piñata until every last piece of candy had fallen from it. In case wordplay was foreplay.

"Flight attendants say a lot of strange things," Rodney said. "They use a lot of extraneous *do*s. You notice that? We *do* request. We *do* apologize. We *do* thank you for flying with us today."

"We *do* hope you'll choose American Airlines if your future plans call for air travel," Mairead said. "I want to shake them and say '*All* plans are *future* plans.' But I'd be arrested by federal marshals."

"It's all hot air," Rodney said, warming to the subject. "Like the recirculated beer farts they pass off as oxygen. 'This will serve as your *last and final* boarding call.' 'Return your *tray table* to its *original, stowed, upright and locked* position.' 'Welcome to Dallas—the *correct local time* is 6:30.' Have you ever stopped someone on the street and asked for the *in*correct time in some distant land? *Correct local time* is the only time I require."

"I like how the seat belt sign is always *illuminated*, never lit," Mairead said. "Like they're prison-educated, trying to use the longest possible word for everything."

"I *do* hope our future plans call for eating," Rodney said. "Because I'm about to pass out."

She had a dimple in her chin that put Rodney happily in mind of a golf ball, her face all latent energy, resting on the tee of her swan's neck.

He recalled Keith's advice. Loosen the grip. Let the club do the work.

"Caroline tell you I have a roommate?" he said.

"She did. How's that going?"

"Great," Rodney said. "Fine, anyway. Part of me won't mind seeing him go."

"Which part?"

Rodney said: "My nose." This morning, Keith took a dump with the door open. But he couldn't tell her that. "His cast," he said. "It smells like a dead cat."

"You dropped a TV on his foot," Mairead said. "The least you can do is give him a sponge bath."

Rodney was preparing a riposte when the hostess announced, "Toole, party of two. Your table's ready."

Mairead fought off her own smile and said, "You told her to say that."

———

Rodney ate pizza but thought about spaghetti, Mairead's spaghetti-strapped shoulders, which she shrugged when Rodney asked her how she liked her job. "It's fine for now," she said. "I don't want to do it forever. How did you like *your* job?"

"It wasn't the worst job I ever had," Rodney said.

"What *was*?" Mairead asked.

Where to begin? When he was sixteen, Rodney said, his father urged him to take a job in a Jolly Elf convenience store: "And by *urged* I mean *forced*." It was one of the most dangerous jobs in America, late-night convenience clerk, and certainly one of the more dangerous in suburban Minneapolis, where there was little call for smoke jumpers or Bering Sea crab fishermen.

Rodney was issued a red smock: short-sleeved and unmistakably game-worn—spumoni-spangled by its previous inhabitant, for they scooped ice cream there. "Rocky Road as dense as Carrera marble," Rodney said. "That summer—and that summer only—I had forearms like Popeye's."

"Just think," Mairead said. "That same summer, kids were calling *me* Olive Oyl."

In the beginning, Rodney worked days. At hourly intervals, the manager—a mustachioed bald man who looked like Super Mario on a three-day bender—told him to "front the milk." Rodney had never heard *front* as a verb before and was afraid to betray his ignorance of convenience store patois by asking him what it meant.

"This was long before *front* became hip-hop slang for *lie*," he told Mairead. That usage, Rodney was sure, was just now reaching his childhood subdivision, like the light from a distant star.

"After a week or so," Rodney said, "I finally guessed the meaning of *front*. I was supposed to keep the oldest milk pushed to the front of the dairy case."

"I didn't know there was a name for that," Mairead said. "I front all the time. I front the underwear in my drawer after I do the laundry. I front the plates in my kitchen cabinets after I do the dishes."

Rodney felt his armpits burst into flames when Mairead said "underwear," but he forged ahead as if he'd scarcely noticed. "It's basically the FIFO principle—First In, First Out—I had just learned about in my high school accounting class," Rodney said. He didn't share that double-entry analogy with his coworkers, who would have replied with a Purple Nurple or a Hertz Donut or any of the manifold other tortures practiced by the teenage Torquemadas of his day— and still talked about by Keith, the Sun Tzu of seventh-grade warcraft.

And then one day Rodney didn't *have* coworkers. Rodney was working nights, by himself, locking up when the store closed at midnight. "When there were no customers," Rodney said, "I'd go sit in the stockroom." He could see, vividly, the stockroom's single club chair. By which he meant à chair made of *Club* and *Oui* and other down-market nudie magazines.

The magazines came shrink-wrapped in bundles that were stacked on a shipping pallet. "You've heard of an educated palate?" Rodney said. "This was an uneducated pallet, a pallet of epic ignorance, a pallet—quite possibly—with a criminal background."

It was the only place to sit in the stockroom, this Pallet of Pornography, whose opaque bundles—obstinately unbrowsable in their cellophane seal—looked like enormous ice cubes.

"I thought they all came in their own little plastic bags," said Mairead. "That's how they are at the airport, anyway."

"This was before that," Rodney said. "The manager was

the only one allowed to stock them. He put them on these shelves that demurely hid all but their title behind a little wall, like a dressing room screen."

"Like the showers on *MASH*," Mairead said.

"Exactly. I don't remember ever selling a single issue of any of them, but every month they were thumbed into pulp by the customers, believe me."

Rodney could still see those customers, standing at the newsstand as if it were the Bodleian Library at Oxford.

"But mostly the customers smoked," Rodney said. Behind the counter, above the register, an infinite variety of cigarettes were racked. Rodney didn't smoke then. "When customers asked for Marlboros," he said, "I'd put Marlboros on the counter." And invariably they'd say, "Hard pack, not soft pack." Or "The One Hundreds!" Or "The menthols!" Or "The filtered ones!" Or "The unfiltered ones!" or "The Lights!" Every adjective set him off on a new search while the customer sighed theatrically and trembled in a trough of nicotine withdrawal.

It was almost impossible to handle cigarettes all day and not want to try them, and so one day Rodney put a Marlboro hard pack in his backpack and smoked one at home, in the garage with the door closed and the window open.

"When the customers would leave," Rodney told Mairead, "I'd try to estimate their height against the measuring tape on the door frame, just to pass the time."

"Those send a lovely message," Mairead said. "They tell customers: You're not always right. You're always a suspect."

"And well they should be," Rodney said. "Half the customers were shoplifting. They'd walk in healthy and walk out with a frozen pizza-shaped goiter under their sweatshirt." Many of them were Rodney's high school friends, waving to him on their way out.

"Or they'd come in drunk and drive away with a twelve-pack," Rodney said. It was only three-two beer, but that plus a three-pack of Skol was a drunk-driving starter kit. DIY DUI.

Mairead said, "Did you call the police, I hope?"

"Only once," Rodney said. "Out of spite, not any sense of civic duty."

"What do you mean?"

"This shirtless guy threw down eight or nine items and I asked him if he wanted a bag. And he looked at me and said, 'No, I'll *juggle* it out the door.'"

Mairead laughed and so did Rodney, who said: "It wasn't funny at the time." At the time, as an abstemious teenager, it offended his moral sensibility.

"I told him, 'You're drunk and I'm calling the cops.' Then I picked up the phone."

"What did he do?"

"He ran out the door with half his items in his hand and jumped in his car. He probably dived through the open window, like Luke Duke. Then he laid a patch in the parking lot. And I called the cops."

Eighteen years later, Rodney could still recall the scene vividly. He returned to the stockroom, settled onto his throne of ice cubes—Jor-El on Krypton—and brooded. About a job in which drunks insulted him, friends mocked him, management smocked him, shoplifters defied him, all while he stood impotent, watching.

He was sitting on sealed bundles of naked women, as if trying to get them to hatch, as if trying to accelerate their arrival, to will them into his existence. He had a pack of butts in his backpack—Marlboros, red box, hard pack, by far the most popular. And that night, after biking home at 1 a.m., he drank a can of his father's beer from the basement fridge.

And then he went to his room and listened to Dexys

Midnight Runners singing "Tell Me When My Light Turns Green" and he lay awake and wondered when—*if*—that would ever happen. In English class that fall he had to read *The Great Gatsby* and he underlined in blue Bic: "Gatsby believed in the green light, the orgiastic future that year by year recedes before us."

And eighteen years later, though he'd kicked the cigarettes, he was still drinking beer and finding portent in lyrics and lines from novels. And he was still trying to hatch a naked woman and wondering when, exactly, his light was going to turn green.

There was one slice of pizza on the tray, a wedge of orange surrounded by silver that reminded Rodney of a *USA Today* pie chart on some hopelessly lopsided issue, with orange representing, say, the percentage of Americans who'd read a book in the last year or could name the vice president.

Mairead insisted they get the slice boxed up so Rodney could take it home to Keith, a clear suggestion, Rodney thought, that he was meant to be going home now.

They walked outside into a gorgeous evening that Rodney didn't want to end.

"Nightcap?" he said.

"No thanks," Mairead said. "I don't wear them."

"*Airplane*," Rodney said, impressed.

They walked a block. Ahead of them on the sidewalk a homeless guy was shaking his change cup like a maraca: "Help a brother out?"

Rodney said, "Want a slice of pizza?"

"What kind?"

"Sausage and green pepper."

Before he took it, the guy lifted the lid on the box and

peered inside, as if checking under the hood of a used car. When they had passed him, Mairead smiled and said, "What a saint you are, giving cold pizza to the hungry."

"It's not that," Rodney said. "I just couldn't bear the thought of Keith eating it."

They approached a bar Rodney had never been in, mainly because it was called Bar None, and he gave it another shot: "Nightcap?"

Mairead exhaled and said, "A quick one. But then I really do need to get home."

"Of course."

The room was dark, not crowded, and Coltrane's *Soultrane* was playing low. They sat at the bar and ordered drinks. It was the kind of place where couples canoodled, Rodney thought, though he wasn't certain what canoodling consisted of, beyond the fact that celebrities were always doing it in the pages of the *Post*.

"Ever canoodled?" Rodney said.

"Not on a second date," said Mairead.

"I don't even know what it means," said Rodney, afraid he'd made some unwitting advance. "It sounds like the name of a canned noodle product. Canoodle brand canned noodles, from Chef Boyardee."

"You should go into marketing," Mairead said. "Between Canoodles and E-Cola, you're a natural."

"Why did *you* go into marketing?" Rodney asked.

"I don't know," Mairead said. "I liked to watch TV. I memorized the commercials. My mom said. 'You like all these jingles, you should go into advertising.'" Mairead laughed. "It probably started there."

She said her mother was always trying to convert her only daughter's childhood interests into reliable, and reliably boring, career ambitions. "So she'd say, 'You like to read, you should be a lawyer' or 'You like to draw, you should be an architect,'" Mairead said. "It never occurred to her that I should be an editor or an artist. It never occurred to me, for that matter. Michelangelo would have been a housepainter if he'd grown up in our house."

For the next hour, Mairead talked about her family. About her three older brothers who had forced her college boyfriend into indentured servitude, making him mow the lawn and take out the garbage whenever he came over. "They called him Schneider," she said, "after the super on *One Day at a Time*. My brother John got him a tool belt for Christmas."

She talked about her father, who died of stomach cancer when she was twelve, and of the classmates who came to the wake, some still in Little League and Girl Scout uniforms on their way home from somewhere else, and about how—in hindsight—she had enjoyed that attention, and still felt guilty about having done so.

"To this day I can't abide people who say they won't let cancer *beat* them," Mairead said. "As if it's a matter of will and my dad was a weakling." In fact, she said, he built houses with his bare hands: "Literally built them. He was a general contractor, but he loved to help out with the framing and dry-walling and shingling. He built our house. If there was an NRA for nail gun enthusiasts, he would have been its Charlton Heston."

A second round of drinks came and she talked about losing herself in the library as a teenager, happily disoriented among stacks that looked like ladders—unscalable ones—to a girl who dreamed of distant places. Even now, she said, whenever she found herself in the financial district, swallowed by its concrete canyons, she felt like she was back in her local library, dwarfed by the stacks.

As she talked, Rodney stole glances at her spaghetti straps

and thought of her underwear fronted in its drawer and still felt a tingling on his arm where she'd touched it for a second, ages ago, while he'd pretended not to notice.

After a third round of drinks, she said, "I should get going," and they left Bar None and walked toward the corner to hail a cab. At mid-block, she put her hand in his and said, "I had a nice time tonight."

They kissed under a second-story air conditioner whose white noise sounded to Rodney like applause.

At the corner, they kissed again, at the stoplight. A taxi appeared, unhailed, and idled impatiently at the curb. They laughed and Mairead got inside. Rodney could walk home from here.

Trouble was, the light was red. If Rodney were to walk away casually, as he wanted to do, he'd have to go in the opposite direction of his apartment. So instead he stood there, next to the idling taxi, Mairead in back, and tried not to look at her for fear it would break the spell.

"This is awkward," Mairead said out the window, and Rodney laughed.

And then the light turned green, all the lights turned green, as far as he could see up Amsterdam Avenue.

6

Rodney couldn't sleep. There was still a tight circle of feeling where her fingertip had touched him on the arm—like a cigarette burn, but pleasant—and what Mairead had said about the safety of her career choice was also loitering in his thoughts.

On his nightstand was a thousand-page biography of Dickens. Rodney liked to say he was working his way through the life of Dickens at roughly the same pace Dickens had worked his way through the life of Dickens, and he was scarcely exaggerating. He bought the book at the Strand five years ago and was still on page 361. Rodney hoped Dickens would die before he did, and he looked forward to the day when he could send the finished book windmilling across the room in triumph. A pyrrhic triumph, he realized, for he had long since ceased to enjoy the tome, and read on out of a grim duty to finish what he'd started.

He kept every book he ever read. Until there were just too many, he had them all out on shelves, their spines displayed as trophies, like the taxidermied heads of big game he had bagged.

On a dare at Boyle's one night, he vowed to read his way

through the entire library of Penguin Classics, alphabetically by author—1,082 paperback volumes from Austen to Zola. But he never made it past the first writer, who turned out not to be Austen but someone named Edwin A. Abbott, author of *Flatlands*, a two-volume novel about geometry. It was about as interesting—and made as much sense as—a geometric equation about literature. So he abandoned the pursuit.

It was a failing, he told Armen, more architectural than intellectual: collectively, the Penguin Classics weighed seven hundred pounds, and his bookshelves—supported by brackets and braces—were affixed to a non-load-bearing wall.

But the fact remained: he loved words—reading and writing. He loved reading about writers, often more than he liked reading the writers' own works. Take Balzac. (It sounds like the slogan for some new pharmaceutical, Rodney thought, perhaps a campaign Mairead was working on.) Or Proust, who wrote, self-imprisoned, in a room soundproofed with cork. Rodney had the solitude but lacked the fortitude for such a life. Proust sent messengers out for the telling details in *Remembrance of Things Past*, the way Rodney sent out for General Tso's Chicken. Such an arrangement held an enormous appeal for Rodney, who saw himself tipping a Chinese delivery man who brought him vivid descriptions of the setting sun.

By junior high, when Aunt Laura found his account of a Twins–Royals game in his wastebasket, he thought he wanted to be a writer. At the time, his literary influences were confined to those he read at the breakfast table: the sportswriters at the *Star* and the copywriters at Kellogg's. He watched *Stand by Me* and saw himself in Gordie Lachance, who also wanted to be a writer, then suddenly didn't, in a line Rodney could quote from memory: "Fuck writing. I don't want to be a writer. It's stupid. It's a stupid waste of time." From what Rodney had read since, all writers felt that way some of the time, and some writers felt that way all of the time.

And why wouldn't they? Franz Kafka wrote on the side while working in insurance. (Like Rodney, he was allowed to compose the annual reports.) His major literary works were published after his death, when Kafka was ill positioned to enjoy his fame to its fullest.

Likewise, Melville's career didn't hit its full stride until after he died. He had early success with *Typee* and *Omoo*, but couldn't live off their proceeds. By the time he wrote *Moby-Dick*, he got the second half of that title as payment: Nothing. Nada. *Dick*. And so Rodney hoped that his career, too, might trace a posthumous arc, of fame and riches in the afterlife.

Alas, these things seldom came to unemployed corporate apparatchiks, especially if they left behind no books, no children to burnish their legacy, nor much in the way of anything else. "I want to leave a little trace," Samuel Beckett said to explain why he wrote. "I don't want this to have happened to me without leaving a trace."

The *this* that happened to him was life.

This happens, Rodney thought when he first read and dog-eared that page: an anagram of *Shit happens*.

But *this* and *shit* were not anagrams on this night. They were antonyms. Life—Rodney's life—was looking up, and so was Rodney, still staring at the cottage cheese of his bedroom ceiling, thinking of what Mairead had said.

It never occurred to her that I should be an editor or an artist. It never occurred to me, for that matter.

Rodney enjoyed solitude, loved words, adored drink, and was desperate, like everyone else, to leave a trace. So why hadn't he become a writer? Was it his desire to please his parents, to have a steady income, to wear a tie? Or was it a failure of nerve?

And why did he behave as if he *were* a writer, a writer who feared the vampiric effect of someone else on his life? As some wanker put it in one of those books on his shelf: "The enemy of good art is the pram in the hallway."

Rodney had neither pram nor art. But he *did* have Keith, and Rodney could see himself wheeling his roommate around the neighborhood in a pram, like the Jamaican nurses on the block, pushing the babies of investment bankers or driving Miss Daisy in a wheelchair.

One night last fall, Keith and Rodney left a bar on Tenth Avenue and couldn't get a cab in the rain. So Keith hailed a pedicab, a bicycle rickshaw. He was entirely untroubled by the arrangement—a West African immigrant serving as his human draft horse. "It's his job," Keith said the next day, after Rodney had refused to ride along and had walked to the subway instead. "*Not* hailing him is the sin. You're depriving him of his livelihood." Rodney thought he was probably right. But he still refused to have his shoes shined in airports.

Tonight, when Rodney had arrived home, Keith said, "Where have you been? I was worried sick." He was on Rodney's computer. He must have retrieved it from Rodney's nightstand. His back was against the wall adjoining the next apartment. Rodney was pirating the neighbor's wireless.

Rodney said, "How long are you gonna be on my laptop?"

"If I had a dollar for every time I said that to a stripper," Keith said.

"You *did* have a dollar every time you said that to a stripper," Rodney replied.

"True dat."

Keith didn't visit strip clubs. Rodney knew that. But the two sometimes affected a frat-brother bravado, wordlessly daring one another to break character. It was a pose even more ridiculous on men of their age than it was on actual fraternity brothers. Keith didn't care that Rodney had gone out tonight. But he still pretended to be hurt when Rodney was leaving. "I thought we were going to Boyle's," Keith said. "Bros before hos, man."

"True dat," Rodney said.

Keith got his slang from sitcoms and movies and iTunes. Ninety percent of urban slang, like 90 percent of gangster rap, was sold to white guys from the suburbs, Rodney knew. It was, in a nearly literal sense, white noise, like talking about golf or baseball or beer—all things Rodney and Keith talked about instead of ever talking about their hopes and fears: the things they thought about while staring at the ceiling at night, as Rodney found himself still doing at 2 a.m.

Rodney had only had one serious girlfriend, and that was the problem with her: what he wanted was an *un*-serious girlfriend, one who laughed, or at the very least didn't fall asleep when he took her to Boyle's, as his serious girlfriend, Rachel, had done two years earlier, on the night before Thanksgiving, the beginning of the end.

The next morning they had driven a rental car to Vermont for Thanksgiving with her family and stayed through the weekend. On Saturday, the Lowrys would put up their Christmas tree, a real one. Rodney had been raised with a fake one and said he liked it that way: "Faux fir," he called it. Nobody laughed.

Rachel's house had a tasteful white light in every window. The house Rodney grew up in was carnival-lit and thrummed: visible from outer space, audible from Outer Mongolia, a joy buzzer in canary yellow aluminum siding.

Rachel's vengeful Santa had left a lump of coal for every

act of naughtiness committed during the year. Rodney believed in a benevolent Claus who bore no resemblance to the temperamental God of the Old Testament, beyond the white beard.

She was Catholic. But their respective holiday traditions exposed fault lines more stressful than the ones Rodney had heard about from married friends and relatives: Private school or public? To spank or not to spank? Toilet roll facing the wall or facing away from it?

You can tell a lot about your family tree from your family's tree, Rodney realized. And he didn't want his future offspring to play beneath a seven-foot Fraser fir that left Rachel's living room floor as needle strewn as William Burroughs's writing room.

In Rodney's house, it was an annual rite to assemble the Christmas tree, whose plastic branches slotted into corresponding holes in the "trunk," a green-painted pole made of real wood. It was a tree trunk made from another tree trunk, a distinctly American kind of genius, Rodney thought.

It also had an artificial scent. It smelled like the Christmas tree air fresheners that dangled from the rearview mirrors of New York taxis. Their facsimile-of-a-facsimile of a tree was perfect for the Pooles, as close to nature as they wanted to get.

"I come from a long line of indoorsmen," Rodney told Rachel's parents, whose smiles looked like grimaces.

The Lowrys were campers. Mr. Lowry split logs that he fed to a wood-burning stove that heated their house. Rodney's father was the anti-Thoreau. He called their next-door neighbor—who would walk his dog each morning along the stream across the street—"the Creek Freak."

None of which boded well that Saturday after Thanksgiving when Rodney and Mr. Lowry went off on a bonding expedition to a tree farm to cull a Fraser. On arrival, Rodney was issued a hacksaw, which he hung around the top of his chosen tree like a lei.

And then he hailed a tractor-driving fifteen-year-old farm-hand, who asked—after a long and baffled silence—if Rodney wanted him to do the sawing. Rodney said yes. The kid's expression said, "Would you like me to saw off your genitals while I'm at it?"

And then Rodney realized that every other lumberjack there was cutting down his own tree.

The tree, he'd been told repeatedly by Rachel and her mother, had to be rushed back to the house by LifeStar and put into water immediately, lest it succumb, in those first critical hours, to something called "sap seal."

When he arrived, Rachel and Mrs. Lowry had lain out the lights for outside: a string of white ones for each of the arborvitaes, which Rodney hung around their necks like a single strand of pearls.

Rodney was seeing the Ghost of Christmas Future. He envisioned his favorite ornament—a sequin-suited elf that he called Huggy Bear—being hidden away against the wall every Christmas, a metaphor for his entire side of the family.

When Rodney came in from hanging the lights, the radio was tuned to a station that played nothing but holiday songs, 24/7, from Thanksgiving Day through Christmas. Which was okay, until the sixteenth Andy Williams song of the weekend came on, after which he wondered if it was possible for a radio speaker to form its own sap seal.

Looking back, he could identify the very moment his relationship with Rachel ended, though neither of them knew it at the time: He was seated at the kitchen table in his girlfriend's house when "O Christmas Tree" came on the radio. And Rodney began reminiscing about the seven members of the Poole family building their own tree on an assembly line more efficient than any Detroit had ever seen.

To this day, Rodney thought there was no more meretricious poem in the Western canon than Joyce Kilmer's "Trees": "Poems are made by fools like me, but only God can make a tree"?

Bullshit. The Pooles made a tree every year.

First Rodney's employer let him go—that's what his boss had said: "We're letting you go"—then Rodney let *himself* go. For seven weeks now, he'd been sitting down to pee. It was easier than standing, and Rodney could read on the toilet until his ass went numb and his legs fell asleep, after which he'd have trouble standing, so that he'd sort of hobble over to the couch and lie down, ostensibly to let his legs wake up, during which time the rest of him would fall asleep.

This happened often, actually, his legs waking as the rest of Rodney nodded off, or vice versa—the two halves of his body on alternate sleep schedules, like a husband and wife who worked the day and night shift, respectively, and only saw each other at dinner.

He certainly wasn't sitting to pee in the hope of keeping the bathroom clean. He didn't need to. Though he couldn't justify the expense—indeed, was less solvent than she was—he still paid Marisa seventy-five dollars to clean his place on the second Thursday of every month, filling 4K with a lemon-scented bouquet of chemicals that Rodney found refreshing. As with the tree, he preferred the facsimile to the authentic, Febreze to a real breeze.

Marisa had her own key, and Rodney found great comfort in coming home to see—just inside the door, next to her purse—her white sneakers. They were tiny things, of the size he'd only ever seen on children or cast in metal, bronzed and hanging from a rearview mirror or pewterized and then pushed around a Monopoly board.

Mostly, Rodney just liked the presence of a woman in his apartment, even if she was a fifty-six-year-old Guatemalan who spoke no English and smelled, though not unpleasantly, of Pine-Sol. His place had a woman's touch even when Rodney did not.

Rodney got out of bed at 10:17 on Wednesday morning and immediately sat down to pee. At Boyle's, he realized, he did the opposite. In the fetid stall at Boyle's, Rodney stood to shit, dropping deuces from a great height and hoping to hit the target, as in the early days of air combat.

Sitting on the john now—numbness advancing from his pelvis to his feet, the epidural effect of his laziness kicking in—Rodney resolved to be a better man.

He would kill two birds this morning: he would (1) go for a run that would (2) take him to East 117th Street, where he could check on Keith's U-Haul. Rodney hadn't run in two months and felt fraudulent swaddling himself in Dri-Fit and Under Armour, an elaborate wardrobe for a production likely to close after a single performance.

At times like this Rodney was glad he didn't have a doorman, who would have had to smile grimly and pretend as if the running were an everyday occurrence, not a biennial one-off.

Rodney didn't stretch. He jogged from the front door of his building to the light at the corner, where he had to run in place for half a minute, a varietal of New York wanker he had always detested, like the man babbling into his Bluetooth or the woman sweeping him into the street with her double-wide stroller, plowing pedestrians out of the way like the cowcatcher on a steam locomotive.

He jayran across Columbus and jogged past Boyle's. Doing so felt like a small act of betrayal. He felt self-righteous and judgmental—superior in a fraudulent way, the equivalent of renting a Bentley for his high school reunion.

And then, thank God, he was in the park on a gorgeous August day, running past the loafers and early lunchers and all the couples—the hand-holders and the pinky-linkers and the high school kids with their hands in each others back pockets.

In Rodney's hometown, it was not uncommon to find oneself in traffic behind a pickup truck in whose cab you could see *two* shadowy figures in the driver's seat, like the silhouette of Siamese twins. That practice, of riding tandem in the driver's seat, was known among his friends as "Riding Hoozh"—short for Hoosier, a slur against the state of Indiana. In Indiana, Rodney imagined, it was called something different. Everyone needs someone else to look down on.

The park was filled with PDAs: both public displays of affection and personal digital assistants. The latter had robbed the former of its acronym, just as the great running back Eric Dickerson's nickname—E.D.—had been supplanted in the public's imagination by erectile dysfunction.

Rodney once overheard a guy who had just been birthday-caked at Boyle's say, of turning fifty, "My semi-annual erection has become an annual semi-erection."

He had seen an ad for a new contraceptive called Yaz, taking the nickname of the Hall of Fame outfielder Carl Yastrzemski. Was the brand name meant to exude confidence in scoring position? Rodney would have to ask Mairead about the marketing philosophy behind that.

Mairead. What was she doing right now?

It was impossible to watch sports on TV without seeing a

commercial for Flomax in which three gray-haired buddies with enlarged prostates went marlin fishing and mountain biking and then kayaked down the Colorado, the rushing river a subtle reminder that your Flomaxed urine stream would soon resemble a Class VI rapids.

Then there was the one for that fiber-rich cereal in which a contractor reviewed blueprints at a construction site while all about him bulldozers and front-loaders were seen dumping operatically.

Rodney ran past a man on a bench yammering into his BlackBerry: he was having a PDA *with* his PDA, holding it away from his ear but close to his mouth.

Rodney thought of all these things—of anything—to avoid looking at his watch, to avoid marking progress on the run, a Vulcan mind trick that worked today: He was lost in his thoughts, with no idea how long he'd been running, so that when he arrived on 117th Street just west of First Avenue and saw a canary yellow Volkswagen Beetle where the U-Haul used to be, Rodney didn't even break stride.

He turned around and headed for home.

Wednesday afternoons Rodney watched live televised English soccer in a gorgeous reproduction of the sort of Irish pub that probably never existed. Everything, right down to the taps, was manufactured in Dublin by the Irish Public House Corporation and shipped—lock, stock, and aged oaken barrel—to Manhattan, where it was assembled into a mirrored Victorian movie set of a pub called the Old Casablanca, which the expat women who gathered there called, not without justification, the Old Catch-a-wanker.

As far as Rodney was concerned, the Wanker was Even

Better Than the Real Thing, whose authors—U2—were in a mural of Irish icons on the wall, along with footballers Roy Keane and Mick McCarthy. It was painted by the Michelangelo of Irish-American pub muralists, Paul Joyce, whose great-grandfather James was up there too, next to Elvis.

Joyce knew a thing or two about leaving a trace. Rodney never read much of *Ulysses* beside the first sentence and the last sentence, but he figured its very opacity vouchsafed its genius. "I've put in so many puzzles and enigmas that it will keep the professors busy for centuries arguing over what I meant," Joyce said. "And that's the only way of insuring one's immortality."

If inscrutability meant immortality, Keith was going to live forever. Rodney hadn't told him that the U-Haul wasn't there this morning—that it had been towed or stolen, that he hadn't been checking on it. Keith was constructing a tower of Sweet 'N Low packets from his chair next to Rodney's, at a table in front of a projection TV that rather spoiled the illusion that they were imbibing in the reign of Queen Victoria.

But then the Wanker was another replica that exceeded the thing replicated, like Camden Yards in Baltimore or the second *Godfather* movie. Yes, it was a bit Disneyfied, but Rodney had read that Disney—specifically, the Rose and Crown pub at Epcot—annually dispensed the most Guinness in the United States.

What was Rodney supposed to tell Keith? *Good news and bad news, mate. Every one of your earthly possessions has disappeared.*

And the good news?

Every one of your earthly possessions has disappeared.

The Wanker also showed English soccer live on weekend

mornings. The 3 p.m. kickoffs in London meant a 10 a.m. start in New York, where beer could not legally be dispensed until noon on Sundays. And so the regulars sat and waited for the Seth Thomas clock behind the bar to chime twelve o'clock.

The bell had the same salivary effect as it had on Pavlov's dogs.

The Wanker had fifty taps and when the soccer was on those taps bowed in unison like a chorus line. They dispensed Pete's Wicked Winter Ale and Theakston's Old Peculiar and Drained Lizard Imperial Stout and Morland Old Speckled Hen. They reminded Rodney, always, that just about any phrase made a superior name for a boutique beer: Valley Forge National Park. Royal Canadian Mounted Police. Heisenberg's Uncertainty Principle. International Date Line Nut Brown Ale.

On those Sunday mornings when he found himself in the Wanker, though, Rodney ordered Guinness. He'd watch the barman tilt the tulip glass at forty-five degrees, fill it three quarters of the way, then leave it on the bar to surge and settle. Keith thought it perverse, waiting two hours for a beer and then waiting another two minutes to drink it. But Rodney liked the waiting often as much as he liked the thing waited for. He liked looking forward to see Mairead as much as he liked to see her.

Seeing someone, he thought, consisted principally of *not* seeing them. At least at first. But those first days were usually the headiest ones.

And so he waited for his Guinness. That was the best part. He always liked the waiting. His Lenten sacrifices—giving up soda, swearing off desserts—weren't sacrifices at all. It was self-indulgence masquerading as self-denial.

At 12:02 the barman would complete the pour, drawing a

115

shamrock in the cream with the last of the draft. Three circles and a stem.

Armen could do an ampersand or Michael Jordan's Jumpman logo or write a sonnet in the top of your Guinness if you cared for that sort of thing. "Like peeing in the snow," he said.

On Wednesday afternoons, Rodney arrived an hour early at the Old Casablanca to get a table. "Guinness," Keith said to the waitress. She was Irish and he had always fancied her. And then, just to fill the dead space at the end of the sentence: "Vitamin G."

Guinness first lapped up at New York's shores in 1842 and New York's shores had lapped it up ever since.

Rodney ordered a Guinness, too.

"Siobhan, right?" Keith said.

"Right." It rhymed with *Hoyt*.

"How do you spell that again?"

Rodney rolled his eyes. For the love of Christ.

"It's spelled the way you pronounce it after eight pints." *Points*.

"But it's pronounced Shuh-BON?" Keith said.

"Shove-ON," she said. "As in 'Shove off.'"

Rodney was certain Siobhan had been constructed in Dublin by the Irish Public House Corporation and shipped to New York as part of its Victorian Pub Package.

Siobhan left for the bar and the other waitress—ten years older—passed their table and said: "As in 'Shove on yer knickers, yer ma's comin' home.'"

Siobhan returned with the Guinness. Rodney took a swig. Spot-on. Six degrees Celsius. The famous Six Degrees of Preparation.

In the sixth minute of the match Arsenal striker Emmanuel

Adebayor headed a cross into the back of the net and Rodney and Keith joined in the singing:

> *HE'S TALL! HE'S QUICK!*
> *HIS NAME'S A PORNO FLICK!*
> *EMMANUEL . . . EMMANUEL.*

And then a regular who called himself Arsenal Wayne yelled, "One–nil to the Arsenal!" Like the rest of the Americans who comprised at least half the audience for televised soccer at the Old Casablanca, Rodney said "nil" instead of "zero" and "football" instead of "soccer" and enlivened his vocabulary with other words and phrases from the British Isles: *one-off*, *shite*, *mate*, *Gents*, *wankers*, *tossers*, *taking the piss.*

He used *fancy* as a verb.

Whenever the words slipped into Rodney's speech outside the Wanker he was given shit about it. His vocabulary at the Wanker was the equivalent of Madonna's bizarre, English-inspired accent, and Rodney knew it. But he didn't care. He didn't give a toss. "I'm gonna have a slash," he told Keith and headed for the bog.

These Gents were a Disney vacation from Boyle's. At Boyle's there was nothing gentlemanly about the Gents. Indeed, the very word on the door had become louche and ironic, as in the phrase "gentleman's club" or the nudie mag *Gent*. Everything that was labeled "adult," Rodney knew—adult content, adult films, adult language—was for children, for people who had never grown up.

By law, you had to be a grownup to get into the Wanker, but by virtue of being here—drinking beer and singing songs and shouting at the TV on a Wednesday afternoon—you really weren't grown up.

He rejoined Keith at their table and continued to celebrate, in shouts and in songs, the "adult" virtues of binge drinking and promiscuity. Rodney recalled his favorite former Arsenal player, the bowl-cut forward Paul Merson, and his most memorable goal celebration, in which he pantomimed drinking pints with both hands. They serenaded him from their seats:

THERE ARE GOOD HAIRCUTS AND BAD HAIRCUTS
BUT I'VE NEVER SEEN A WORSE 'UN.
HE RUNS ALL DAY
HE SHAGS ALL NIGHT
ARSENAL'S PAUL MERSON

Nobody in the Old Catch-a-wanker could be accused of skiving off work because nobody here had a visible means of employment. Rodney had read a book called *The Great Good Place*, by an urban sociologist named Ray Oldenburg, who coined the phrase "the third place" to describe informal public gathering spaces—bars—that are neither home nor job. Rodney had no work and home was a way station, where he kept his books and his bed. For him, bars were the *first* place. Home was the second. There was no third.

And so he sat there—among the paper hooligans in their replica jerseys in a prefab pub—and roared at the set in somebody else's slang.

There was no place else on Earth Rodney wanted to be. But he couldn't concentrate on the match. In his career—he thought of it in the present tense, though it was rapidly receding in the rearview—Rodney hadn't written so much as he had *replicated* writing. It occurred to him, sitting in the Wanker, that he found safety in a facsimile of writing—

speeches and press releases, devoid of his byline and delivered in somebody else's voice.

Always in somebody else's voice. He aspired to journalism but settled for ventriloquism.

Rodney made a silent vow to write something, anything, in the first person. If he still had—if he ever had—a first person. Perhaps the first person, like the third place, didn't exist for Rodney.

Even revising his résumé, at this point, would be a comparative model of creative writing. It would have to be. His only job as a grownup was at Talbott, where his bosses first encountered Rodney's gift for written obfuscation on his résumé. On his résumé, Rodney hadn't worked in a Jolly Elf convenience store. He had facilitated the fronting of calcium-based consumer goods and chaired a high school journalism course. He justified the latter entry on the grounds that he had *made* a chair *out of* journalism, including a magazine called *Coarse*.

Rodney wondered if it might still be possible to break into magazine journalism at age thirty-four. He then wondered if that was the right phrase, "break into": you didn't break into journalism, as you did a bank; you were more apt to break out, like an escaped convict or a case of acne. Journalism was, according to everything he had read, low paying, oppressive, disfiguring.

He began composing a new résumé in his head, in case— God forbid—things didn't work out with BM. Résumé writing was neither first-person nor third-person. It was person-free. It consisted entirely of sentences that had been guillotined of their subjects: *Presided over fourteen magazine titles.* Rodney *had* presided over—in fact, sat on—a vast inventory of "traditional media." It was the industry euphemism, Rodney saw, for what younger people slagged off as "old media"—words on paper, newspapers and magazines and, most antiquated of all, books.

The truth was, Rodney had never held down a magazine job. He had never held down anything, save a barstool and a *Club* chair. He didn't hold down the Talbott job; the Talbott job held him down.

It held him down the way concrete shoes keep a Mafia hit victim from bobbing to the surface. But it also held him down in a way that averts chaos, the way you hold down a beach blanket in a sudden gale.

And now Rodney was untethered. For the first seven weeks, he felt free, a balloon floating away to God knows where. But then passengers on the *Hindenburg* must have felt like that, too, right up until touchdown. He now physically ached to get a callback from Curt Mayhew at Banco Marinero.

From his room, Rodney called the impound lot. He felt like a petrified parent calling the ERs at 2 a.m. on prom night. Except that he *wanted* confirmation, a voice to say "Yes, we *do* have what you're looking for." But they didn't. The U-Haul was AWOL.

Sat there on his unmade bachelor's bed, its fitted sheet scored with zebra stripes of blue ink—he often fell asleep doing the *Times* crossword—it seemed an absurd notion: Rodney as parent. For a long time he'd thought, vaguely, that he'd like to have children. Someday. *Eventually*. And then one day he was walking into an R-rated movie when a boy, maybe twelve years old, approached him and said: "Can you pretend you're my dad so I can go in there?"

That was two years ago and it nearly killed Rodney, the notion that he was old enough to have a twelve-year-old son.

He told the kid to fuck off, but still: that word, *Dad*—it stabbed him in the chest.

For a time he consoled himself that he would leave a tiny legacy of books. Of *a* book. But he never even started one, never had the slightest notion how to start one. He wanted to give birth to a book, fully formed, like the would-be son who materialized at age twelve outside the theater. But Rodney had read enough of writers' lives to know that it's easier to conceive children than books.

He hadn't found a way to tell Keith that his shit was gone, either at the Wanker or during the cab ride home. But Rodney, personally, would welcome such a purging of his possessions. Not that he had any. His books excepted, Rodney kept very few things. It made Marisa's job easy and offered him the illusion that reinvention was perpetually possible. Without possessions, Rodney was always starting over, a tabula rasa. He got that from his father, who threw everything away, who wanted to expire not after spending his last dime but after pitching his last piece of household clutter.

Rodney's anti-materialist bent didn't signify asceticism so much as an unreadiness to start life, to commit: Why buy new silverware, he figured, when he'd one day get it for a wedding present? Never mind that he didn't even have a girlfriend and had eaten, for years now, with plastic forks and knives from the Chinese takeaway, so that he wouldn't have to wash what few knives and forks he owned.

The blank page induced in him this same kind of paralysis: hope and despair in equal measure. It's no wonder he'd never started a book.

But then Rodney didn't know if he wanted to write or just *be* a writer, just as he didn't so much like reading writers as he did reading *about* them.

In college, he read a Philip Larkin poem, "The Life with a Hole in It," about the kind of writer he thought then he'd like to be. In a few lines, there was everything he wanted—drink, women, the French Riviera. It even indulged Rodney's weakness for alliteration. "The shit in the shuttered chateau" wrote in the morning, and divided the afternoon "between bathing and booze and birds."

But Rodney was not the Shit in the Shuttered Chateau. He was the Wanker in the One-Bedroom Walkup. Rodney had never hung anything on his walls, save the braces and brackets that supported his bookshelves. In his father—in anyone of his father's age—such austerity was a virtue. They called it downsizing. Empty nesters used the same word as the people who fired Rodney—as if Rodney hadn't been let go but rather was sent off to college by his bosses, who then converted his room into a den.

Whenever Rodney visited his parents' house, they were urging on him some space-wasting token of his childhood: a baseball trophy or photo album. "Take it," his dad would always say, "or it's getting pitched." His father didn't want cremation or burial, Rodney thought, but to be thrown in a bin and rolled to the curb the first Wednesday after he expired.

His father didn't need to leave a trace. He had the opposite obsession: He needed to leave *no* trace, unlike the needy writers and rock stars and chanteuses in the Père Lachaise cemetery in Paris, where Oscar Wilde and Jim Morrison and Edith Piaf were still accepting admirers backstage.

Five years ago Rodney attended the funeral of a quiet coworker he barely knew who was T-boned by a drunk on the Fourth of July. Rodney rented a car and drove thirty minutes north of New York, to another vast metropolis—to a vast necropolis—of contiguous cemeteries. Afterward, he had a wander around their green hills, rubbernecking at gravesites. The permanent residents of that gated community included the villainous (James Cagney) and valorous (he paused over Billie Burke, who played Glinda the Good Witch of the North in *The Wizard of Oz*). Dorothy Kilgallen, if she weren't already there, might have filled her gossip column with the boldface names inscribed on the headstones: Danny Kaye, Tommy Dorsey, Rube Goldberg, and David Sarnoff, founder of NBC and the first person to receive a distress call from the *Titanic*. Inside those gates, Rachmaninoff stopped composing and started decomposing.

That cemetery was called Gate of Heaven, and for a long time, you wouldn't want to be caught dead anywhere else. Magazine baron Condé Nast was interred immediately next to Billy Martin, so that the former Yankee manager appeared hounded by the press even unto eternity. On Martin's grave, when Rodney visited, were weather-beaten Yankee and Indians caps, a pair of his signature sunglasses from the seventies and a shriveled hot dog, smothered in sauerkraut and sealed in the stale sarcophagus of its bun.

Rodney strolled into the adjacent Kensico Cemetery. Eleanor Gehrig's headstone contained the ashes of her husband, Lou. Nearby lay Harry Frazee, the Red Sox owner who sold Babe Ruth to Jacob Ruppert, the Yankee owner, who was also there, in a massive four-columned mausoleum that suggested very strongly that you *can* take it with you.

Fifty yards down a gentle slope from Martin's grave Rodney literally stumbled on the Babe and his second wife, Claire. On Ruth's headstone, Jesus held the hand of a little boy in a baseball uniform. Rodney stepped over the Yuengling can on his grave and found a riot of other tokens left behind by visitors:

two American flags, three Yankee caps, a bat and a baseball on which was inscribed, in a shaky hand, "Take Care of the Boys, Babe." More than fifty years since the Hearse of the Bambino stopped there, Rodney marveled, Ruth was still receiving fan mail.

He thought of Elvis, buried in the backyard for the benefit of Graceland tourists; of Lenin, in his Plexiglas penalty box. These men did not let death cramp their lifestyles. No sir. They did not take death lying down.

Rodney's father didn't need—he didn't want—his voice to be heard from beyond the grave, like that animatronic Lincoln in Disney World's Hall of Presidents. Lincoln was the only man who wore a higher hat than Rodney's father. Rodney's father wore a baseball cap precariously balanced on the crown of his head, in the manner of Joe Torre, whose Yankee cap all those years seemed to be secured by hatpins. Everything—hats, socks, belts—rose with age, climbing to the rooftop to forestall the floodwaters of mortality.

Rodney's father now had to unzip his fly to blow his nose.

But his father was also sane and secure, untroubled by the rising tide of time. He didn't need to leave books. He left sons. "Books are immortal sons deifying their sires," Plato wrote, conflating books and children, and Rodney wondered if he would ever issue either one of them.

In a college journalism course, he witnessed the public humiliation of a fellow student who asked a visiting writer if he had any advice.

"No," said this bald eminence, to nervous laughter.

"None?" the professor prodded.

"Writing is neither profession nor vocation, but an incurable illness," the writer said, and Rodney's Bic, poised above his spiral notebook, was set in motion. "Those who give up are not writers and never were. Those who persevere do so not from pluck or determination, but because they cannot help it. They are sick, and advice is an impertinence."

He was a pompous buffoon, Rodney thought at the time. But now he'd read enough to know the guy was right.

Asked why he wrote, Beckett said: "Because I can't help myself."

From his bed, Rodney could see into the closet, whose bifold doors were open just enough to expose—on the top shelf—the Gatorade bottle full of coins. All those presidential faces, pressed up against the plastic, as if gazing down through an airplane window, gave Rodney the sensation that his money was flying away while he remained rooted to the tarmac, waving goodbye to his savings. Which is precisely what he was doing with every passing day.

Rodney told himself he needed books more than he needed beer and when he headed to Boyle's with Keith that night, he considered himself a kind of Gatsby in reverse. Gatsby said, "I've been drunk for about a week now, and I thought it might sober me up to sit in a library." Rodney, on the other hand, lived in his private library and went to Boyle's to unsober himself.

At Boyle's, they could talk about anything, of grave consequence or none at all or both at the same time. At the bar, eyes were naturally drawn to that bottle of Frangelico, a Rorschach test that Rodney likened to an alcoholic Oscar. It put Wanamaker in mind of a bottle of Mrs. Butterworth's and had Keith thinking of another famous Franciscan, the cartoon cleric swinging a baseball bat on the sleeve patch of the San Diego Padres' uniforms.

"He's called the Swinging Friar," Rodney said. "Some years he bats lefty, some years righty."

Keith said, "He's called the Swinging Friar and he swings both ways? Can't he get defrocked for that?"

Rodney reflected that defrocking was both the punishment and the crime at the root of the priest scandals.

"I thought their mascot was the San Diego Chicken," Wanamaker said, crashing the conversation.

"They have two," said Rodney. "The Chicken and the Friar."

"Maybe that's why the Chicken crossed the road," said Armen. "He was running from the Swinging Friar."

Rodney bolted for the can, took a leak, and washed his hands. Turning the rusted spigots of the sink at Boyle's, you acquired as many germs as you killed. It was a wash, washing your hands there. And there was always some pasty waster watching you in the mirror, someone who looked like you on a very bad day.

Rodney had a look at himself. He had a good long goo, as the Irish said at the Wanker. It was unforgiving light—light that had a chip on its shoulder, light that held a serious grudge—but even so, this was ridiculous. In the fluorescent mirror of the Boyle's bathroom, his nose looked bulbous—not a nightlight bulb, but a 150-watter, something to read by. His cleft chin was a miniature ass, his full clown lips like two night crawlers in flagrante.

The eyes were all right. He'd been told he had "kind eyes"—brown, receptive, the eyes of a listener. His eyes were all ears. But his eye*brows*—circumflex and circumspect— were always expressing doubt. His eyes and eyebrows played good cop, bad cop—the eyes inviting confession, the brows conveying suspicion.

Beneath both eyes sagged twin hammocks of flesh, and beneath both hammocks sat his rouged cheeks. The redness evinced good health but was, to Rodney's way of thinking, evidence of its opposite: some kind of skin condition. He had plenty of salad, plenty of hair, but it was strawlike and undomesticated and sprang from an oval head that sat atop a long straight body, so that Rodney, on bad days, thought he resembled a toilet brush. What did Mairead see in him? She had to see something *in* him, because she couldn't possibly see something *on* him. This book, judged by its cover, wasn't selling a single copy. It required a long browse in a bookstore aisle, and even then it wasn't for everyone.

Mairead. The thought of her gave Rodney a tingling in his pants that he did not instantly recognize as his phone, on vibrate.

On his way from the can to the curb, he passed Keith and Wanamaker at the bar and told them, "I gotta take this call." He recognized her number and answered the phone— "Hello?"—in a heightened state of sobriety, the same way he acted hyperawake whenever a caller woke him up. Which was often, given Rodney's schedule.

"Hi, it's Mairead."

"Hey!"

"Is this a bad time?"

"No, I was just . . . no. What's up?"

"Let me shut the door."

"Are you still at work?" Jesus, what time was it? Rodney checked his phone. It was 8:07. "What are you *doing* there?"

"Working," she said. "Believe it or not, I'm in my office trying to figure out how to sell more Certs."

"Certs?" Rodney said. "Does it still have Retsyn?" Certs

had forever boasted that it contained Retsyn, even though—
rather, *because*—no one had any earthly idea what Retsyn
was, anymore than beer drinkers knew the meaning of "cold-
filtered."

It seemed that part of Mairead's job was to entice con-
sumers with wondrous product descriptions whose come-ons
featured amenities so seductive—Rodney thought of "Beech-
wood-aged" Budweiser—that further explication was unnecessary.

"It still has Retsyn," Mairead said.

"Do dry cleaners still practice the dark art of One-Hour
Martinizing?" Rodney asked. It was a process at least as
ancient—and every bit as arcane—as the coming of beef or
the deviling of ham.

"I don't know," she said.

It was an equatorial August evening. Rodney was leaning
against a car whose owner was unlikely to return anytime
soon, as a boutonniere of blaze orange parking tickets was
pinned to the windshield.

"And what is Hall's Mentho-Lyptus?" Rodney said.

"I'm guessing it's a kind of mentholated eucalyptus?"
Mairead said.

"Is Mentho-Lyptus related to Mentho*latum*, as in Mentho-
latum Deep-Heating Balm?" And here Rodney impersonated
the baritone voiceover of the commercial: "There's no beating . . . *Deeeeep Heeeeating.*"

"I can't tell you," Mairead said. "I used to work on the
Always account." She laughed. "Panty liners. Always with Dry-
Weave. I never figured out what Dry-Weave was. It sounds like
something they'd offer at my hair salon, you know?"

But Rodney didn't know. Like the eddying plastic grocery
bag corkscrewing skyward from the sidewalk, Rodney was
afloat—adrift on summer and beer and infatuation, and the

sound of a woman's voice, of *this* woman's voice, saying *panty*.

It was one more thing they had in common, Rodney and Mairead—they both loved words but had used them for evil, to enshroud rather than enlighten: Rack-and-pinion steering. Steel-belted radials. Viscosity and thermal breakdown. Rodney had no earthly idea what any of these things meant, which is why they were always touted as salutary features in car commercials.

"Is Vicks Formula 44 in any way related to Formula 409?" Rodney said.

"I'll ask around at our next staff meeting," Mairead said.

"You do that. And find out if the less famous formulas between 44 and 409 have any marketing potential, either as cold medication or kitchen cleaner."

"Or perhaps both," Mairead said.

Rodney thought of the commercial for Scrubbing Bubbles shower cleaner, whose thickly-eyebrowed bubbles "work hard so you don't have tooooo"—that last monosyllable chillingly drawn out as the bubbles were sucked down the shower drain, having evidently worked themselves to death, a concept the Japanese call *karoshi*.

Rodney wondered, looking back into Boyle's, if it was possible to do the opposite: if you could die from lack of work.

He kept a few books going in his head at one time, circling the air-traffic tower of his brain, more books joining the holding pattern than would ever be allowed to land. At the moment, he was reading novels by Martin Amis and Roddy Doyle, whose main characters, John Self and Jimmy Rabbitte, Sr., were unemployed and haunting libraries in London and Dublin, respectively. But Rodney wasn't going to the library. He was jobless, not *home*less. In New York, the jobless sat in the aisles at Barnes & Noble, and fell asleep with

their backs propped up against bookshelves. They used literature as a drunk does a lamppost: for support rather than illu-
mination.

Rodney gazed into the louvered eyes of Boyle's. In there was
his future, his fate. Jesus made the link between death and
drinking when he said, "Father, take this cup from my lips."

"Your father . . ." Rodney said to Mairead.

"Yes?"

"How did you cope?"

"When he died?" she said. "I don't know." And then: "I'll
always remember riding from the church to the cemetery. We
were at the head of the funeral procession and I turned to
look out the back window, as kids do. I knew enough not to
wave. But there was a line of cars behind us that snaked all
the way to the horizon. It was like this conga line of grief. And
it made me happy, to know how many friends he had."

There was a momentary silence before Rodney spoke.
"With my Dad, there won't be a trip to the cemetery," he said.
"He's compulsively anti-clutter. His pallbearers will be two
guys in waste management jumpsuits tossing him in the
back of a recycling truck. Or he'll have the Salvation Army
pick him up and put him in the collection bin behind the
church."

"Lovely."

"Some people donate their body to science," Rodney said.
"My dad will donate his body to Goodwill."

"You've got problems," Mairead said. "Can you hang on?
One quick second."

Rodney was staring across Columbus when he saw a guy
walking down the opposite sidewalk, lowering a Blimpie down
his neck. And what a neck it was. Rodney had never seen Longneck before last Saturday night at Boyle's. Or perhaps he'd seen
him plenty but never noticed him. Rodney never noticed

Honda Civics until his mother started driving one, then he began seeing them everywhere.

"I know how I want to go," Mairead said when she came back on the line. "I want my ashes stuffed in a confetti cannon, then fired in the face of the woman who was just in here."

"Your boss?" Rodney said and watched Longneck recede down Columbus, his bobbing head periscoped above the crowd. What a daffy-looking bastard. Rodney spent a solemn interlude wondering what the guy must look like in the fun-house mirror of the Boyle's bathroom. Perhaps it served as a corrective lens and turned Longneck into Cary Grant.

"*One* of my bosses," Mairead said. "She likes the word *whizbang*, as in 'We're looking for a *whizbang* idea from you.' I really need to get out of here." Whether she meant for the night or for good Rodney didn't ask.

"You want to get a drink tomorrow?" Rodney said.

"I'd love to."

Rodney resumed his lean on the parked car and looked into Boyle's. It was like spying on his own life. He was having an out-of-Boyle's experience. Through the window he could see the back of Wanamaker, for whom cremation was out of the question. His liver would burn for centuries, an eternal flame lighting Boyle's like a Freebird or a birthday cake.

"The inventor of the Frisbee wanted his ashes placed in a Frisbee mold," Rodney told Mairead. "His last wish was to be thrown onto his neighbor's roof. I wouldn't mind spending eternity that way myself."

Back in the bar, Rodney swiveled and sat sidesaddle on his stool to get a furtive look at the college kids in the booth behind him, their conversation going round and round like a sock in a dryer. The guy doing all the talking. His hair was moussed into a gently sloped A-frame, and Rodney said to Keith: "Everywhere he goes, he has a roof over his head."

A-frame was talking about America's handgun laws and Keith said to Rodney, "There should be a Brady Bill for breakups. Like, you get seven days' written notice if a chick is breaking up with you."

What a strange thing to say, Rodney thought. He wondered if Keith and Caroline had had a fight.

A-frame ducked outside for a smoke, bitching about it. Rodney turned to Keith and said, "They just banned public smoking in France. In *France*! The French gave us the word *cigarette*. They gave us Jean Nicot, the diplomat for whom nicotine was named. They gave us Gauloises, the cigarettes smoked by Picasso and Sartre and Camus . . ."

Rodney knew Keith enjoyed these rants, even though his friend pretended to detest them, especially in bars, especially around chicks. Keith once told him, "Rodney, you're boring the pants *onto* women."

But Camus, that chain-smoking absurdist, knew his shit. He thought the true university was "a collection of books" and culture was "the cry of men in the face of their destiny" and that "great works are often born on a street corner or in a restaurant's revolving door."

In other words, he believed in books—that books could transform, that books were a retort to death, that books could be born anywhere.

Rodney and Keith settled up with Armen and stepped outside. On cloudless nights outside the house he grew up in, it was impossible to look at the sky and think that humans were alone in the universe. Last Christmas, Rodney stood in his parents' driveway and gaped for a full minute at Orion's Belt. It would make a great name for a shot, he thought. O'Ryan's Belt.

But in big cities you can't see the night sky, can't see—just by looking up—your own cosmic insignificance. Or perhaps big cities just attracted people with an inflated sense of their own importance.

Camus wrote: "At thirty, a man should know himself like the palm of his hand, know the exact number of his defects and qualities, know how far he can go, foretell his failures—be what he is. And, above all, accept these things."

On Saturday, Rodney would turn thirty-five.

7

He returned from breakfast to see the toy boats of her two clogs just inside the door, and Marisa hoisting up the living room blinds as if they were mainsails. Was it the first Thursday already? The air conditioner was still on, rattling with emphysema, but Marisa had opened the windows anyway, and let in not *fresh* air, exactly, but *different* air—the dogs'-breath of a New York August displacing the bachelor-pad bouquet of beer breath and B.O. and Permafart. She had just arrived.

Marisa spoke almost no English. She periodically passed Rodney a note, written by her niece, announcing a change in schedule for the following month, but beyond that, Mister Poole and Señora Aguilar's only exchanges were of cash and complicated hand signals and the smallest of pleasantries, which they found themselves trading—"Good morning, Marisa" "Hello, Mr. Rodney"—when Keith abruptly stepped out of the bathroom, towel-less and still shining like a seal from the shower.

He was naked save for the cast, kept watertight in the polka-dotted clown costume of a Wonder Bread bag secured around the shin with duct tape.

Marisa shrieked, then held a dust rag in front of her face with two hands, the way Rodney hid his eyes with a newspaper whenever a panhandler entered his subway car.

Keith modestly crutched his way into the kitchen—the nearest hiding place, to his credit—and emerged a minute later, apologizing, wrapped in an apron Rodney had gotten as a gag Christmas present. On the front it said CAT: THE OTHER WHITE MEAT.

The nakedness of Keith, like the nakedness of Adam, could not be covered by clothes. Indeed, clothes—the ridiculous fig leaf of the cat apron—only called more attention to his shame. And so three faces were aflame with embarrassment when Keith, wearing his apron like a hospital dressing gown, open at the back, withdrew from the room like a butler at Buckingham Palace. He was bowing, too, with every abject apology.

"I come back?" Marisa asked Rodney. But they both knew the question was rhetorical. She was in her clogs and out the door on a summer wind of Windex, a mistral of lemon mist.

"You can come out now," Rodney said to the bathroom door, and Keith did, reluctantly—Punxsutawney Phil looking for his shadow.

"I'm sorry." They said it simultaneously, but Rodney was the first to fill the ensuing silence: "I forgot to tell you she was coming," he said. "I forgot she *was* coming."

"No biggie."

"That's what she said."

But Keith felt the need to say what he said next: "I didn't do it on purpose."

In other words, this wasn't college, where Rodney and Keith's freshman dorm resembled a ten-story beer can, both in shape (a cylindrical silo for storing freshmen) and content (robustly alcoholic).

A single corridor ringed each floor, so that visiting parents, searching for their son's room, had nowhere to run when encountering Keith in the hallway. Indeed, running would only return them to Keith—freeballing his way back from the shower stalls, toothbrush in one hand, soap dish in the other, towel slung over his shoulder like a military sash. Mothers blushed and fathers seethed, but their embarrassment was never reciprocated.

The contrast between Keith's exhibitionism and Rodney's *in*hibitionism was—what better word?—stark. ("Forbidding in its bareness and lack of ornament": Rodney had looked it up.) There were two kinds of creatures, as far as Rodney was concerned: those who were exceedingly comfortable with nakedness—their own and other people's—and those who were self-conscious in their own showers. The clinical name for Rodney's fear of nudity—again, he had looked it up—was gymnophobia. Perfect, really, because that's where Rodney feared it most—at the gym. From the Greek *gymnos*, or "naked." In ancient Greece, the Olympics were contested in the nude. Gymnastics were quite literally "naked activities." As an Olympic sport, nude gymnastics couldn't survive the introduction of the pommel horse, but naked activities carried on. They were all around Rodney.

It was nudity, as much as cost, that made him cancel his gym membership. And what a word that was: *membership*. That's all Rodney saw at the gym: other members' members. The amount of casual nudity—of unnecessary nudity—always astonished him. The elderly, especially. Rodney saw them through the window of the steam room, like plucked chickens in a refrigerated display case. Talking about the weather with legs splayed.

On his last day in that locker room, as Rodney watched breaking news on a wall-mounted TV, an eighty-year-old nude toddled over to him and stared up at CNN. He looked like some character from Greek mythology, with a man's head and a sheep's body, so covered was he in white wool. He and Rodney were practically touching elbows.

"Earthquake?"

"Yeah," said Rodney. And the mythical Mansheep squinted at the set and flossed his undercarriage with the towel he was straddling. Rodney resigned from the gym in a sales associate's office, behind a door marked "Members Only." For years Rodney had seen that sign—MEMBERS ONLY—and wondered if it wasn't just another of the gym's specialized workout rooms for those obsessed with isolating individual muscles: Abs Only, Pecs Only, Members Only.

So Keith was a gymnophile—a gymno*mane*; a gymno*maniac*—and Rodney was a gymnophobe. Keith was famous on the fourth floor of their freshman dorm for a steady rotation of female visitors to the upper berth of his bunk bed; even then he had a thing for the aerial artists and the mountaineers. Rodney pitied Keith's roommate, looking up at the buckled ceiling of that writhing mattress, bowing to within a foot of his nose, as when Gilligan had to sleep beneath the Skipper in bunked hammocks on *Gilligan's Island*.

As for Rodney, his face slowly shrank throughout that first semester, constricting with every pull of the drawstring on his hoodie, from which Rodney surveyed the campus like Death.

When Rodney had arrived on campus, his randomly assigned roommate, an ROTC from Cincinnati, had already been in residence for a week. He had commandeered the top bunk, papered the room with Marine recruiting posters, and stocked the fridge with forty-ounce Schaefers, which were Rodney's introduction to daily beer drinking. They required a commitment, when forty ounces were the least you could drink, and two beers meant the equivalent of a seven-pack.

Beer was a social lubricant that drew him out, literally drew him out from under the hood of his sweatshirt. To say that it brought Rodney out of his shell was no mere metaphor but a vivid description of beer's effect, so much did Rodney resemble a turtle in the Reaper cloak of his black Celtics hoodie.

"Beer is proof that God loves us and wants us to be happy," Benjamin Franklin said. Or was said to have said. When the killjoys at the Ben Franklin tercentenary in Philadelphia digitized all of Franklin's writings and failed to find any such quote in a computer scan of his entire oeuvre, Rodney consoled himself that the sentiment—emblazoned on a foam-rubber can cozy he still had in a kitchen cabinet—remained true.

Franklin was a Francophile who thought the elbow was perfectly positioned by Providence for lifting a wineglass to the mouth.

Rodney thought of something Mairead had said on their second date, when she idly scanned the wine list: "Who am I kidding, pretending to have a discerning palate? In college I drank beer out of a boot."

"I've done that," Rodney said. "You have to finesse that air bubble before it hits the heel or—"

"Not a *glass* boot," Mairead said. "A steel-toed Timberland work boot."

Rodney thought about all the receptacles from which he had imbibed beer. From can cozy and Solo cup, pilsner and pint glass, beer bong and Partyball. From longneck, shortie, and tallboy. From shot-glassed samplers at brewpubs, arrayed in a tray like test tubes, and yard glasses moored to wooden towers, as if ready for launching at Cape Canaveral. From two cans holstered to either side of a construction hardhat and conveyed to the mouth by clear rubber tubes and from the filter of his own T-shirt, when straining out the glass of a broken bottle.

Ben Franklin was not just a drinker but a gymnophile, too, who liked to sit nude in front of an open window, a practice he called an "air bath."

If science ever proved a link among genius and drink and gratuitous nudity, Keith would be remembered as a veritable da Vinci. Rodney was banking that books and beer were the engine of intellect, and he sometimes dreamed of opening a bar and bookstore that he'd call the Bibulous Bibliophile.

Keith came out of the bathroom, dressed in clean clothes for the first time in days.

"What are *you* all dolled up for?"

Keith crutched his way to the door: "Doctor's appointment. I have seven minutes to get to Ninety-second and Lex."

Of course. Keith had showered and shampooed and deodorized and put on a crisp blue Oxford in the same way that Rodney flossed only the night before he went to the dentist or others attended Mass exclusively on Christmas.

"My last clean one," Keith said, picking lint from his sleeve. "I'll grab a couple out of the U-Haul while I'm over there."

Rodney still hadn't told him it was gone.

The phone rang. When Rodney was still employed, a ringing telephone—be it bleating cell or shrieking cordless—instantly activated the acids in his stomach. Even someone *else's* phone, crying out in an airport, could make Rodney ache with anxiety. *The office is calling.*

Now that he was unemployed, Rodney had another reason to fear the phone. He had become the Friend Who Had Time to Talk. His buddies knew: No secretary would screen his calls, no wife would answer his phone and demand a transitory moment of small talk, no pressing appointment awaited him. Rodney was never in a meeting. And so he'd spent many afternoons in the last two months listening to monologues that began, "It's a five-hour drive to my next sales call" or "I've got a six-hour layover in Atlanta . . ."

Rodney had begun to see himself as an accessory to murder: he helped others kill time.

"Hello?" Caller ID displayed Mairead's home number.

"Hey, it's me," she said.

"Not at work today?"

"I called in sick."

"Well that stinks."

"But I'm *not* sick," Mairead said.

"I beg to differ," Rodney said.

"You do?"

"I do," Rodney said. "You drink beer out of other people's work boots. That's pretty damn sick if you ask me."

She was already laughing. "In Michigan, that's like drinking champagne from a glass slipper," she said.

"There's a Marx Brothers movie," Rodney said. "*At the Circus?*"

"Never saw it."

"Groucho's whispering sweet nothings to this lady. Something like 'Remember that night I drank champagne from your slipper? Two quarts. It would have held more, but you were wearing insoles.'"

"Are you saying I have big feet?"

"I didn't say that," Rodney said.

"You didn't *say* that. But you're thinking it."

"I am? No. What I *said* was . . ."

Mairead howled. "You're tongue-tied," she said. "I made you stammer. How sweet."

"You *are* sick."

"I am," she said. "It's because of my huge feet. Try fighting off a bunch of transvestites for the last pair of size-twelve heels at Nordstrom Rack."

"What makes you think I haven't?" said Rodney. And then: "Did you say *twelve*?"

"I did."

"Wow. I've heard of ten-gallon *hats*. But you've got the matching *shoes*."

"Apparently."

"Forget champagne," Rodney said. "Your slipper could serve one of those blue drinks that come with five straws and a rubber shark."

There was a smile in her tone when Mairead said: "Are you finished?"

"Yes," Rodney said in the smallest possible voice, as if he were a chastened child.

At his Newstead Abbey estate, Lord Byron imbibed from a chalice fashioned from a human skull. A skull—"from which, unlike a human head, whatever flows is never dull." He wrote "Lines Inscribed Upon a Cup Formed From a Skull," from the point of view of the skull's departed spirit:

> *I lived, I loved, I quaff'd, like thee:*
> *I died: Let earth my bones resign.*
> *Fill up—thou canst not injure me*
> *The worm hath fouler lips than thine.*

Rodney thought, *this* was the way to spend eternity, having your head turned into a pint glass or beer stein: raised in toasts, swung in song, filled with frothing Guinness—over and over and over again. Lather, rinse, repeat.

Maybe he'd mention it to Armen. In the event of my untimely demise, I'd like my head turned into a beer glass at Boyle's.

It would be, as they said at the Wanker, good *craic*: lotsa laughs. *Hey, would you look at the beer on that head . . .*

"Want to get out this afternoon?" Rodney said to Mairead. He had nothing in mind. The only spontaneous thing his ex-girlfriend ever did was meet him at the Metropolitan Museum of Art in the middle of one rainy workday, a rendezvous that resulted in Rodney feeling sad. They were in the Charles Offin Room, Rachel lost in some medieval masterpiece, when Rodney said in his best Carnac impersonation: "Charles Offin."

Rachel ignored him, and rolled her eyes when he repeated himself: "Charles Offin." But she wouldn't play along.

Rodney said, "What does Chuck's wife do when she's horny?"

She didn't even smile. She just chewed her cheek from the inside, as she always did—as if her tongue were trying to tunnel out of prison—and walked on to the next painting.

"I was going to go to the Strand this afternoon," Rodney told Mairead. "There's a couple of books I was looking for." This wasn't true, but he had a sudden urge to go there with her. "Wanna join me? You could pick me up."

"I don't have a car."

"On the subway. You could pick me up on the 1 train, at Seventy-second Street. I'll wait for you. On the downtown-most part of the platform."

"Is that even a word?"

"Of course it is. It's a thing you stand on to wait for the train."

"Not 'platform,' smartass."

"*Downtownmost*? If it isn't, it ought to be," Rodney said. "See you in thirty minutes?"

"This is absurd," Mairead said. And then, laughing and sighing—the happy exhale of an accordion—she said: "Make it an hour."

Keith came in as Rodney was leaving. Over one shoulder, he wore a new sling. Over the other, a canvas duffel bag—white with burgundy stains—that Rodney recognized from the move. He remembered schlepping it down the stairs and heaving it into the U-Haul and wondering out loud if he was ditching a corpse for Keith: "You didn't whack a midget, did you, Keith?"

"Is that what you call it?" Keith said. "'Whacking the midget'?"

It was just shirts and a few free weights. The stains were from a bottle of wine that had broken in the bag in an over-head bin years ago. But Rodney wondered of the bag, as with all of Keith's stuff: Why keep this piece of shit?

Keith now set the bag down just inside the door. "That doesn't *still* have weights in it," Rodney said.

"I took 'em out," Keith said. "It's just some clean clothes in there now."

Rodney couldn't fathom where Keith had found the bag if the U-Haul had in fact vanished. And it *had* vanished, Rodney was certain of that. He had seen it—he had *not* seen it—with his own eyes. The U-Haul had been *annihilated*—Latin for "something reduced to nothing." Annihilation had its antithe-sis, but that was a tougher trick to pull off: *exnihilation*—turning nothing into something. Exnihilation was the province of God and authors—of God and his *fellow* authors. Rodney and Armen once debated that: whether they were God's creatures or God's *characters*, unwitting bit players in an epic novel.

"God's not a novelist," Armen said. "Or not a very good one. I can't follow the plot."

"And everyone knows how it ends," Rodney said.

God traded in epic nonfiction. There were days when Rodney wanted to flip ahead a few pages and see what happened to him next. Tell me when my light turns green.

"What'd the doctor have to say?" Rodney asked Keith.

"He said I'll be fine," Keith said. "But I'll be wearing a boot in my wedding, which Caroline will hate. 'It'll ruin the pictures.' You know how she is with that stuff."

"You found the U-Haul all right then?"

"Yeah," Keith said. "No problem."

"Where was it?"

"Where we left it," Keith said.

"On 117th?" Rodney said.

"Yeah."

"Any tickets?"

"No."

"For *real*?"

So the van had vanished and returned from nothingness. Disapparated and apparated like Harry Potter. Exnihilated, like the universe: the Big Bang Theory of Keith's U-Haul.

Rodney had no time to solve that riddle. He was running late. Mairead would be looking for him on the downtownmost part of the platform. They were playing hooky: Mairead from the stresses of work, Rodney from the stresses of non-work.

Maybe after the bookstore they'd find a bar and get annihilated.

———

If they should ever remake *Fantastic Voyage* and a microscopic Raquel Welch were to steer the *Proteus* submarine through Rodney's bloodstream—a river of beer rivaling the lake of St. Brigid's—then the Strand is what his brain would look like from the inside: fifty-five thousand square feet of literature and trivia and air, the precious and useless given equal weight, the whole of human knowledge under one roof, but just try to summon what you need on a moment's notice—without getting lost in Sports or Sex or Food or any of a thousand other headings.

Rodney liked to think of books as everlasting, a conversation across the ages. But here was proof that they were not. The Strand was an assisted-living facility whose residents, with ravaged spines, faced extinction. And these were the lucky ones.

Just outside, geriatric books were forced to sell themselves on the street, beckoning from plastic milk crates and station-wagon tailgates and blankets spread on sidewalks—surrounded by elderly, emaciated *Life* magazines. Better to die in the remainder bin at Barnes & Noble and suffer the cremation of pulping than to pimp yourself on the streets like this, Rodney thought.

"Look at that," Rodney said, pointing to a sandwich board across the street. "Spectacular."

The sign outside the diner read: TODAYS SPECIAL'S.

"Brilliant," Mairead said. "Two words, both mispunctuated."

Why did people find the apostrophe so vexing, Rodney wondered, especially when it was used as the stand-in for a missing letter? Why was the shortened version of "and"—'n'—so troublesome? It's not *this 'n that* or *this n' that*. It's *this 'n' that*, dammit. For those attempting to abbreviate 2007, it was

'07—not 07', as he had seen spray-painted on so many Minnesota bridges by so many members of the classes of 2007 on his last trip home.

It was a conversation that had started on the subway, where they'd seen ads tout "Ticket's" and "VIP's." "The apostrophe shouldn't be used by everyone," Rodney had told Mairead. "It ought to come with a warning label signed by all future surgeon generals. Or surgeons general."

"I know that's right," Mairead had said of *surgeons general.* "But I can't stand the sound of it. It's like Johns Hopkins or Ruth's Chris."

He wanted to kiss her right there.

A minute later, they stopped at an ATM and the screen asked for her "PIN number," and Mairead pointed out the redundancy of the phrase: "A PIN is a Personal Identification Number," she said to Rodney. "So this thing wants my Personal Identification Number . . . number?"

"You're beautiful when you're pedantic," Rodney said. And he meant it. He would never forget the day Magic Johnson—movingly but redundantly—announced that he had the "HIV virus."

"This reminds me of being at the library as a girl," Mairead said when they were lost in the hedge maze of the Strand's stacks. The children's section of that library, she said, had a chair that looked like a giant leather catcher's mitt: Rodney pictured her as a soft pop foul, falling into the sweet spot to read *The Secret Garden* or *Jane Eyre* or the Betsy-Tacy books. Every book Mairead mentioned was half a century old or older. They looked for those books now.

Mairead riffled the pages of *Little Women* as if it were an animation flip book. And it was, in a way, for just flipping the pages—and inhaling their scent—brought the contents to life.

"What's that about?" Rodney said.

"It's about this girl, Jo," she said. "She wants to be a writer, and she—*why are you snickering?*"

"I'm not snickering."

"You snorted," Mairead said. "Or chortled. Or *something*."

"I wasn't snorting or snickering *or* chortling," Rodney said. "I was doing all three. I was . . . snorkeling."

"And what were you snorkeling *about*?" Mairead asked.

"Just that every other character in every other book I've ever read dreams of being a writer," Rodney said. "When you were a kid, reading *Little Women*, I was reading *David Copperfield*. *He* wants to be a writer. Stephen Dedalus in *Portrait of the Artist as a Young Man*—*he* wants to be a writer . . ."

"So does Betsy," Mairead said. "In the Betsy-Tacy books. Is there something wrong with wanting to be a writer?"

"Yes," Rodney said, though he couldn't at the moment think what. "All these writers," he finally said. "They can dream up any fate they want for their creatures. And all they ever think of is . . . *writer*?"

Mairead laughed. "That's it? *That's* your objection?"

They were standing in front of a table marked PAPERBACK FAVORITES. Rodney began to slap his palm on various covers as if they were Bibles and he were preparing to testify for the prosecution in some literary trial.

"*Confederacy of Dunces*," he said. "Guy wants to be a writer. *Bright Lights, Big City*—wants to be a writer. *The Kite Runner*: aspiring writer . . ."

"*The Devil Wears Prada*," Mairead said, slapping her palm on another paperback. "Or as my mom pronounces it, *The Devil Wears* PRAY*da*. Either way, the chick in it wants to be a writer."

"See?" Rodney said.

Mairead tapped another cover with her index finger. "*Breakfast at Tiffany's*," she said. "The guy in it—George Peppard in the movie?—wants to be a writer. This is fun."

"Told you," Rodney said.

"I see your point," Mairead said. "Or half of it. I still don't know what's wrong with wanting to be a writer."

Rodney exhaled. He knew he wasn't arguing with Mairead. He was arguing with himself, justifying his own choices. "It's just kind of precious and indulgent and *wussified*, is all," Rodney said. "Your father didn't aspire to write poetry. He chewed nails and mixed concrete and fell off roofs."

"He never fell off a roof," Mairead said. "He *did* fall off a scissor-lift. He was replacing a window."

"My point exactly," Rodney said. "James Joyce didn't know what a scissor-lift *was*, much less how to fall off one."

"I don't think they existed when Joyce was alive," Mairead said. "And I'm not sure *you* know what a scissor-lift is yourself."

"It's a pro wrestling maneuver," Rodney said. "The signature finishing move of the Undertaker."

"It's a motorized scaffold," Mairead said. "Though we nearly required an undertaker when my dad fell off his. He cracked two vertebrae, but went to work the next day. He believed in the Protestant work ethic."

"You're Catholic," Rodney said.

"But he never went to Mass," Mairead said. "He always said he was 'self-made,' whatever that means."

"Nobody's self-made," Rodney said. "Not literally, anyway."

"He thought he was," Mairead said. "He took credit for all the good things that happened to him. And blamed God for all the bad things."

Rodney told Mairead a joke he'd heard at Boyle's or St. Brendan's—he often confused the two. It was about an Irishman—late for an appointment and frantically circling the block—who promised God he'd stop drinking and attend Mass every morning if He would just help him find a parking space. At which time a parking space opened directly in front of the Irishman, who looked up and said, "Never mind, God— I found one."

Mairead smiled—it was too hot to laugh. As Rodney told the joke, she idly picked up a Paperback Favorite and fanned herself with it. *The World According to Garp*. "Guess what Garp wants to be," Rodney said.

"Writer?"

"Yep."

If literature was a mirror, Rodney held that mirror to his mouth to see if he was still breathing. Looking at all these books about aspiring writers, Rodney concluded that the answer was no. He wasn't alive, he was a cliché, preserved in amber: The Guy Who Wanted to Write.

In his old job, when they needed to fill a vacancy fast, they gave prospective employees a pro forma interview called a mirror test: as long as the candidate was breathing, he got the job.

Rodney wondered if he was getting mirror-tested for the job at Banco Marinero.

"You told me on the phone there was something you wanted to look for," Mairead said. "A book?" He decided now to look for Byron, for "Lines Inscribed Upon a Cup Formed From a Skull." He wanted to show Armen, suggest they have their heads turned into pint glasses. He thought of a neologism: *skullmuggery*.

What Rodney found first, in a volume of Byron's poetry, were these lines from *Don Juan*:

But words are things, and a small drop of ink,
Falling like dew, upon a thought, produces
That which makes thousands, perhaps millions, think;
'Tis strange, the shortest letter which man uses
Instead of speech, may form a lasting link
Of ages; to what straits old Time reduces
Frail man, when paper—even a rag like this—
Survives himself, his tomb, and all that's his.

That Rodney was standing a continent and two centuries removed from where and when Byron wrote those words was proof of their veracity.

This wasn't an old folks' home. It was a place of eternal life. The bookstore was a kind of heaven.

Rodney bought a volume of Byron and, attracted by the title, something called *The Earnest Drinker: A Short and Simple Account of Alcoholic Beverages for Curious Drinkers*, published by Allen & Unwin of London in 1950 and filled with margin notes made in impeccable Palmer script. Mairead bought a Nancy Drew, *The Scarlet Slipper Mystery*. Then she and Rodney walked out into the boiling afternoon. New York in August was the engine room of a burning tugboat.

Rodney fancied a cold beer in a dark place.

"I have this idea," he said, and told Mairead about the Bibulous Bibliophile, his pub-slash-bookstore where people could drink and read, browse and booze.

H. L. Mencken wrote, "I know some men who are drunk on books, as other men are drunk on whiskey." But Rodney now wondered out loud: "Why should anyone have to choose between the two?"

They walked up to 18th Street, to the Old Town, and rested

their forearms on its cold bar, fifty-five feet of marble and mahogany backed by an acre of beveled mirror. As in a cathedral, Mairead's eyes went straight up—to the ceiling, sixteen feet high and covered in tin. "I have to remind myself not to genuflect," Rodney said as Mairead surveyed the heavens and he surveyed her neck.

"How old is this place?" she asked the barman.

"Eighteen ninety-two," he said.

Like the Byron on the bar, the Old Town was another immortal, speaking across the centuries. The dumbwaiters worked, and so did the legendary Hinsdale urinals, born the year Mark Twain died, in 1910. Mark Twain could have whizzed in one of these, Rodney thought, as the ice cubes at the bottom of the urinal hissed and steamed like a locomotive.

"Looks like they beat you to it," Mairead said when Rodney returned.

"Beat me to what?"

"Your bar-slash-bookstore," Mairead said. She was pointing to the book jackets framed on the back bar. They were signed by Billy Collins and Frank McCourt and Nuala O'Faolain and Seamus Heaney. And Mairead was right: this *was* a pub-slash-bookstore. Rodney ordered a second round of beers and looked in the Byron for "Lines Inscribed Upon a Cup Formed From a Skull."

When he found it, he told Mairead: "Forget turning me into a Frisbee and throwing me on a roof. This is how I want to spend the afterlife: as a pint glass in a place like this." He splayed the book open in front of Mairead and she read aloud by the light of the lamps overhead.

"You want strangers to drink from your skull?" she said a moment later.

"Like Vikings," said the barman, bringing another round.

"They drank from the skulls of the vanquished. That's why their toast is *Skol*. It means skull."

Rodney raised his glass and said, "Skol."

Mairead said, "What's with you and death?

"Me and Death?" Rodney said. "I mean, Death and I?"

"You talk about it a lot."

"Do I?"

"You're not sick, are you?"

"Not that I know of," Rodney said. "Not in the medical sense. I think about dying sometimes because I like living. Did you ever read a book that you didn't want to end? You get depressed when there are more pages in your left hand than in your right? I turn thirty-five on Saturday and . . ."

"Happy Birthday!" Mairead said. "You didn't tell me."

". . . and I'm getting to the tipping point of the book. Pretty soon there are more pages in my left hand than in my right. That's all. I just don't want the book to end." He meant it, too.

Mairead put her hand on his. Rodney said, "When it's just starting to get good."

"I told my mom I met someone," Mairead said.

"Congratulations," Rodney said. "Someone I know?"

"Someone you love."

"How did you describe me?"

"I told her you were really into books."

"Did she ask what I do for a living?" Rodney said.

"No," Mairead said. "But I'm sure she'll say something like 'If he likes books, he oughta be a meter reader. They get to read all day.'"

"I'm working on it," Rodney said, even though he wasn't. He wasn't working, and he wasn't *really* working on working, unless you counted the one pre-interview interview. So he was grateful when Mairead didn't ask about his job search. But then he didn't think she would, or he wouldn't have brought it up.

"No rush," Mairead said. "You're thirty-five. You got thirty more years until retirement."

"I know," Rodney said, taking a pull off his pint. He held it up as if making a toast and said, "In fifteen short years, I'll be a member of AA *and* AARP."

"I love a man who knows where he's going," Mairead said.

"By then I should be ready to settle," Rodney said. "Like Keith and Caroline."

"Settle, or settle *down*?" Mairead said. "Because 'settle' I could take as an insult."

"Settle *down*," Rodney said. "Guinness settles. Speaking of which." He drained the rest of his pint glass.

They'd been drinking for much of the afternoon when Mairead said, "*Are* Keith and Caroline settling down? Because Caroline thinks Keith might be cheating on her."

Rodney said, "*What*?"

Mairead said, "Is he?"

It was dark when they left the Old Town. My God. How long had they been drinking? They took the subway to Mairead's place. At the door to her building, Rodney said, "Can I come in for coffee?"

"I don't have any," Mairead replied. "I don't drink coffee."

"Neither do I," said Rodney as Mairead let him in. "It's always made me feel a little left out, not drinking coffee when there's a Starbucks on every corner. Like living in Vegas, with no interest in gambling."

She lived by herself in a studio apartment. For all the

houseplants and family photos, Rodney thought, these apartments were little more than hotel rooms, a single space dominated by a bed.

The few times Rodney had been alone in a studio with a woman, the bed seemed to leer at them, and he always found himself unable even to sit on it, as if it were radioactive.

But this studio had no bed. Rodney sat on the sofa, which he presumed was a foldout, while Mairead used the bathroom. The wall opposite him was dominated by a floor-to-ceiling cabinet, melamine with a cherry veneer, that Rodney hoped to God concealed the TV. Surely she had a TV.

He wanted very badly to put his head down and go to sleep to the lullaby of a late baseball game.

Rodney rose, walked to the cabinet and pulled on its bifold doors. At the instant Mairead emerged from the bathroom, a Murphy bed fell from the closet like the cartoon tongue of a dog in heat.

"What do you think you're doing?" Mairead said.

Rodney felt the rush of blood to his cheeks and said, "I was looking for the TV."

There was something about their antique afternoon together—with its musty books and working dumbwaiters, its Hinsdale urinals and Murphy bed—that made Rodney feel part of a courtlier age. He had no intention of sleeping with Mairead on this night and abruptly tried to stuff the bed back into its cabinet. But she said, "Leave it."

Rodney eased the bed to the floor—it reminded him of lowering a drawbridge, the portal to a fortress—and Mairead sat at its foot. She said, "You didn't think . . . ?"

"Of course not," Rodney said, looking around the studio. After a pause he added, "Though I have this fantasy of doing it in every room of your house."

She lay her head on a pillow. "I do want to sleep with you," she said. "I want to fall asleep with you right now."

And so Rodney lay next to her. They were both fully dressed. It was just as well, he thought. He must have had a dozen Guinness and would be suffering from Brewer's Droop, one of a thousand urological plagues that concerned him. There was a lineman on the Giants named Bentley Johnson and whenever Rodney heard the name it sounded to him like an affliction—something that chauffeurs contracted after prolonged sitting in a luxury automobile.

"Tell me a bedtime story," Mairead said dreamily. Her eyes were already closed.

"You're living in a bedtime story," Rodney said, braiding his fingers behind his head.

"I am," she murmured, turning her back to Rodney and pulling her knees to her chest. He couldn't tell if it was a question or confirmation.

"Once upon a time," Rodney said, "there was a man named William Murphy. He lived in a single room in San Francisco. He wanted space to entertain, so he invented the Murphy bed. Which is how Mairead Quinn came to sleep in this giant pop-up book that she opens every night and closes every morning."

Mairead didn't say anything for a very long time. Rodney thought she was already asleep when she whispered, "That's lovely," her voice fading like a radio station.

She was already off to the Land of Nod.

Rodney lay awake and thought of many things. He listened to her breathing in and out like a bellows. What a strange phrase for sleep, "the Land of Nod," that place in Genesis—"East of Eden"—to which Cain was exiled for slaying Abel.

He thought of Abel and exile and "Able was I ere I saw Elba"—that palindrome of Napoleonic exile—until his stream of consciousness became a trickle of consciousness, and then a dry creekbed of consciousness. He turned away from Mairead, and in two hours he was asleep.

8

Rodney woke to the water-cannon sound of the shower. Mairead evidently had better water pressure than he did. He couldn't wait to give it a go, that shower: it sounded like the delousing station in a prison.

There was a drawer in the Murphy cabinet next to the bed, and Rodney opened it. He didn't know why. In it were pens and a scrunchie and a pair of oversized glasses that called to mind Larry King or Harry Caray. Rodney shut the drawer when he heard Mairead's hand on the bathroom doorknob, just before she made her rock star's entrance—surrounded by steam.

She wore a cream-colored towel. Rodney said, "Good morning." Then he reached into the nightstand drawer, removed the glasses, sat up in bed, and put them on, saying: "I need a better look at this."

Mairead turned and howled.

"That's my emergency backup pair," she said.

"I see," said Rodney. "If your apartment gets broken into in the middle of the night, the burglar will tremble at Tootsie's approach."

Rodney watched her pad around the room leaving puddled footprints on the laminate floor.

"In my nightstand," he said, "I have what appear to be the love child of John Denver's glasses and John Lennon's glasses."

"I didn't know glasses could procreate," Mairead said, gathering clothes in her arms.

"They can," Rodney said. "In fact, they print up little bumper stickers that say, 'Glasses Do It in About an Hour.'"

Mairead reached into a drawer in the Murphy cabinet and removed a pair of underwear. "I hope you've fronted those," Rodney said, peering over the glasses. She was standing above him, one hand securing her towel. Still supine, Rodney held the wrist of her other hand, and she had to lean over him to kiss him, as if administering CPR. She smelled of oatmeal soap and lilac shampoo and detergent. Rodney held on to her wrist but she said, "I'm going to be late for work."

"I have no problem with that."

She gathered the rest of her clothes and said, "Plus, you look like Charles Nelson Reilly." As she returned to the bathroom to dress, Rodney removed the glasses.

Five minutes later, she came clicking across the laminate in patent-leather shoes and a pinstriped suit and said, "I had a wonderful time playing hooky yesterday."

Rodney reached up to pull her onto the bed but she resisted and said, "Call me this afternoon. The door will lock behind you when you leave." And with that, she went clicking out of the apartment.

Still wearing yesterday's clothes, Rodney got up to take a leak. He clocked himself in Mairead's vanity mirror. As at Boyle's, this wasn't a vanity at all, but vanity's opposite. Beneath bare dressing-room bulbs, the mirror induced self-loathing more than self-love. Thank God Rodney's contact lenses were still soaking in saline in two water glasses by the bed. He preferred to greet himself, and the day, in gauzy soft focus, a Barbara Walters–meets–Barbra Streisand TV interview.

He made the Murphy bed, removing the pillows then tucking in the sheets and blanket so that it all stayed together when he pushed it back up against the wall. Then he pulled the bed down again, just enough to see that the bed remained made, in the same way that he always reopened the door of a public mailbox to make sure that his letters had slid down. He did the same thing with the door on his garbage chute after throwing a bag down. As a kid, he did it with the refrigerator door, to see if he could catch it with the light off inside.

Rodney put in his contacts. His colleagues at work were always proselytizing for laser eye surgery. People who were newly Lasiked, like people who were newly married, weren't happy until all their friends had joined them. But Rodney *liked* glasses. All his colleagues who'd had laser surgery said the same thing: "Now I can see in the shower." Rodney the gymnophobe thought: Visual acuity is the *last* thing I want in the shower.

His vision was bad enough that he would not have survived adolescence had he been born into that benighted world before corrective lenses kicked in, sometime after the Middle Ages. Even now, though he usually wore contacts, Rodney sometimes found himself in that Gordian knot: unable to find his glasses because he was not wearing his glasses.

He got his first pair in eighth grade and spent the ride home from the optician seeing the world as if for the first time, reading street signs and billboards with his head out the window like a dog's. That's exactly how the world looked now, with Mairead in his life, everything sharp and new and clarified. Maybe that's why they called it *seeing* someone.

Rodney resisted sandblasting himself in the shower—he had nothing to change into, he realized—or having a rummage around Mairead's studio to see what he could see. He liked the slow striptease of a relationship, the time-release revelations. He never flipped ahead in books; he had no intention of starting now. Just seeing Mairead fresh from the shower—hair wet, water beaded on her bare shoulders—was an intimate act. And though he'd deflated it with the jokes and the glasses, Rodney was moved in an almost spiritual way by the sight of her still wet from her morning ablutions.

Ablutions: a priest's ritual washing of hands during Mass.

His lenses were still soaking in two water glasses on the nightstand: the ocular equivalent of dentures, it occurred to Rodney as he brought them to the bathroom to put his eyes in. The toothpaste he squeezed onto his index finger reminded him of the Polident commercials, in which denture cream was applied to a prosthetic gum line. Rodney brushed his teeth with his finger. They looked fine, his teeth. But then his front two were not original. They were as porcelain as the Hinsdale urinals, his incisors having been broken off just below the gum line by a thrown baseball when Rodney was thirteen, about the same time he got his glasses. For two weeks, his smile looked like a two-car garage with the doors up.

You don't keep the factory parts for very long in this life before the after-market upgrades are installed. Rodney looked at himself in Mairead's anti-vanity and wondered what his Blue Book value would be, with all the miles on his clock.

His clock. To hear them talk, you'd think only women had biological clocks. Yesterday, at the bar, when Mairead asked him about dying, Rodney said he heard his clock ticking all the time. "That's a good thing," he said. "I try not to waste any time." If Mairead noted the irony of this, after eight consecutive hours of book browsing and beer drinking, she didn't say so. What she said was "A woman's clock ticks louder. When our alarm goes off, we can't bear children."

True, but Rodney could hear his own ticking as clearly as the mantel clock Mairead kept on a shelf, the only sound now in the apartment. He heard it in her heels, ticking across the laminate and out the door—and out of his life, he feared, if he didn't find a job.

And he heard it twenty minutes later, across town, when he saw the U-Haul: it was at the other end of the block from where'd he parked it, and when he walked over to touch it, to see if it was real, he heard the loud tick of its engine, cooling.

So the U-Haul was disappearing and reappearing, annihilating and exnihilating, like some large-scale magic stunt by David Blaine or David Copperfield.

Rodney had cabbed it over from Mairead's to see it for himself, the mysterious return of the prodigal van. Then he walked home through the park, thinking of David Copperfield. Or rather, *David Copperfield*. When he saw the book for the first time, at thirteen in the public library, he thought it was about the magician. Then he started reading about the boy whose father—dead before David was born—left him a small library to keep him company, books that "kept alive my fancy" and gave hope of a better place than home and school.

And though Rodney didn't have an evil stepfather, like David's Murdstone, or attend a nineteenth-century English boarding school, like David's Salem House, the idea that books could transport—of books as rapid transit—resonated. In the end, David Copperfield fell in love and became a father and was elevated—the other Copperfield might say *levitated*—above his circumstances. Maybe he was a magician after all.

Walking clockwise against the flow of runners at the Reservoir, Rodney saw the rain. Saw it before he felt it, a heavy raindrop stirring up dust in front of him like a bullet in a Western. Almost instantly came the car wash of an August thunderstorm, and Rodney on foot, in the center of Central Park: Out of Murphy's Bed and into Murphy's Law, he thought.

Rodney wore a short-sleeved cotton shirt that buttoned up the front and didn't tuck in, a style favored by dictators in tropical climates. And even though it was now translucent with rain, and he couldn't possibly get wetter, Rodney began to run.

Edward A. Murphy was an American aerospace engineer who conducted rocket-sled experiments for the air force in 1949 to test the human limits of acceleration. It was he who posited that anything that can go wrong will go wrong, and Rodney reflected, while testing the limits of his own acceleration, that it really *shouldn't* have taken a rocket scientist to make this observation on the cosmic conspiracies against man. But it did.

He ran into the oncoming runners, many of them two and three abreast, a chain of paper dolls linked at the elbows. It was hammering down now—"Like a horse pissing on a flat rock," Keith always said—and rainwater was already spider-veining out from the running path and seeking lower elevations.

His mouth was paste: dehydration—though water, water everywhere. He couldn't stop thinking of various Murphys. Rodney's train of thought was a local. It made all stops; it often stalled between stations. But it was without end. He read a novel by Alexander Theroux about a guy whose "trains of thought had no cabooses." Rodney recognized himself in the description.

So he thought of Murphys, of James J. Murphy, who founded the Murphy's brewery in Cork in 1856, making stout near a holy well, at once a spring and shrine, a devotional site called Our Lady's Well. In 1913, the Number Five vat at Our

Lady's Well brewery ruptured and twenty-three thousand gallons of porter flooded into Leitrim Street. The Cork *Constitution* told of a worker swimming forty yards to save himself from drowning in this Amazon of alcohol—a tributary, perhaps, of St. Brigid's Lake of Beer.

A hundred years earlier, in 1814, the vat atop the Henry Meux brewery in Banbury Street, London, burst and flooded the streets of London's West End with 3,530 barrels of beer. Two houses were swept away and nine people died—one, according to legend, from alcohol poisoning.

Rodney watched the water sluicing into the gutters and imagined it was porter. In his mind he was singing along with Springsteen to "American Land," in which city taps dispensed lager.

He ran with his plastic-bagged books beneath his right arm, as if carrying a football against the kickoff coverage of joggers coming at him, including a group of five in identical sausage casings of long Lycra tights—in this heat, for God sake—and all of them abreast, like the Rockettes. They cursed at him in German while breaking rank. At least he thought it was cursing.

Rodney used his left index finger to windshield-wipe the water from his forehead, a combination of rain and last night's Guinness: His skull was already a sweating pint of beer.

When at last he washed up at his apartment, lungs in flames and sneakers squishing, Rodney had a powerful thirst on. He realized how Keith must have regarded him: sweating and sodden and sucking wind after leaving 4K at lunchtime yesterday. "What happened to *you*?" Keith said when Rodney, making his sitcom entrance, stood dripping in the door frame.

"I feel like the skeleton who walked into the bar," Rodney said. "Bring me a beer and a mop."

"You look like you just came back from Guadalajara."

Keith was referring not to the Mexican city but the down-market Mexican restaurant just off campus in college, and the night Rodney got caught in a biblical deluge while returning to their dorm with dinner. His takeout bag, already wet with grease, ruptured in the rain and Rodney's dinner fell into a filthy puddle in the parking lot of a laundromat. He paused for a moment and watched his dinner disappear: his chimichangas were two U-boats, his nacho chips a tortilla flotilla. Then Rodney reached into the puddle, picked up the chimis, and sprinted back to the dorm with them, one in either hand, the anchor on a relay bearing twin batons, battered and fried.

Rodney dried the chimis on the radiator and then ate them. For the rest of the semester, his room and those that adjoined it—Keith's included—smelled like deep-fried dogshit.

"What happened to *me*?" Rodney said, removing his sneakers with his feet and pulling his shirt off over his head. "What the hell happened to *you*?"

Keith was clean-shaven and clean-shirted, spruced up, hosed down, deodorized, maybe even Martinized—made over by some miracle barber.

He had also tidied his little area of Rodney's living room. The coffee table, temporarily exiled against the wall to make room for the air mattress, had been covered in crumbs—twice Rodney had swept them into his own hand with the postage-paid subscription card from a magazine. They called this act, in the restaurant trade, "crumbing the table." Rodney overheard a waiter say it once and he'd never forgotten that—*crumb* as a verb.

T-shirts had drooped over chair backs like Dali clocks. The unmade mattress on the floor cried crack house.

Now the mattress was gift-wrapped in clean sheets, the

clothes laundered and folded. Rodney got down in a push-up position, like the pope kissing the tarmac, and skeptically sniffed the AeroBed. It was redolent of fabric softener.

"Snuggle?" he said to Keith.

"I'd love to," Keith said. "But I'm saving myself for marriage."

Rodney had forgotten: Caroline was coming tomorrow. "What time does she get in?"

"Noon."

"Excited?"

"Excited to stop sleeping nine inches off the floor," Keith said. "No offense."

"You preferred sleeping nine *feet* off the floor?" Rodney said.

"I did, actually. It made me feel like a Berenstain Bear."

"They slept in a loft?" Rodney said.

"They lived in a tree."

"Like the Swiss Family Robinson?" Rodney said. He always envied that treehouse—that penthouse, with all mod cons—that the Robinsons built in the Disney movie version.

"If you say so," Keith said.

The word *penthouse* made Rodney think of Keith's magazines, moldering in the U-Haul. He wondered if there was a nudie magazine called *Treehouse*. But then they never name magazines for the places people read them, or newsstands would be teeming with titles like *Crapper* and *Waiting Room* and *Middle Seat*.

"I saw the U-Haul today," Rodney said. "I was at a used bookstore over there." Keith would buy this. He was oblivious to the location of the borough's bookstores.

"How's it look?"

"It's across the street and down the block from where we parked it," Rodney said.

"Right."

"Keith, I haven't moved it. I know I said I would, but I never did."

"I know," Keith said. "Because a friend of mine's had the keys since Monday."

"And he's been moving it?"

"Yeah."

"Good," Rodney said. "Does he at least live in that neighborhood?"

"Yeah," Keith said, turning away from Rodney and beginning to pack a suitcase. "She's five blocks away."

"She?"

"A friend of mine from work," Keith said, without inflection. He kept his back turned, in a way that dissuaded further discussion.

Rodney picked up the phone, heard the perforated dial tone that indicated a message. He called his voice mail and heard Curt Mayhew inviting Rodney back for a second interview at Banco Marinero on Monday. "We'll kick your tires," Mayhew said. "You can kick ours. Have a great weekend."

It sounded to Rodney like a mirror test. He had a job if he wanted one.

At 10 a.m. Rodney retired for a nap. He hadn't slept well last night, lying next to Mairead, on top of the covers at first, then under them when the AC became too much to bear. He couldn't arrange himself in a way that was both comfortable and chaste, and so he spent two hours creating a kind of anti–Kama Sutra, contorting himself into every conceivable nonsexual position.

It was nearly 3 a.m. when he finally fell asleep, his back to Mairead, the two of them making the beast with two fronts.

Then he'd had to get up every hour, and stumble blindly to the bathroom—twice to pee, twice to fart. There was nowhere to cropdust in that tiny studio, and so he went into the john, as if he were sneaking a smoke. He turned on the fan but it sounded like a jet engine, so he fanned the air with his hand.

When he finally did drift off, Mairead was breathing softly, a slight whistle in her nose, and Rodney dreamt that the two of them were a pair of pills on the stuck-out tongue of the Murphy bed. Rodney was dreaming of ecstasy, but in the metaphysical, not pharmaceutical, sense of the word.

Lying down to take his nap, Rodney reached for the paperback dictionary on his nightstand. He noted a third definition of *ecstasy*: "A mental state, usually caused by intense religious experience, sexual pleasure, or drugs, in which somebody is so dominated by an emotion that self-control and sometimes consciousness are lost."

So those were the three sources of bliss: religion, sex, mind-altering substances.

God

Woman.

Beer.

He set the dictionary aside and picked up *The Earnest Drinker*. Flat on his bed, he opened the book, a raised roof above his face. From its fanned pages fluttered a flaking brown newspaper clipping—a United Press tidbit headlined ADVISES A DRINK TO EASE TENSION—on the salutary health benefits of an evening cocktail. Rodney set the clip on the nightstand.

The book looked to have once been a gift, for it was inscribed, on the title page, in the fastidious hand of another epoch, "To Frank—Hic!" Taking up the entire back endpaper was a an epigraph of sorts, written in the same hand:

> Alcohol, to indulge in an understatement, has had a conspicuous position in the history of the race. It fathered religion and science and agriculture, produced more human confidence, and promoted good will toward men. It is the most efficient and practical relaxer of the driving force in the brain; it offers an immediate method of personal enjoyment. It is the greatest medium known for the purpose of permitting man to forget, at least for a little while, the shortness of life and the ludicrously helpless and infinitesimal part he plays in the functions of the universe.
>
> —*Liquor, the Servant of Man*
> Smith and Helwig

It was not lost on Rodney, as he lay there on the bed, that all of the people associated with that statement—its authors, the author of the book in which it was inscribed, the original buyer of that book, and its original recipient—were, almost certainly, dead.

And yet here they all were, gathered in his bedroom, speaking to him.

Keith was gone when Rodney woke up. But he'd left a note. How sweet, Rodney thought, Keith leaving that note. Made the place feel like a proper home almost.

Rodney was happy. Not ecstatic, exactly, but not depressed. He saw a cable news segment the other night that said unemployment often caused depression. But not in his case. Quite the opposite, if anything: *em*ployment had caused him depression.

Still, he was aware that drinking, sleeping till noon, dwelling on death—his daily routine—were often thought to be acts of despondency. That's how they sometimes appeared, on the unshaven face of things. But in Rodney they were affirmations. He was sure of that.

Keith's note, written in a kid's block letters on a white lunch sack—yesterday's carryout—said: "Back around 5." In case Rodney was worried.

It didn't say where he'd gone. Was it possible that Caroline was right, and Keith was not monogamous, was in fact—was there such a thing as omnigamous?

For what seemed a very long time now, Rodney had been something more exclusive than monogamous, his only action an occasional wank: the *ménage à . . . un*. Rodney took two years of high school French and knew that phrase literally meant "household of one," which is precisely what he'd been before Keith's convalescence, and to which he would return in the next forty-eight hours. He didn't know if he was ready for that.

Rodney called Mairead's office number. Her assistant said she was "out of pocket," Mayhew-speak that briefly inflamed the acids in his stomach. But he envied Mairead the inane meetings and off-site excursions that gave shape and purpose to her day, and he was at once comforted and made anxious by the prospect of going back to work himself. Rodney was just getting up at two, and he knew *that* only by the seagull-squawk of the students just released from St. Brendan's School.

He was about to leave a message when Mairead's assistant said, "Could you hold on one second? Here she comes now." A moment later, Mairead was on the line and Rodney said, "You're back in pocket."

"What?"

"Your assistant said you were out of pocket," Rodney said.

"That means I was in the bathroom," Mairead said.

"I'll need a refresher in corporate cryptography," Rodney said. "Because I might be going back to work."

"Really?"

"Don't sound so surprised," Rodney said, while thinking: Why couldn't she just say "Congratulations"?

"I'm not," Mairead said. "I think it's great."

"Yeah, I have a second interview on Monday," Rodney said.

"*For?*"

"A job," Rodney said. "In banking."

"Great," Mairead said. But to Rodney's ear, "Great" sounded like "Gross" or "Grody" or "*Groan*"—an ugly utterance, and one of surprise.

"You don't sound thrilled," Rodney said.

"I don't?" Mairead said. "Didn't I just say it sounded great?"

Rodney held the receiver at arm's length for a second, something he used to do to calm himself on his old job. When he returned the phone to his ear, Mairead was saying: "Is it something you want to do?" Keith had asked him the same thing. It was starting to get on Rodney's tits.

He puffed his cheeks like a chipmunk's and blew all the air out of his lungs before replying.

"If by *it* you mean drawing a paycheck, then yes, it *is* something I want to do," he said. "I'd prefer to make a banking salary while writing book reviews, but I didn't see that listing on shitjobs.com."

"Are you getting angry?"

"I'm not angry," Rodney said. "But you're responding to everything I say with a question. It's like talking to Alex Trebek."

"He gives the answers," Mairead said. "On *Jeopardy*, it's the *contestants* who say everything in the form of a question."

She was right, and it irritated him, and he should have just laughed, but Rodney didn't feel like laughing right now. "I meant Socrates," he said. "It's like talking to Socrates."

"Socrates, Trebek, what's the difference?" Mairead said.

Rodney didn't respond. She was trying to engage him in one of their tetherball games of banter, but he wasn't punching the ball back.

"Hello?" Mairead said.

"I'm here."

Mairead said: "Socrates said the only thing he knew was that he didn't know anything. Whereas Trebek—he knows he knows everything. So I guess they're really not the same at all."

Rodney said, "It's a good job."

"It *sounds* like a good job," Mairead said. "Who said it wasn't?"

"Everybody's asking me if it's what I want to do, like *I* might not know what *I* want to do," Rodney said.

"What do you want me to say?" Mairead said. "I told you it sounded like a great job. I'm telling you that I'm happy for you. I will assume that it's something you want to do."

"It is," Rodney said. "But then you've known me for a full week, so you might know better than I." He knew as soon as he said it that he shouldn't have. But he was powerless to stop.

"I'm going to hang up now," Mairead said.

"That would be a grown-up thing to do," Rodney said.

Mairead remained silent for a moment. Rodney waited her out. Finally she said, "This isn't a very pleasant conversation."

"This isn't a conversation, period," Rodney said. "You're not telling me what you really think. Do you assume I'll hate my job because you hate yours or do you not like the thought of dating a banker or . . ."

"Is that what you think?" Mairead said.

"God*damn* it—speak a declarative sentence."

"Okay," Mairead said. "Here's a declarative sentence: You're an asshole. If you think I'm so shallow as to *care* what you do for a living, then you're mistaken about me. And I, apparently, was mistaken about you."

Rodney wanted to take back everything he said, suck the words back into his mouth like spaghetti. Instead he said, "You're the one always talking about your dad's work ethic so I thought you might appreciate the fact that I'm at least looking for—"

"I'm not finished!" Mairead said. And then, in a shouted whisper: "*I'm not finished.* If I'm not embarrassed that you *don't* have a job, why would I be embarrassed that you might *get* a job?"

"Well you don't seem very happy for me," Rodney said.

"Because *you* don't seem very happy for you," Mairead said. "*You're* the one who talks about my dad. But since you bring him up—yes, he *did* work all the time. But he loved what he did and he died at forty-two. Life's too short to hate your job, especially if you hate yourself because of it."

"Is that an ad slogan you're working on?" Rodney said. "*Life's too short to hate your job*? Let me tell you, life's a lot shorter when you don't *have* a job to pay for groceries. So if I take a job that I don't necessarily love, it's only because—and this is just me—I like to *eat*."

"Don't speak to me as if I'm an idiot," Mairead said. "If I don't sound thrilled for you, it's because *you* don't sound thrilled for you. Otherwise, I don't give a shit if you go to work for Banco Marinero or Franco-Americano or whatever it is."

After a long silence Rodney said: "Franco-Americano?"

Mairead said nothing while Rodney tried to defibrillate the conversation. "I *wish* I could get a job at Franco-American," he said. "Meetings catered with Ravioli-Os? Can you imagine lunch in the executive dining room? *Would sir like the meatballs or the sliced franks with his Spaghetti-Os?*"

After a full fifteen seconds of silence Mairead said: "Are we done?"

Rodney said, "You tell me."

She hung up.

So Mairead was not impressed with his desire to work. Why was he surprised? Rodney thought of the time, two years ago, when Armen had an awning put up outside Boyle's—burgundy with "Boyle's" in script—because he thought it would class up the joint. He got so many complaints from the regulars that he eventually took it down. Nobody wanted it. You never could tell what another person wanted.

Rodney looked at Curt Mayhew's business card, at the word *Banco*. Every time he saw it he thought of Banquo, whose ghost, chains rattling, came back to haunt Macbeth.

9

Outside he saw the summer-school kids, Quasimodoed beneath their bookbags. Hunchbacks with backpacks, walking headlong down the sidewalk as if into a gale.

Rodney was going to Boyle's to blow off steam. The city sympathized, its streets seething, steam rising on Columbus from two open manholes. They resembled the nostrils of a cartoon bull.

He was walking fast—*he had a good head of steam going*—when he reached the threshold of Boyle's in mid-stride, his right hand reflexively reaching for the brass push plate. But the door didn't yield and Rodney ran into it. He was reminded of walking down basement stairs in the dark, expecting one more step when in fact he'd reached the bottom.

Boyle's was locked. On a Friday afternoon.

Rodney hoped this really was the bottom of the basement stairs, that there was no metaphysical crawl space, no spiritual sub-basement, into which he could still descend.

A sheet of paper was taped to the door, a color-xeroxed photograph of a young man in a short-sleeved white shirt and gray tie. His black hair was beginning to recede, a narrow finger of baldness encroaching above either temple, what Keith (who was just starting to lose his hair) liked to call "power alleys."

The man in the photo smiled, and his smile was framed by a goatee, and his goatee was flanked by two flushed cheeks, which in turn were bookended by two women, in profile. The women were kissing the guy on either cheek. The three were at a party somewhere, perhaps a wedding reception. Rodney couldn't tell.

Above the photo was a headline: WE LOVE YOU GARY. Below the photo was a single block of text, done up on a computer in what Rodney recognized as Times New Roman. He read:

Gary, our beloved brother/son/uncle/father/friend, passed away unexpectedly on Thursday. While we mourn our loss, Boyle's will be closed indefinitely, but friends of Gary are invited to join us here on Saturday night @ 7 p.m. for a celebration of his life. In lieu of flowers, the Garabedian family asks that you make a donation to St. Gregory the Illuminator Armenian Church. And tip your bartender ☺.

It was ninety-two degrees. Rodney felt his skin chill, as if he'd stepped, sweating, into the walk-in freezer at the Jolly Elf. Gary was Armen and Armen was the young man in the old photograph on the flyer, a flyer that looked identical to the "Missing" posters that papered every lamppost after 9/11.

Armen was dead. Rodney had just seen him the night before last behind the bar at Boyle's, where the Venn diagram of their lives overlapped in two feet of polished rosewood, the common ground in otherwise separate circles of existence.

Columbus continued to smoke volcanically. He thought of the daughter Armen seldom got to see, of the two anonymous girls kissing him in that photo—how they were now middle-aged.

Inappropriate jokes made forced entry to his brain. He imagined cocktail umbrellas flying at half mast in Armen's honor, a marine folding a bar rag into a tight triangle before placing it on Armen's casket.

He wanted to cry but he couldn't. Rodney hadn't cried as an adult, except at the end of *Cinema Paradiso* and when the Twins won the World Series. Otherwise, he was a stranger to what Saint-Exupéry called "the land of tears." He hadn't cried when his Aunt Laura died. Instead, grief triggered in his tear ducts a kind of dry-heaving. But he *wanted* to cry, he really did.

A truck backed up, its *beep-beep-beep*s sounding to Rodney like censored expletives.

Rodney walked to Cliffs of Moher, the Irish bar on Amsterdam, where sitting at the bar felt like an act of betrayal, like sleeping with another woman the day after his wife died.

Still, he was cheered by the motley row of tap handles, a chorus line waiting to take its curtain bow. Rodney asked for a Harp. The barman held a glass beneath the tap and pulled the pearl-white ceramic paddle without ever looking away from CNN.

Rodney had come to Cliffs of Moher because Armen's friend tended bar there. A guy named Cliff. At least that's what everyone called him, ever since the night some drunk walked into Cliffs of Moher, looked at the two barmen on duty, and said, "Which one of you is Cliff?"

Rodney laughed every time Armen told that story. It gave Cliffs of Moher a glamour (and a possessive apostrophe) it didn't merit: "Cliff's of Moher," like "Frederick's of Hollywood" or "Lobel's of New York," the lingerie emporium and butcher shop whose respective store windows specialized in artful displays of flesh.

"Excuse me," Rodney said. The place was nearly empty, the white-shirted barman leaning on the back bar, looking up at the TV, sipping Coke through a straw. "I'm not trying to be funny, but is Cliff here? The guy they call Cliff?"

The barman looked at Rodney and said, "That's me."

Rodney said, "Are you a friend of Gary's, by any chance? Garabedian?"

"I am," Cliff said. "I was."

"So you know?"

Cliff didn't say anything. Rodney said, "You know what happened to Gary?"

"Who are you?" Cliff said. His eyes were almost biolumi-nescent, the blue of a Bombay Sapphire bottle.

"My name's Rodney. I'm a friend of Gary's. Except I know him as Armen. *Knew* him. I'm sorry—I'm still stunned. I just saw a notice on the door at Boyle's and . . ."

Cliff put both hands on the bar, leaned forward, exhaled—it was *rum* and Coke—and told Rodney everything.

Armen had a heart attack while taking a beer delivery, dead-lifting a keg of Bass into place in the Boyle's basement. The guy driving the beer truck called 911. The EMTs had to bring Armen up the steel service ramp and through the cellar doors that opened onto the sidewalk. It was 9 a.m.

Rodney could see those cellar doors opening, the morning pedestrians hustling to avoid them, the rubberneckers stop-ping to get a good goo. And Armen—dead on a stretcher—ris-ing from the Earth's surface like a submarine-fired Exocet missile.

In his exhaustive ruminations on how he'd like to go, Rod-ney never conceived of this possibility: hugging a half barrel of Bass, embracing 136 pounds of ale in his final earthly act. He persuaded himself that Armen died happy, and not—or not just—in a basement, with a stranger, too young.

Rodney was the only patron in Cliffs, a server-to-drinker ratio that made him uneasy. Worse, Cliff seemed to see through him with those eyes, those cool-blue halogen headlamps. Rodney felt more sorry for himself than he did for Armen, whose death he'd begun to think of as noble: ascending that ramp at a forty-five degree angle, as if pointed at heaven, as if bracing for launch. Armen had achieved escape velocity.

Not Rodney. A mantel clock ticked on the back bar. On CNN, a small graphic in the lower right corner of the screen silently shuttled between Eastern and Pacific time, forcing those sods between the coasts to do the math if they wanted to know how late or early it was. Black-and-white photographs of ancient Ireland tatted up the walls: thatched cottages, donkey carts, old men in flat caps. Everything about Cliffs was a lesson in time's passage—the shadow spreading like a stain across the ocher tiles, the Republic of Ireland football shirt fading in its frame, the born-on dates on those bottles of Bud Light that Cliff was loading into a Rubbermaid trash barrel full of ice beneath the bar.

Rodney asked for one of the bottles. He saw his reflection in it, in every sense of the phrase. The bottle had a born-on date. It had a sell-by date. When its contents were consumed, it left an empty shell. Its afterlife was a mystery: It might get redeemed, it might get recycled.

He peeled the label off in one piece. It reminded Rodney of peeling the dead skin off a sunburn as a child. He thought of Longneck, the physical manifestation of this longneck bottle of Bud Light, then of Armen intervening on his behalf that night. He handed the bottle back to Cliff and said, "I'll be right back. I have to make a phone call. I lost track of time." But in fact that's all he could think about: time.

From the sidewalk, he called Mairead's home machine, secure in the knowledge that she wouldn't pick up. Rodney didn't apologize for their previous conversation—*she* had called *him* an asshole—but he did say: "A friend of mine just died." It was unfair, he knew—she would have to call back and feign sympathy, at the very least—so he tried to close on a more jocular tone. "Do you want to get a beer tonight? There's a place near me called Cliffs of Moher. You'll want to have your inoculations topped up, but otherwise it's all right."

Inoculation came from the Latin *inoculatus*, which sounded like a Catholic saint or his grade-school principal: Sister Inoculatus.

Rodney was summoned to Sister Immaculata's office in sixth grade. It was the only time he ever played hooky in grade school, and then only from recess. He and his friend Frankie Collins went AWOL on the playground and walked to the record store a block away. It was actually a head shop, though they didn't know that at the time, despite its name— the Record Joint—and its heady aroma of incense and fringed suede.

Rodney ordered another Harp and thought about the Record Joint for the first time in years.

Frankie had led Rodney straight to the "O" bin, where the cover of *Honey*, by the Ohio Players, captured a naked woman slathered in the title substance, presumably just before she was attacked by bees or bears.

Rodney asked Cliff for a bar menu. New York's afternoon traffic was just beginning to clear its throat.

Rodney and Frankie had been busted when some parent driving past the Record Joint phoned the school to report two uniformed kids in a strip-mall parking lot at ten thirty in the morning. Which was fine, because the whole point of hooky was someone might catch you. Hooky—it came from *hoejke*, the Dutch name for "hide and seek"—lost its illicit thrill if nobody was looking for you. And that's the kind of hooky Rodney was playing now, two decades later in New Amsterdam: Nobody cared that he was on the lam from work all day. No one was looking for him.

In one of his earliest memories—he must have been three or four—Rodney fell asleep in his parents' bedroom closet while playing hide and seek with his cousins. He woke in the dark, looking up at his father's Oxford shirts in their dry-cleaning bags, a dress shoe digging into his back. One side of his face was dimpled from the carpet pile. And he realized what had happened: His cousins had stopped looking for him.

His parents found him softly snoring on the floor of the closet and let him sleep there. But he didn't know that until years later, at his high school graduation party, when they were telling baby stories to embarrass him. When he was four, Rodney just thought nobody cared if he was hiding.

That's what it was like yesterday, playing hooky when he was unemployed. Or right now, in the Cliffs of Moher. He didn't have to phone in sick and nobody came looking for him on the streets of Manhattan, where there were always crowds of people blowing off something. When he got rightsized Rodney had instructed Keith to punch him in the nuts if he ever spent the day in Starbucks, on his laptop, making a frappuccino last six hours.

Being out of work felt the same as sitting at home on Saturday night. He knew it wasn't rational, but it seemed like everyone else on Earth was doing something that he was missing out on. The same with insomnia. Whenever Rodney woke in the middle of the night he was certain that he was the only one in the world who was awake, even though he could see lights on in other apartments. Even though everyone in Europe was eating breakfast.

Rodney tucked into a chicken pot pie. He pierced the top crust with his fork and the surface steamed like the city streets. The shadow that was on the floor was now climbing the wall. Even Keith, if he really did have a squeeze on the side—on the East Side—was showing an entrepreneurial spirit. He was doing something. Some*one*, maybe. Was that possible?

Forget the morality of it. Was it *physically* possible that Keith was having a farewell roll in the hay—in the hay*loft*, if Keith had his way—with his "friend"? His "friend," from "work," who was free to move the van today at midmorning?

Rodney had seen a guy on TV who did two thousand one-armed push-ups in an hour, so he supposed Keith, in his condition, could consummate the affair.

Employment was vertical, everything about it aspiring upward, to "the top": You were *on* the job. You held *down* a job. There was a corporate ladder and you climbed it.

Unemployment was horizontal, a flat line. Rodney was not yet flat broke, but he was, for astonishing amounts of time, flat on his back: reading, filling in crosswords, or staring at the ceiling like Michelangelo, a Michelangelo of lethargy.

His parents sometimes worried that he was sitting around all day, but the truth was something far worse: He was *lying* around all day, on the couch, on the bed, on a bookstore floor. Rodney read about a woman who spent two years sitting on the toilet, until the seat became fused to her rear end and had to be surgically removed in an ER. Rodney wondered if he might rise from bed one of these days and take the mattress with him, buckling beneath its weight like the kids question-marked under their St. Brendan's backpacks.

And so he walked home, not quite pie-eyed but comprehensively pot-pied, in the hair-dryer heat of the afternoon. He went straight to the shower. Then he dried off and lay naked on his bed, his arms and legs spread like da Vinci's Vitruvian Man.

The light on the phone next to the bed was flashing red like a traffic light at midnight. Rodney had a message.

He never heard it ring. Maybe when he was in the shower, singing into the soap.

They were doing Carnacs at Boyle's one night and Rodney held a cardboard coaster to his forehead and said, "Sing Sing."

"Sing Sing," repeated Armen, acting as Ed McMahon.

"What does Ruben Boumtje-Boumtje do in the shower?"

Armen laughed. Wanamaker said, "Who the hell is Ruben Boomchay-Boomchay?"

"Basketball player," Rodney said. "From Georgetown."

Rodney could reach the phone on the nightstand without sitting up. His dad often told him in high school to get off his lazy ass. But Rodney was one step down from that now. He didn't have the energy to get *onto* his ass prior to hoisting himself off it. And so he lay there on his side and picked up the phone and waited for the perforated dial tone.

First he called Mairead's machine again. He'd forgotten to say where Cliffs of Moher was. "Sorry to keep playing phone tag," he said. But he knew, even as he said it, that they weren't really playing phone tag. Or if they were, he was always "It."

Then he retrieved his message. It was from a woman. "Miss Terodney," it began. "This is Marisa's niece. My *tia*, she left her sunglasses in your apartment. Could you send them to me in the mail?" She left an address somewhere in Queens. It had an implausibly high street number—257th Street?—and a house number with a hyphen in it.

"My *tia*, she cannot clean your house anymore, Miss Terodney. I am sorry."

Marisa was devout. She always blessed herself before dusting the crucifix in Rodney's bedroom and shuffled the magnets on the fridge to give St. Brigid's prayer card pride of place.

He couldn't blame her for bailing. She probably thought he was running a bathhouse.

So he would have to clean the place. Caroline was coming to visit, which meant Mairead might come, too. He hadn't ruled that out, and Rodney would not let either of them contemplate the dire state of his toilet bowl.

He pushed the Dirt Devil around the living room. The vacuum had a single headlight on the front, like a motor scooter, in case he ever needed to Hoover the carpet in the dark. Rodney didn't think vacuuming made a difference: The speckled, commercial-grade carpet could never come clean and would never look good. It was a living tapestry, the woven remnants of every creature who had walked its surface these last twenty-five years. Whenever he regarded it at eye level—lying in front of the TV after a long night at Boyle's, one cheek pressed to the ground—Rodney saw their toenail trimmings and dog dandruff and curled black hairs.

But vacuuming did have a placebo effect. It made Rodney feel cleaner. So when the vacuum bag filled, Rodney removed it. It was three feet long and the smallest squeeze brought a cloud of dust, like a pitcher's resin bag. That's three feet of me, Rodney thought—sloughed-off skin cells and fallen hair—as he sent his old self Geronimo-ing down the trash chute.

At the grocery store he bought a three-pack of Dirt Devil bags and a pair of rubber gloves. They didn't have them—apparently didn't *make* them—in Rodney's size. This was the last vestige of sanctioned chauvinism. They were yellow and far too tight—he had to O.J. them onto his hands with a proctological *snap!*—and his hands were sweating in them before he could unroll them. But he wasn't cleaning his bog without protection.

In the same aisle he bought Comet. It came in a can the size, shape, and color of Kraft Parmesan Cheese, right down to the little holes in the top. He bought a bag of purple sponges and an orange pail. His shopping basket hung from his elbow as if he were picking daisies, and into it he tipped Pine-Sol and Fantastik and Windex, the jewel-toned liquids mimicking the back bar at Boyle's.

The Windex was the deep blue of Barbicide, the stuff combs floated in at the Italian shop where Rodney got his hair cut, the stuff Rodney raised, to disastrous effect, on his first date with Mairead.

Later, when Rodney was on all fours in front of his toilet, shaking Comet out onto the tiles, he thought of the Clubman talc the barber shook onto his neck and brushed off with a wood-handled whisk of horsehair, called a neck duster.

Rodney hadn't had a haircut in two months. Now that he had a job interview lined up, maybe he needed to go someplace where they didn't give you change from your ten. Maybe he'd get it styled, like one of those post-college pricks who drank at Boyle's for the irony of it.

He tried that when he dated Rachel, getting a decent haircut. He went to a place where some chick massaged shampoo into his temples, then toweled off his head while Rodney looked up and she leaned over him, the crown of his head nearly slotting into the space between her breasts, like a puzzle piece. In hindsight, they must have done it intentionally, and probably had a name for it—the Neck Duster, maybe. All the while he was getting his hair cut he had half a loaf on, under the smock.

He went back a second time and got a sixty-year-old lady and that was it for the forty-dollar haircuts.

"Last time I saw you on all fours in front of the toilet, you weren't cleaning it."

It was Keith. Rodney hadn't heard him come in. He'd come straight to the bathroom for a slash. Murphy's Law. Just as the tiles were starting to look like brushed teeth.

"There's no place to piss in this city," Keith said. He was moving to the City of Ample Bathrooms.

That was Keith—enviously oblivious, like the Chicago of the Sandburg poem: *Under the terrible burden of destiny, laughing as a young man laughs.*

Rodney did a push-up to get off the floor. Keith set a twelve-pack of Miller Lite on the sink while he took a leak. "Thanks," he told Rodney, nodding at the beer. "For everything."

Rodney popped the top on a can and said, "I've got some bad news, man."

Keith looked at the toilet and said, "Should I be sitting down?"

"Armen," Rodney said. "He died yesterday."

"*What?*"

"Heart attack. Lifting a keg in the basement of Boyle's."

"You're shitting me."

"I wish I were."

They drank the beer in the living room, Rodney still in his yellow gloves. Keith put Rodney's iPod in the docking station and said, "Let's make a playlist for Armen." And so they began with Pink Floyd's "Wish You Were Here" and added Nick Cave and Shane McGowan's cover of "What a Wonderful World" and then Keith went online to download Frankie Yankovic's "In Heaven There Is No Beer," after which he cranked Queen.

"You sick bastard," Rodney said.

As "Another One Bites the Dust" issued from his speakers, Rodney heard a *bang-bang-bang* from the other side of the wall. He turned down the music, knowing what three bangs meant in the Morse code of apartment living. Keith banged six times on the same wall: "I see your three bangs and raise you three more!"

Rodney didn't mind. She was a pain in the ass. Never said hi in the hall. Rodney walked in off the street right behind her once and she pulled her jacket tight around her like he was a rapist. He let the vestibule door shut behind her first just so he could unlock the door again himself, to prove he had a key.

"She plays opera at eight o'clock in the morning," Rodney said. "Screw her."

The thing was, she wasn't bad looking. Rodney had no idea how old she was—somewhere between thirty and forty-five. He couldn't get any closer than that. Lived alone. Traveled a lot. Rodney got her phone bill one time and knocked on her door and she took it and thanked him with the chain lock still on. Another time, he was on the couch, watching TV at two in the morning, when he heard voices in the hall, a key in her lock, then the stereo, the squeaking of bedsprings, and snoring like a ripsaw—all in the span of two minutes, takeoff to touchdown, like one of those speeded-up time-lapse films of flowers blooming or people filling an arena before the auditions on *American Idol*.

Keith turned the volume back up as U2 began to belt out

"Some Days Are Better Than Others." Rodney got off the couch and turned it back down.

"What happened to 'Screw her'?" Keith said.

"I don't need her knocking on the door," Rodney said. "Seeing you with the twelve-pack, me with the one rubber glove? She'll find out about the discount prostate exams. I could lose my license."

Rodney opened another beer. "Look at you," he said. "You look like a walking medical malpractice suit."

"Except I can barely walk," Keith said. "People were crossing the fucking street when they saw me crutching up Columbus this morning with a coffee cup."

Rodney rolled off his rubber gloves. His fingertips were pruned and cadaver-colored and smelled like chlorine, as if he'd spent all day in a pool instead of ten minutes cleaning the can.

He put the cleaning supplies in the orange pail, which he'd emptied into the bathtub, and stashed it under the kitchen sink. From the kitchen he called Domino's—he knew the number by heart—and when the pizza arrived he buzzed the guy in and greased him. There were four more pizzas in his thermal bag.

"The guy who invented the delivery bag should be a billionaire," Rodney said. He set the pizza on the ottoman and Keith pounced on it as if it were a wounded animal.

Keith reduced his first slice to a crust and said, "I tell you who's a billionaire: the guy who thought of the little plastic stools that prevent the box from crushing the pizza." Domino's didn't need those stools because their boxes were made of thick, corrugated board that folded in a way both beautiful and ingenious, like an origami crane or something.

Rodney was auditing Keith, making sure he didn't take more than his fair share of four slices or six beers. The beers were easier to keep track of, because Keith was making a pyramid from the spent shells of his empties. He had the base of three, the two on top of that, and was now drinking the one that would make the pyramid's point. Rodney watched him drink the last beer and couldn't help but think of it as a cheerleader.

"It's called a Top Flyer," Rodney said.

"What is?"

"The cheerleader who goes on the top of the pyramid."

"How do you know this shit?" Keith said.

"I read."

"Cheerleader magazines?" Keith said. And then, after a moment of reflection: "Not that there'd be anything wrong with that."

Rodney didn't like where this was going.

"I met this High Flyer once," Keith said.

"Top Flyer."

"Whatever."

Keith was engaged, all but a married man. She'd be here tomorrow, his fiancée.

Fiancée, from the Old French *fiance,* "a promise, trust."

"Does Caroline trust you?" he asked Keith.

"What?"

"You heard me."

"Of course she trusts me."

"Should she?"

"Why shouldn't she?"

"I don't know," Rodney said. "All these women you talk about—they were before Caroline?"

"What are you driving at?"

Rodney was not one of these language snobs who had to be Heimliched when someone ended a sentence with a preposition. So he let it go. Likewise, when he heard someone scold a child for using a double negative, he always pictured the prick in some karaoke bar singing "I Can't Get Any Satisfaction."

"I'm not driving at anything," Rodney said. Keith had completed his pyramid—his beeramid—and Rodney admired it for a moment.

Then he said to Keith, "Though now that you mention driving: the girl you work with, parking the U-Haul every day . . ." Rodney had begun to think of her as Carlotta—for Carlotta Tendant, a burlesque stripper's name he'd heard somewhere and never forgot.

"Yeah?" Keith was working his jaw muscles though there was no more pizza to chew. He hadn't eaten the crusts, and Rodney silently counted them up. Five, the fucker. And he never offered to pay.

"You seeing her?" Rodney asked.

"I see her at work," Keith said. "I told you. We work together."

"I know," Rodney said. "It's just that when I checked on the van this morning, the hood was still hot."

"You *felt* the hood?"

"I heard the engine ticking."

"It's ninety-five degrees, Encyclopedia Brown. Did you think the hood might be cool?"

"I heard the engine ticking, Keith. At ten o'clock in the morning. So she must have been late to work this morning."

"Your friend, Mairead, she must've been late for work, too," Keith said, as if he'd caught Rodney in a lie. "This morning."

"No," Rodney said. "She left on time. And I slept on her couch." It wasn't strictly true about the couch, but the spirit of it was.

"And did you tell her about the other night," Keith said. "About the chick you met in Boyle's?"

"The one whose friend you were hitting on?"

"Yeah," Keith said, not rising to the bait. "That one."

"I'm not engaged to Mairead," Rodney said. "I've only known her eight days, and I'm not even sure we're still dating. If we ever were." So why was his face suddenly engulfed in flames? "Last time I talked to her she hung up on me."

Silence and darkness seemed to fall simultaneously. Rodney was on the floor with his back against the sofa front. Keith was opposite him, his back against the wall.

"Nothing happened with that girl from Boyle's," Rodney said. "Just so you know." It was important to Rodney that Keith knew that.

He was holding the last unopened can from the twelve-pack, and now he bowled it across the carpet, toppling Keith's beeramid. It sounded to Rodney as if the cans were clattering behind a limousine, "Just Married" shoe-polished in the windows, Keith and Caroline pulling away from the church, everything irreversible, an unhappy marriage, an eventual divorce.

"Right," Keith said. "If you say so."

"I do say so," said Rodney. "We went to her place. She lived twenty fucking floors up and her elevator was out. I felt like Shrek going to rescue Fiona."

"So what happened?"

"We finally get to her apartment," Rodney said. "We're both sweating and wheezing. We get inside, I sit on the couch, she curls up next to me"—Rodney was milking this, enjoying the embellishment—"and she . . . *projectile vomits* over every square inch of the place."

"She did *not*," Keith said. He was laughing. "She did *not*."

"Like she was applying stucco," Rodney said.

"Get *outta* here."

"Swear to God."

"What did you do?" Keith said, except it was all one word:

Whajadoo? In college, Keith could reduce two sentences—
"Did you eat? Let's go eat"—to two words: *"Jeet? Skweet."*

"I did a runner," Rodney said. "Five minutes later, she
opens her door, sees me still pushing the elevator button and
says, 'It's out of order, remember?'"

Keith howled.

Outside, the glacial procession of taxis honked their way
to Broadway theaters. Rodney went to the kitchen with the
empty pizza box. When he returned, Keith retrieved the last
full beer from the floor and said, "Just so you know, it's over.
Between me and"—Rodney saw Keith catch himself—"and
the one parking the U-Haul. I broke it off last night."

Rodney didn't know what to say. Keith looked a mile past
Rodney and popped the top on the beer.

"Jesus!"

The beer went off like Old Faithful, first in a single spume
that hit the ceiling, then in sixteen different directions, like a
hose with a thumb on it. It scared the shit out of both of them.
First Keith held the can above his head, like Liberty's torch,
then he clapped his mouth over the hole. But beer had
already beaded on the ceiling and run down the walls in little
teardrops.

Rodney was roaring. "I hope you got the keys to the
U-Haul back," he said.

"First thing I did," Keith said, "before I told her."

Rodney believed Keith. And he was relieved. Still, he didn't
want to toast him at his wedding, knowing about Carlotta, or
whatever her name was. Rodney dragged the armchair five
feet across the room, stood on it, and dried the ceiling with
paper towels. The beer was dripping, as if the apartment
above his had burst a pipe.

Keith pointed out another spot on the ceiling that Rodney

had missed, and then another. The beer was dripping onto the carpet. "Half cavern, half tavern," Rodney said.

He blotted those beer spots, then threw twelve empty beer cans into a garbage bag, followed by the beer-soaked paper towels, and said, somewhat redundantly: "What do you say we get a beer?"

10

So even before they got to Cliffs of Moher Keith was three sheets to the wind. Rodney hadn't spent any time at sea—he got motion sick just reading in taxis—but there must be a hell of a lot of drinking going on out there, he thought, to judge by the number of nautical synonyms for *shitfaced*.

Keith still had trouble walking on his crutches. He couldn't support the one crutch properly, the one that fit under the armpit of his injured shoulder. Even when he was stone sober he appeared to be three sheets, lurching all over the sidewalk, crutches splaying like the legs of a newborn calf. Rodney hoped the drink might cause a counterlurch that would help Keith walk straight, in the way the warped Boyle's mirror might make Longneck look like George Clooney. But it wasn't happening. It was like following his five-year-old nephew on a bicycle, Rodney rushing to his side every time he wobbled, waiting for him to fall over.

Negotiating these sidewalks was difficult enough for the clear-headed and healthy. Rodney tried to avoid an oncoming pedestrian. The man's black mustache underscored a nose that required no additional emphasis. Rodney and The 'Stache mirrored one another in attempting to step out of the way, and the two repeated these hostile courtesies in the opposite direction until Rodney held still and The 'Stache walked past.

Trouble was, everyone walking toward them thought Keith was blind or drunk—possibly both. The wide berth he was given steered more foot traffic into Rodney, who had managed to fall behind. From ten paces back, Keith looked like an untethered Macy's balloon, ropes flailing in the wind as it veered toward disaster at a stately pace akin to slow motion.

That was the origin of three sheets to the wind. A sheet wasn't a sail but a rope that held a sail, so that three ropes loose in the wind made a three-masted ship move as Keith was now moving. Like a drunken sailor. People were always drinking like sailors and *spending* like drunken sailors and *cursing* like sailors—or the guys who loaded and unloaded sailing ships: longshoremen.

Drunk, profligate, profane. Maybe Rodney missed his calling and should have sailed to sea, like Melville. But no. Rodney could get sick on an express elevator. He tried scuba diving on a family trip to Hawaii and was green before the boat made it to the dive site. Fifty feet under water, he barfed through his rented regulator, attracting hungry fish in a technicolor riot.

Keith had stopped to rest at a newspaper coin box. He was leaning on it like a lectern. His eyes were closed, as if in prayer, as if he were about to start a sermon. "Are you *asleep*?" Rodney said when he caught up.

"Resting my eyes," Keith said.

Rodney didn't fancy having a catatonic Keith draped over his shoulder all night, lugging his lifeless form around in a *Weekend at Bernie's*–like deception.

"I'll hang you on the coat rack when we get to Cliffs," Rodney said, referring to the three locker hooks outside the can that comprised the bar's cloakroom. "I see your shirt has a fag tag."

In fifth grade, Sister Catherine hung Chuck Varda on a hook in the closet and let him dangle there for an hour from his fag tag, a little fabric loop that was sewn to the backs of their uniform shirts between the shoulder blades, apparently for just such a purpose.

"We called 'em Fruit Loops," Keith said, coming to at the coin box. "Or ripcords. You could sneak up from behind and fit your fingertip in there and *yank*"—and here he pantomimed doing so—"an inch-wide strip down his back. Rest of the day, the kid looked like a goddamn . . ." He lost the plot for a moment, then regained focus. "Like a fuckin' *skunk*."

The more Keith drank the more he swore. Rodney said, "You'd make a hell of a sailor, Keith." He even walked like he didn't have his land legs.

"We called 'em fuckin' pulltabs, too."

"What?"

"Fag tags. We called 'em pulltabs, too."

Keith was a Torquemada of these preteen tortures: of Purple Nurple and Hertz Donut, Noogie and Nipple Cripple, Wedgie and Wet Willie, Dutch Rub and Indian Burn—of Sudsy and Swirly and Snuggy.

"These fuckin' crutches," he said. "They're givin' me a wicked Pit Viper."

They were walking again. Rodney thought about giving Keith a Flat Tire. He admired that Keith, at thirty-four, could still catalog these playground acts of terror. He was still a child in that way. Like a child, Keith never thought about mortality, was oblivious to oblivion.

There were two sides to that coin, of course. Rodney

recalled all those things labeled adult that were really for children, for people who had never grown up—adult magazines, adult films, adult language—and suddenly thought of another: adultery.

When it came to perpetual adolescence, this was the other side of that coin. This was tails. That's what Keith was chasing: tails. And the coin was sure to keep coming up tails, over and over in Keith's life, whether or not he was still seeing Carlotta.

They washed ashore at Cliffs of Moher. Rodney went to push the door open for Keith just as Keith was leaning into it. There were cheers when Keith fell into Cliffs. Rodney helped him off the tiles and the bar applauded again, as if an injured basketball player had just gotten to his feet. By the time they made it to the bar, there were already beers waiting for them. Then Keith said to Cliff, loud enough for everyone to hear: "Just thought I'd drop in."

There followed immediately another round—of applause first, then of drinks.

It was going to be that kind of night.

Of course she wasn't coming. Rodney had been naive to think she might. It was only 9:15, but still: He'd been looking at the door every thirty seconds starting at a quarter till, so it seemed like forever. He made a silent vow to stop checking the door, the way he always vowed to stop checking his watch during Mass.

To kill the time, Rodney watched a guy hit on a chick with long black hair. The chick had this nervous habit of tucking her hair behind her ears with both hands, the way Steve Nash does on defense. The guy bet her he could walk the length of the bar without his feet ever touching the floor. Rodney couldn't hear what the stakes were.

"What about your shoes?" she said.

He said they wouldn't touch the floor either.

"You'll just walk on your hands," she said, which was precisely what Rodney was thinking.

"I won't," the guy said. "Though that would be pretty impressive, don't you think?"

Steve Nash batted her eyelashes at the guy. He had longer lashes than she did. They were black and luxurious, like something you'd drive through at a car wash. The kind of eyelashes Snuffleupagus had.

Steve Nash stuck out her right hand and said, "Okay. Shake."

Snuffleupagus came over to Keith and asked to borrow his crutches. Keith said, "What for?" and Snuffy said, "To win a bet," and Keith looked at Rodney, who told him, "I think you have to do it."

"Why do I have to?"

"Some kind of man code to do with bar bets."

So Keith handed over the crutches and Snuffy carried them to the far end of the bar, near the Gents. His hands on the crutch handles, he hoisted himself up like a gymnast on the parallel bars. He pulled his feet up behind his ass and took a couple of tentative hops. Rodney was thinking, no way this guy makes it the length of the bar when Mairead walked in, twenty-five minutes after nine.

He waved to her. A little too eagerly, but he couldn't help it. She was with another woman, which made Rodney feel better about being there with Keith. In the absence of his crutches, Keith was Chang-and-Enged to Rodney's right shoulder. He didn't even have a barstool. Nobody gave up his just because

Keith couldn't walk or stand. Maybe if he was a hundred-year-old man or twenty-one-year-old woman. And even then, probably not.

Mairead nodded her head to acknowledge Rodney. She couldn't get to him because everyone in the place had cleared a path for Snuffy. He was surrounded on all sides, like Tony Manero in *Saturday Night Fever*, only this freak was making his way toward the door on Keith's crutches, using them like a set of stilts for his arms.

An agonizing interval passed between each step. It was like watching a man on a tightrope. By the time Mairead entered, the crowd was counting out each step for Snuffy:

"Five!"

There was silence while the guy swayed and took a couple of tiny bunny hops to regain his balance, the crutches acting as twin pogo sticks.

Someone yelled, *"Five and a half!"*

Snuffy forged ahead.

"Six!"

Rodney watched Mairead watch the crowd. She was smiling. So was her friend. How could they not? There was a new CD on the stereo. The Proclaimers were banging on about walking five hundred miles. For all Rodney knew, every night at Cliffs was like this.

"Seven!"

Rodney didn't see how the guy could possibly make it. His arms were starting to spasm. The whole stunt was like something out of Cirque du Soleil. All around Rodney people were making their own side bets. Somehow Snuffy kept going.

"Eight!"

Mairead and her friend remained just inside the door. Someone pointed out a small puddle of beer on the floor. Cliff tossed a bar rag to Rodney, who got down on both knees and wiped it up before Snuffy could stick a crutch in it. He felt like a ball boy cleaning sweat from the floor at a Knicks game, then dashing back behind the basket, just ahead of the fast break.

"*Nine!*"

One long step to go.

Snuffy's face was going red with the effort. He stuck out the right crutch and planted it. He lifted the left, swung himself forward and—

"*Ten!*"

He stuck the landing.

The bar went batshit.

And then Cliff cranked "We Are the Champions." Rodney thought of the poor prick who lived above, the floor vibrating his furniture all over the apartment, like the players in an old electric football game.

Keith's crutches were passed back to him, hand over hand across the heads of the crowd, as if they were bodies at a concert. The hand grips of the crutches were still slick with sweat. Keith cleaned them with his shirttail. It had been out all week. Tucking it in with one hand was too much trouble.

Mairead made her way through the crowd. He wanted to kiss her like it was V-E Day. It felt like V-E Day in Cliffs. But she didn't even give him a peck on the cheek.

She said hello. Then she said hello to Keith, literally said, "Hello," with a formality—and an upward lilt on the second syllable—that suggested she knew: Keith was two-timing her best friend. Perhaps three-timing her.

Rodney hoped she knew. No way *he* was telling Mairead about Carlotta Tendant, though it bothered him to be keeping a secret from her.

For the moment, conversation was impossible. A figure flew

across the TV: in tandem, Rodney and Keith looked up at the glow of the flat-screen, as if at an alien spacecraft in a Spielberg movie. It was the Mets game, made inaudible by Freddie Mercury. A Pirate was thrown out attempting to steal second and someone, in the sliver of silence between songs on the stereo, shouted: "Where's Hookslide?"

Cliff turned down the stereo. Or rather, the stereo was shouted down by a growing chant: "HOOK-*slide*! HOOK-*slide*! HOOK-*slide*!"

Hookslide stood and stretched his arms in front of him, fingers braided and palms facing out, the way a concert pianist does before flipping his tuxedo tails and taking a seat in a Tom and Jerry cartoon. And thus began the elaborate pantomime of stretching—of failed toe touches and shallow knee bends—until finally, hands on hips, Hookslide stopped rotating his torso on the pivot of his waist and took, to great applause, his starting position outside the men's room.

"You know this guy?" Mairead said.

"Hookslide?" Rodney said. "Not really. I know *of* him, more like." He had heard of this guy but never fully believed that he existed.

As it had with Snuffy, the crowd again cleared a narrow alley of floor space. Rodney couldn't figure out where the space came from. Cliffs was full before the space was cleared, and yet, with no one leaving the bar, there was this base path created for Hookslide. It was as if the bar had collectively sucked in its gut, the way Wanamaker did when a woman walked into Boyle's.

In fact Wanamaker was in Cliffs, standing in the corner like an alcoholic hatrack. Of course he was here. It was the nearest Irish bar to Boyle's.

There used to be more. But Rodney had seen so many bars turned into bistros and boutiques. They haunted him, these ghost bars. He still recognized their eyes, even behind the Botox and sunglasses that turned, say, Mother Machree's into an airy place to eat tapas. The windows—they were always the giveaway.

Boyle's was next. It seemed obvious to Rodney all of a sudden. Armen was its engine, the energy that kept it alive, in motion. He was its soul and now *his* soul had departed, leaving behind two empty shells. One would be buried this weekend. The other—the bar itself—would be turned next spring into a Jamba Juice or Banana Republic.

"HOOK-*slide*!"

The chant was building again. Cliff placed the Manhattan Yellow Pages on the bar and then turned his back, a pro-wrestling referee pretending not to see whatever was going to happen next. A guy in a Dropkick Murphys T-shirt removed the directory from the bar and placed it just inside the front door of Cliffs, twenty-five feet from Hookslide.

The space cleared on the bar floor reminded Rodney of a wedding reception, of a bride about to dance with her father, everyone standing around watching.

How was he going to watch Caroline dance with her father after she married Keith? He'd make sure he was at the bar or buffet table when that happened.

Hookslide raised his palms and fanned his fingers toward himself, as you would when guiding someone into a parking space. It made Rodney think of Keith's U-Haul, which made him think again of Carlotta, which made him think again of Caroline. But Hookslide was simply calling for the chant to grow louder.

"HOOK-*slide*!"

Hookslide took a cautious lead, three slide-steps away from the Gents.

"HOOK-*slide!*"

Rodney noticed that Hookslide let his fingers twitch the way Rickey Henderson did when he was about to steal a base, as if base stealing involved actual larceny and he was preparing to grab something that was literally hot.

"HOOK-*slide!*"

When the chant reached a crescendo, Hookslide sprinted— it was only three strides—then executed a flawless Lou Brock hook slide along the linoleum and safely into the Manhattan business listings. A great cheer went up in Cliffs, and Rodney looked at Mairead looking at the crowd. She was smiling. So was her friend.

"Sometimes he goes on his chest," Rodney said. "Like Pete Rose."

"Who?" said Mairead's friend.

"Hookslide."

"No, like Pete Who?"

"Pete *Rose*," Rodney said. He looked in disbelief at Mairead, who shrugged by way of apologizing for this chick's ignorance of Charlie Hustle.

"Nice circle of friends you have," Mairead said.

"It's more like a triangle of friends," Rodney said. "Me, Keith, and the bartender, Cliff, who I just met today. And I don't even know if Cliff has legs. He could be some mythological man-beast with a bartender's upper body and the legs of a goat."

"That would explain the smell," Keith said.

It was just now quiet enough to be heard without shouting. "This is Gwen," said Mairead, though it might have been Gwyn—Rodney wasn't sure. "She works with me. Worked with me. It was her last day today. Lucky bitch." Gwen-or-Gwyn laughed.

Mairead hadn't said, "This is my friend Gwen" or "This is Gwyn, we went to college together." All she said was "She works with me." This was the coworker, Rodney inferred, who wouldn't go away after the going-away party. Gwen or Gwyn probably asked to share a cab uptown and then took Mairead up on her polite, though hollow, offer to join her in Boyle's for a drink.

But Rodney conceded that he could be wrong. He'd had at least twelve beers, and while he thought himself a spiritual descendant of the mystical pintmen of Dublin, growing more insightful by the glass, what if he wasn't? What if he—and every one of those pintmen he'd read about—was really just a drunk?

"Excuse me," said Gwen/Gwyn. "Where is the ladies' room?"

"I'm guessing straight back," said Rodney. "That's where the men's room is." He admired her courage. He'd seen plenty of women on their first visit to Boyle's walk three blocks to Barnes & Noble and ascend three floors once there just to take a leak. And Cliffs didn't look any cleaner.

"So," Rodney said when Gwyn/Gwen had gone. "How long have you known Gwun?" He merged *Gwyn* and *Gwen* into a third name he thought could pass for either.

"Gwen?" said Mairead, and then, smiling: "Did you just call her . . . *Gwun*?"

"Maybe," said Rodney.

Mairead looked him in the eyes and said, "Have you ever heard of anyone called Gwun?"

"No," Rodney said. "But I'd never heard of anyone named Mairead 'til I met you."

"I don't know *Gwun* very well," Mairead said. "Or Gwen, for that matter. We just shared a cab from Midtown. She was getting out a block from here. It seemed rude not to invite her in."

"Of course," Rodney said.

He *was* a fucking pintman. It was possible. There was a group of prostitutes in Nairobi who developed, through constant exposure to HIV, an immunity to the virus. Rodney had read about them. So why couldn't he, under more or less equivalent circumstances, have built up a tolerance for Guinness?

"Gwun," Rodney said, when Gwen had returned. "What are you drinking?"

She thought for a moment.

"Go on, Gwun," Rodney said. Mairead was laughing. Rodney pronounced it "G'wan, Gwun."

Gwen wanted a Bud Light. Cliff got it, then told Rodney the story of Hookslide's famous hook slide that won Cliffs of Moher the beer-league softball championship in Central Park three years ago, a highlight Hookslide had replayed, like a Civil War reenactor or walking YouTube video, ever since. Cliff described Hookslide evading the catcher's tag attempt, the eternity that passed before the umpire shouted, "Safe!," the happy hogpile at home plate. He described the long red raspberry on Hookslide's right thigh, the result of sliding in shorts. "Like the thing on Gorbachev's forehead," said Cliff, pouring Rodney a beer he hadn't asked for.

Rodney, Keith, Mairead, and Gwen made way for Wanamaker, sliding by sideways to get to the can. In passing, he offered a courtly nod of his head and said, "Ladies."

Mairead and Gwen nodded at him in acknowledgment, a barely perceptible upward tilt of the head, the kind that usually precedes a sneeze.

Rodney said to Mairead: "He was referring to me and Keith."

"Ah," she said. "Of course he was." And then, swigging from a longneck, sweeping the room with her eyes: "I like this place."

So did Rodney. But it wasn't his and never would be, no matter how many Boyle's regulars made this their new local. When Keith went to college, his parents moved out of his childhood home and into a condo, where Keith spent the next four summers, never thinking of the place as home. This, Rodney thought, is how Keith must have felt.

"I like it too," Rodney said. At the bar, a man was picking his teeth with a matchbook cover and checking his reflection in a butter knife. "It's a classy joint," Rodney said. "As you can see."

Rodney drained half a pint in a single go and said to Mairead, "I'm glad you came."

She said: "I only came because you said your friend died. I'm sorry. But you seem to be coping all right."

Keith squinted at the clock behind the bar: "Shit. It's midnight? Already?" Rodney looked at the clock, its round face emblazoned with GUINNESS TIME beneath a pint full of stout. He said: "Keith, man, it's twenty after *two*. In the morning."

There were manifold maritime analogues for drunkenness, but even more for aimlessness. Rodney looked at the clock hands—if they held semaphore flags, they'd be signaling "X"—and saw Keith for what he was: At sea. Adrift. Going under.

"I was supposed to call Caroline," Keith said. "By ten. Her time."

Gwun had gone, two hours earlier. But Mairead hung in there, eight hours after leaving the office. She'd put in a full workday of drinking by the time she looked at Keith and said,

"If you *ever* hurt Caroline, I will hunt you down." It was probably meant to sound playful, but Rodney heard something new in her voice—or new to him, anyway: real menace.

"Hunt me down and what?" Keith said.

"It doesn't matter," Mairead said. "Because you're not going to hurt her."

"If you say so."

Keith was pissed. Rodney could see him flexing his jaw muscles.

"You want to call her now?" Rodney asked Keith. He felt compelled to say something, a third-party effort to calm things down, as when a baseball manager calls a conference on the mound.

"That's not what I'm suggesting," Mairead said. "She's got a nine o'clock flight in the morning, which means leaving for O'Hare by seven, which means getting up at six. He can call her in the morning."

Keith didn't reply. There was only one other group in Cliffs now, two guys and two girls. They were paired off on either side of a booth. Rodney couldn't tell if they were two couples or arranged platonically, the conversational equivalent of a mixed-doubles tennis match. One of the girls, Rodney couldn't help but overhear, was a Juilliard ballet student. Now she stood and formed an "O" with her arms, her hands nearly meeting at her waist, as if she were hoisting an invisible beer belly above her belt, something a Boyle's alumnus named Walt used to do, only his wasn't invisible. What ever happened to Walt? Whenever Walt walked in, Rodney was reminded of the Wodehouse line, about the guy who looked as if he'd been poured into his trousers and forgotten to say "When."

"That's called first position," Mairead said of the ballerina. "See how her feet are pointing out, like Fred Flintstone's?"

"How do you know that?" Rodney said.

"I took ballet as a kid," she said. "Now she's doing a demi-plié." Juilliard was half-bending at the knees, as if she had to pee in the woods.

Her friends applauded. Juilliard demonstrated second position and then third: right hand over head, left hand extended straight out to her side, a human timepiece. "Good Lord," Rodney said to Mairead. "Is it three o'clock already, or is that ballerina fast?"

Mairead said to Juilliard, "You're supposed to face the bar when you plié." Juilliard smiled, then turned toward the bar and pliéd, as if curtsying.

Rodney asked Mairead, "Was that a ballet in-joke you just shared?"

"That handrail you hold on to in ballet class, it's called a barre," Mairead said. "B-A-R-R-E. You're supposed to face the barre when you practice your pliés."

"That's too, too funny," Rodney said. "That's *tutu* funny." He wanted to go to sleep. He tried and failed to suppress a yawn.

Keith put his good arm around Rodney's shoulder and said to Mairead: "This guy loves the Nutcracker."

"Here we go," Rodney said.

"Not the ballet," said Keith. "His ex-girlfriend. Rachel. It was her nickname."

It wasn't true. But just the mention of his ex, in front of Mairead, inflamed Rodney's armpits. He knew Keith was trying to make a joke. And they *had* been drinking for nearly ten hours at this point. But that was merely a half-marathon in Rodney and Keith's shared history, which included a full day and night of uninterrupted imbibing in Montreal ten years ago, immortalized by Rodney (and fondly recalled ever since) as "The Twenty-Four Hours of Labatt's."

Mairead turned to Keith and said, "I hope all *your* girl-friends are exes."

"What's that supposed to mean?" Keith said. Only he wasn't looking at Mairead. He was looking at Rodney. Keith said, "What did you tell her?"

Rodney hadn't told Mairead about Carlotta, but he didn't expect Keith to believe that. Keith would think Rodney had sold him out, his best friend, to a woman he'd known for eight days. Worse—far worse—a woman who had his fiancée's ear. It was an inversion of Keith's worldview, in which life was a game of Rock Paper Scissors, bros trumping hos.

Keith stood and grabbed one crutch. The other had fallen to the bar floor. He appeared to have both a surplus and a shortfall of limbs, a stick figure in an ongoing game of Hang-man. Keith leaned in close enough that Rodney could smell his aftershave. Christ almighty: This guy was applying alcohol to the outside of his body as liberally as he splashed it on the inside.

Rodney suddenly felt superior for not wearing the stuff. He was like a housepainter who only did interiors.

Keith said, "You better not be bad-mouthing me just because she's good-mouthing you."

Rodney grabbed Keith by the T-shirt. In doing so, he pulled out a fistful of Keith's chest hairs. Like plucking grass blades and tossing them to the heavens to test the wind on a golf course—that's how it felt to Rodney. For Keith, it was much worse, to judge by the tiny blood spots that seeped up through his white T-shirt, then joined each other to form a red circle, so that Keith appeared to be wearing the Japanese flag on his chest.

Keith screamed, "Fuck!" and Rodney said, "Sorry" and Mairead—not looking at either of them—said: "I want to go home. *Now.*"

Two taxis rolled up barren Amsterdam like tumbleweeds. Both beelined to the curb, fighting for the fare. Rodney saw Mairead into one of them and motioned for the other cab to wait. He told Mairead, "I'll call you." When she didn't reply, he said it again, but she kept her eyes locked on the surcharge sticker in the Plexiglas panel in front of her. So Rodney closed the door.

When he turned around, Keith was already in the other taxi. How Keith had managed to get himself in, Rodney couldn't say, for Keith was legless in every sense of the word. More impressively, he had managed to close the door. But Keith's greatest feat was this: Incapable of locomotion, bleeding from the chest, approaching catatonia, he had nevertheless persuaded the cabbie to *put the taxi into drive*.

Rodney shouted, "Wait!" But the driver was inching away from the curb, and Rodney couldn't blame him. The poor bastard in his backseat was fleeing a beatdown, by the looks of it. So Rodney just yelled at Keith through the open window: "You better not bleed on my couch!"

"Fuck your couch," Keith said from the black-vinyl oblivion of the backseat. "I'll sleep on *mine*." And with that, the taxi pulled away from Rodney and went rocketing up Amsterdam.

It took Rodney another ten minutes to get a taxi. By the time he got out on 117th Street, Keith was snoring in the back of the U-Haul. Rodney was relieved: Snoring meant breathing.

Even at 3 a.m. it was eighty degrees. Mercifully, Keith had had enough sense to prop open the roll-up door of the U-Haul with two boxes marked BOOKS. Rodney knew, from moving day, that these were really magazines. He hadn't understood then why Keith was holding on to them. But damn if Keith wasn't right: *Swank* and *Bra Busters* were saving his life.

Rodney rolled up the door and beheld: Beneath a quilted blue blanket meant to cushion furniture, Keith was asleep on his fermenting futon.

On approach to that futon, Rodney had to climb over Keith's toaster and microwave and boom box, each in its original packaging. When Rodney finally reached him, and tried to shake him awake, Keith didn't move. Anyone discovering him in the morning would have mistaken him for a corpse, if not for the snoring.

He certainly smelled like one. Keith's apartment had been foul enough. But this was far worse, a *concentrate* of Keith's apartment. Rodney couldn't leave him here. And he couldn't carry Keith back to 4K. Taxis seldom stopped for men carrying cadavers. And so Rodney began a complicated Tetris game, moving boxes, an ironing board, a set of golf clubs, until he reached Keith's mattress, propped in its protective plastic against a side wall. He lay it on top of Keith's coffee table and climbed on. Keith was next to him, two feet away, beneath a sticker that read: RETURN CLEAN OR PAY $20.00 SERVICE CHARGE.

Rodney considered sleeping up front, in the cab of the U-Haul, but that would have meant frisking Keith for the keys and sleeping in a seated position, something Rodney had never been able to do, though he'd come close during his phoned-in pre-interview with Curt Mayhew at Banco Marinero.

Up front, his sleeping form would be on full display in the aquarium-like windshield for any passerby to have at. Of course, that was true now, too, with the back door rolled up.

But he would cook with the door down. So Rodney found the first weapon close to hand—an acoustic guitar Keith had never learned to play—and propped it against the coffee table. If someone climbed in during the night, Rodney was going to go Pete Townshend on his ass.

Keith's coffee table wasn't wide. Or perhaps it was, as coffee tables went. Rodney couldn't say for sure. But it wasn't wide *as a bed*, of that Rodney was certain. About half the width of a twin. He spent a full hour listening for sounds on the sidewalk and pressing the Indiglo function on his watch to check the time. But all he heard were garbage trucks and mewling cats. He dozed, and dreamt that he'd fallen asleep on a beam while working construction one hundred stories above Manhattan.

He woke at 4:39 a.m. and recalled an interview he'd once seen on TV with a perfume maker. She had described the two qualities of a scent as "intensity" and "longevity." Keith's beer farts had both.

Rodney rolled onto his side. The plastic mattress protector rustled in reply. His back was beginning to ache. He pulled a duffel bag beneath his head as a pillow. It was full of sneakers. He rolled onto his other side—slowly, methodically, so as not to trigger an avalanche of boxes and black garbage bags. Somehow Keith looked comfortable, at home. Of course, he *was* at home, when Rodney thought about it.

Outside, someone began hosing down the sidewalk. The sound soothed Rodney into slumber. He dreamt of Mairead: They were picnicking on the top wing of a Fokker Dr 1, the triplane made famous by the Red Baron. Even by the lurid standard of his dreams, Rodney was horny. Perhaps it was the word *Fokker*, but he was doing his best to join the mile-high club—to *invent* the mile-high club, this being the dawn of aviation. Alas, every time the Baron banked, Rodney rolled away from Mairead, to the edge of the wing and the brink of oblivion.

When at last the Fokker leveled off, and they were reunited at the center of the wingspan, Rodney leaned in to kiss Mairead. And she leaned in to let him. Which is when a pocket of clear-air turbulence threw Rodney off the wing and into the blackness beyond. For a moment he seemed to float. And then the ground struck him with the flat of its hand.

Rodney woke up, face down on the floor of the U-Haul, with a backache and a boner.

He had fallen into the foot-wide space between the coffee table and Keith's futon. It was morning. He freed his right arm to check his watch: 6:03 a.m.

"Keith. Keith, man. Get up." Rodney stood and shook Keith until he opened his eyes. Keith looked at Rodney with incomprehension. His blackout had upgraded only slightly, to brownout. Keith pulled the furniture pad up under his chin and rolled away from Rodney.

"*Keith!*" Rodney was finished dicking around. "Wake *up!*" He pulled an L-wedge from Keith's golf bag and began rousting him from the futon with the blade end. Keith sat up. He didn't say anything. He looked disoriented by his surroundings, but not entirely surprised to be waking up in the back of a mover's van.

They didn't speak. Keith was not dead to Rodney. Not exactly. But he was a dot fast disappearing behind an ocean liner, the drunk who fell overboard at midnight, when no one heard the splash. Keith, drunk and drowning at sea—he was every maritime metaphor come to life.

They walked five blocks looking for a taxi. It took fifteen

minutes, Rodney having to Weekend-at-Bernie his buddy across intersections before the lights changed. All the while Rodney thought of the Stations of the Cross hanging in St. Brendan's, and Jesus dragging to Golgotha the instrument of his own demise.

11

He was supine in bed when the tears came. Rodney felt his eyes burn, then pool, then spill over. And as the tears ran into the storm drains of his ears, he thought of all the reasons he had for crying. For Armen, of course. Rodney never loved anyone whose phone number he didn't have as much as he loved Armen. For Keith, for Caroline, for Keith-and-Caroline. For Boyle's. For Mairead. For himself.

But the tears weren't for any of them, Rodney realized. What was it, he wondered, that brought grown men to grief at 6:30 in the morning?

Hay fever. The official Opening Day of the season wasn't until Monday, but already ragweed pollen was throwing out the first pitch. When Rodney moved to New York, he couldn't believe his nose: The pollen was worse here than in his Minnesota hometown. He wanted to pluck his flaming eyes from their sockets and plunge them into a ball-washer on the ninth tee of some golf course. But stepping onto a golf course in August would kill him.

He went to the bathroom, blew his nose into toilet paper, loosed a sneeze that spattered the mirror. Already his eyes were swollen by pollen. *Pollen* and *swollen* ought to rhyme,

Rodney thought, and not just because they looked alike. They were partners in crime. One led to the other, the way *laughter* sometimes led to *slaughter*.

Rodney could still hear the crowd at Boyle's horse-laughing at Longneck as he was frog-marched to the sidewalk last Saturday. And he guessed Longneck still heard that laughter, too. But Rodney didn't fear retaliation. He did at first. But no one, as Keith pointed out, would return to the scene of such humiliation.

Then again, *Keith* did.

But Longneck had been barred from Boyle's—"Locked out with his cock out," Armen had said—and such bans were always taken seriously, though Rodney wondered if a dead barman was really in a position to enforce such a thing.

Rodney brought a roll of toilet paper back to bed. He sneezed convulsively, and again, then four more times in succession, until he heard Keith stir in the next room. On the job, these sneezing jags would enliven Rodney's excursions in a rental car, rendering him blind for ten seconds on some unfamiliar interstate. They got him thrown out of a Ponderosa steakhouse in Pennsylvania, when the salad-bar Sneeze-Guard could not contain the seltzer-bottle fury of his serial sneezing.

He passed another hour sneezing and honking and itching and burning. He fell asleep. When the sun woke him two hours later it seemed to have sought him out specifically, vengefully—the beacon on a police chopper.

Keith hadn't bothered to close his blinds, either: Through the wall, Rodney could hear the oaths and thrashings of a one-armed man trying to pull the covers over his head. He would have a hangover of biblical scale, Rodney knew—his head shattering to the sirens now sounding.

Rodney lay in bed, sinuses constricting, and ranked his

favorite hangover scenes in literature, starting with Kingsley Amis: "His mouth had been used as a latrine by some small creature of the night, and then as its mausoleum." Rodney didn't have hangovers. In the world of hangovers, he was an armchair traveler.

He must have dozed while editing this literary anthology—*The Wrath of Grapes*—because Rodney awoke to his ancient intercom, buzzing.

Keith cursed loudly from the next room: For the second time today, morning had broken. Broken Keith, by the sound of him. And it was damn near breaking Rodney, who couldn't see the numbers on the nightstand clock, surrounded as it was by a snow fort of wadded toilet paper into which he'd been blowing his nose all morning.

Rodney threw off the bedclothes, scattering more toilet paper to the floor. The intercom kept up its sickly buzz, a noisy toy with a dying battery.

He pressed the button. It always made him feel like Bosley on *Charlie's Angels*.

Rodney cleared his throat and said, "Who is it?"

"It's me! Caroline!"

There was a short silence, during which Keith—to judge strictly by his face—appeared to excrete a concrete breeze block. Then he sprung from the AeroBed as if ejecting from a blazing aircraft.

"Come up!" Rodney said. He unlocked his door, stuck his head in the hallway, and inhaled a control sample of the building's air. Then he popped his head back in 4K and tentatively inhaled again: stank breath and passed gas. He stuck his head in the hallway one more time—wearing the door as a figleaf to obscure his naked torso—as the sixtysomething woman who lived two doors down came in with her shopping.

"Morning," Rodney said.

"Good afternoon," she replied.

Rodney and Keith raced to get dressed, like Japanese game-show contestants who get to keep all the clothes they can wriggle into in sixty seconds.

While Caroline knocked urgently, Keith hopped on his good leg, trying to pull on jeans. Rodney jumped into shorts already on the floor and impaled a T-shirt on his head. And still Caroline knocked.

Rodney opened the window and fanned his hand in front of the screen, a teen smoker in his bedroom. Then he and Keith scrambled for the door, as if taking their places at a surprise party. Keith turned the knob and gallantly swept open the door to 4K.

Caroline kissed Keith on her way past him and said, "I'm sorry honey but I really have to tinkle."

"First door on the left," Rodney said, but Caroline was already inside. Rodney had hoped to tidy up. But the bathroom, like the bedroom and the five feet of carpet that linked the two, was littered with balls of toilet tissue, as if Rodney had just hosted the World Series of Wanking.

Emerging from the bathroom, Caroline assessed Keith's cast and crutches and said, "Next time you'll hire movers." Only then did Rodney remember that he'd dropped a TV on Keith's foot, causing him to cartwheel down a flight of stairs.

Rodney sneezed a Pollock painting onto his palm.

"So I'm not the only one," Caroline said. "I was fine in Chicago, but as *soon* as we touched down at LaGuardia, my head exploded. I was sneezing before we got to the gate."

"That's happened to me," Rodney said. "You're barking before you're disembarking."

And then, when no one responded: "It's ragweed season. Every flight into New York is a red-eye."

"This is why you're perfect for Mairead," Caroline said.

"Why's that?"

"She gets your jokes."

Caroline still seemed to think a sense of humor was something like left-handedness: an inconvenience, something people were born with and bonded over when society marginalized them. It's why Caroline had set them up. Mairead was Rodney's left-handed scissors.

"I'll leave you lovebirds alone for a minute," Rodney said. "I'm going to grab some breakfast. Can I bring you anything?"

"Not me," Caroline said. "I ate a couple of hours ago."

"Lunch then?" Rodney said.

"That's what I ate a couple of hours ago," Caroline said. "Lunch. On the plane. I bought the snack box."

"Of course," Rodney said. "Excuse me." He opened his cell phone as if checking for messages and looked at the time on its screen: *1:57.*

He took the stairs two at a time and speed-dialed Mairead from the street. She picked up as he was halfway across Broadway, marooned on the median. "Hello?" She didn't sound happy and she didn't use his name.

"It's me," he said, sitting down on the bench. It looked onto a patch of grass. A tiny park, in the middle of Broadway. Like most of Manhattan's parks, it was half bucolic, half bubonic. A sign warned of a recent rodenticide application.

"I know it's you."

"I wanted to apologize about last night," Rodney said. "Or this morning, I guess it was."

"Apologize for what?" Her flat tone suggested she'd been waiting all day for an apology.

"For Keith. He insinuated that you . . ." Rodney didn't know how to put it, and Mairead wasn't about to help him.

"That I what?"

"You know—"

"I'm listening."

"That you good-mouthed me."

"Right," Mairead said. "I still don't know what that means."

"Neither do I," said Rodney. "But I don't want you to think I told him we slept together."

"We *did* sleep together."

"Right," Rodney said. "He might have inferred something more from that. But I certainly didn't imply it."

Mairead didn't say anything. For the moment, neither did Rodney. He suddenly felt alone, sitting on this median strip in Manhattan. He was on an island that was on an island, making his isolation more acute.

"I don't want to lose you," Rodney said, sniffling. His red eyes began to water and he felt a sneeze coming on.

"Check it out!" a teenager shouted to his buddy. They were waiting for the light to change. "Dude's *crying*!"

"Don't *cry* . . ." Mairead said.

"They're allergies!" Rodney said, to the punks and Mairead and anyone else within earshot. "It's ragweed season!" He attempted to sneeze in verification. He couldn't. Sneezes were like cabs. Widely available when you didn't want one, impossible to conjure when you did.

". . . because I don't *want* to be lost," Mairead said. "You're the first guy I've ever met who knows *imply* from *infer*."

Rodney sneezed twelve times in response.

"Good Lord," Mairead said. "Are you all right?"

"Histamine," Rodney said. "This fucking histamine. Sneezes and orgasms have the same trigger. Did you know that?"

"I did not."

"It explains Sneezy and Happy," Rodney said. "But what about the other five dwarfs?"

They were laughing. "Keith had no business bringing up my ex-girlfriend," Rodney said. "That really pissed me off. Makes it sound like I have a bunch of them."

"Who cares," Mairead said. "We've both dated one or two freaks at this point. My ex-boyfriend used to pee in the shower."

"A lot of guys do that," Rodney said.

"When they're not showering?" Mairead said.

"That's not good," Rodney said. And then: "I'm glad you're not mad. I wanted to call you earlier. To make sure you were okay. But I just got up."

"I know," Mairead said. "Caroline called me. She was standing outside your building. She said Keith wasn't answering his cell and you weren't answering your buzzer, and could she cab it down to my place. She had to use the bathroom."

Rodney wondered how long Caroline had been out there, buzzing, before he'd woken up. "I let her in eventually," he said. "She's at my place now."

"That's a relief," Mairead said. "The way she was talking, her bladder was about to rupture. I could see the ticker on New York 1: 'West Side Bladder Explosion Kills Three.'"

"Are you free tonight?" Rodney said. "There's a memorial service for my friend. But it's in a bar, so it won't be like a wake or anything."

"She didn't tell you?" Mairead said. "Caroline had this whizbang idea that we should double date. You and me and the two of them." Mairead couldn't say Keith's name.

"*Whizbang*," Rodney said. "Describe the sound of a bladder exploding."

"Good one, Carnac."

Rodney was on the 1 train, head down, heading downtown. He was looking at his shoes to avoid eye contact. But not *only* to avoid eye contact. He could see his reflection in his patent-leather Adidas. They were his favorites, Celtic green with shamrocks on the insole and an angry leprechaun on either heel.

He got out at 42nd Street and walked uptown, toward Foot Locker. Rodney had decided to get Keith a pair of sneakers as a going-away present—what game shows used to call a "parting gift"—to replace the shoe ruined in the bar fight. It was an extravagance Rodney could scarcely afford. But he didn't care. He planned to have the ruined shoe bronzed, as a wedding present, a memento of their drinking days in New York.

It was less memento than memento mori, a reminder of mortality, like Byron's skull cup. Only Keith's soiled shoe betokened the passing of a friendship.

Staring at the subway floor, Rodney marveled at the endless variety of footwear. He remembered when there were only two kinds: church shoes and tennis shoes. The former were always black and the latter were always white. Until he mowed the lawn, after which they were green.

In the window at Foot Locker, Rodney saw a single blue Adidas Gazelle. He tried on a pair of twelves. They were like crushed-velvet smoking jackets for the feet. He walked a lap around the store, stopping for a full minute to admire the shoes in the foot mirror. Rodney regarded them as if he were a shih tzu or a supine drunk or anyone else who viewed the world from six inches off the ground.

This is what the world looked like to Edith, from under the bar at Boyle's.

For Keith he bought a pair of shell-toed Superstars with black stripes, the kind Run-DMC used to wear. Rodney knew

Keith wore eleven-and-a-halfs because he had held his shoe in the ER when they examined Keith's foot.

"Wanna drive 'em off the lot?" asked the guy in the referee shirt after ringing up Rodney. But Rodney wanted his shoes boxed up, just so he could take them out when he got home, remove the wadded tissue paper, and take a deep drag from each shoe, fitting them over his nose and mouth like an oxygen mask.

That's what he did as a kid. Then he'd save the shoebox for a class diorama. Did kids still make dioramas? To judge strictly by the kids hanging out in Times Square, Rodney didn't think so.

Buying the shoes instantly made him feel better. Rodney was like a woman in that way. Or maybe it was just that new-shoe smell that carried him, Proust-like, back to childhood.

In grade school, sneakers and haircuts were the only form of self-expression ungoverned by the uniform code. And so Rodney saved his paper-route money for the black Converse Weapons that Larry Bird wore. He would never want anything in life as badly as he wanted those shoes. It was a testament to Bird's greatness that he won three consecutive MVP awards while playing in those ski boots. They were bulky and leaden, something you'd fit a Mafia hit victim with before throwing him into the East River.

Even today, basketball shoes were Rodney's only concession to fashion. Shoelaces were a statement of personal style. Even on a shoestring budget, Rodney could afford shoestrings. He remembered feeling a frisson of happiness when Tony Randall told Johnny Carson that the plastic tip at the end of a shoelace was called an "aglet." Rodney couldn't have been older than six or seven. In the same appearance, Randall said the groove that runs from one's nose to one's upper lip is called the "philtrum." Rodney once mentioned it to Keith, who said, "I always called it the snot gutter."

To the ancient Greeks, the philtrum was an erogenous zone, and Rodney was a philtrum man himself. He loved the spot where Mairead's philtrum met her vermilion zone—the med-school term for the lips themselves. Doctors also called it the red zone, a phrase borrowed by football for that part of the field in which men are trying to score. And other men are trying to stop them from doing so. Like Keith, last night.

Rodney sat on the 1 train with a bag under each arm in a classic subway pose: the exhausted old woman with her shopping.

He was heading back to 4K, to give Keith his shoes. Rodney could never tell Caroline about Carlotta Tendant. Marriages failed. They failed all the time—Keith's would be no different. But there was something ineffably sad about a failed wedding. *That's* what Rodney didn't want on his conscience.

Ragweed pollen found Rodney underground. His snot gutter had filled with mucus, forcing him to lift his head. He raised his gaze from other people's shoes to the ads above their heads.

In the womb, the angel Gabriel whispered to Rodney all of the wisdom in the universe. And then Gabriel pressed an index finger to Rodney's top lip, as if to shush him. In doing so, the angel wiped his memory clean, but left a groove in the flesh, a reminder of man's eternal quest for knowledge.

Or so Rodney's mother told him when they knelt at his bedside to pray. It's probably why he read so many books, pined for Mairead's upper lip, and worried that he was not a man blessed with divine drinking powers but was, instead, a run-of-the-gin-mill drunk. Or worse, that he was dating one.

He had met Mairead over drinks and spent every waking

moment with her drinking. Rodney liked a woman who liked a few beers. But only a few. It was a common double standard at Boyle's, like the way Wanamaker always judged the Miss Universe pageant from his stool, his brutal swimsuit assessments issuing from a face like a dropped pizza.

Still, it bothered Rodney when he saw women binge-drinking at Boyle's. In his doctor's waiting room, last time he got a physical, he read it in a brochure: Children with fetal alcohol syndrome are born without philtrums. From the Greek *philos*: "Love."

"What's this?" Keith said when Rodney handed him the shoebox.

"Just open it," Rodney said.

Keith shook it gently from side to side and said, "If you brought your hamster to show-and-tell, it's dead."

"Open it," Rodney said.

"What's it for?"

"It's a going-away present," said Caroline.

"More like a Go Away present," Rodney said. He was no good at giving gifts. Keith was no good at getting them.

"You didn't have to wrap it," Keith said.

"I know," Rodney said. "Which is why I didn't."

Keith opened the lid slowly and turned his head away, waiting for the novelty spring snakes to deploy. When they didn't, he reached in and removed the Superstars. For a full five seconds, nobody said anything. And then Keith, who looked as if he might cry, said: "Thanks, man. For everything."

Caroline *was* crying, though it could have been the ragweed. Rodney wasn't sure. "That is *so* sweet," she said. And then, hugging Rodney's neck: "You are *such* a great friend."

"It's a toddlin' town, Chicago," Rodney said. "He'll need something to toddle in."

He knew they were communicating through Caroline, but Rodney didn't care. It was easier this way. Like the men and women he saw in the park, talking to each other through a dog.

He (to the shih-tzu): And what's your name?
She (to the shih-tzu): Your name is Sophie, isn't it?
He: And where are you headed, Sophie?
She: You're going to the boathouse, aren't you?
He: Well, Sophie, you are one beautiful creature, you
    know that?
She: Can you say thank you to the nice man?

Keith said to Caroline, "I now kind of wish I'd gotten Rodney something."

"You can get dinner," Caroline said. "For the four of us." And then, turning to Rodney: "Did Mairead tell you? We thought it would be fun to double-date tonight."

Rodney was going to miss Keith. Perhaps he was suffering from the Stockholm syndrome, in which a hostage grows to admire his tormentor, but Rodney felt profoundly sad when he saw Keith's stained white duffel in the hallway, a canvas sausage casing packed full. Caroline slung the bag over her shoulder and said, "Maybe we should register for luggage."

Caroline was the one with Stockholm syndrome, Rodney realized. She loved Keith. Rodney was sure of that.

The couple were staying at Mairead's tonight. Rather, Caroline was staying at Mairead's and Keith was staying with Caroline, who had only stopped by Rodney's to help her fiancé with his luggage. Her fiancé *was* luggage: He was literally leaning on her as they left. Rodney was touched by Caroline's mothering. It's exactly what Keith wanted. Maybe he'd develop the corollary to Stockholm syndrome, what was called Lima syndrome, named for a militant group's takeover of the Japanese ambassador's residence in the Peruvian capital during a party the week before Christmas in 1996. The siege lasted four months, but most of the hostages were released within days because the captors had grown to admire their captives. It could happen to Keith. He could love the object of his torment. Or so Rodney rationalized.

Rodney and Caroline helped Keith down the stairs, then they carried his bags to the curb. Caroline dropped the duffel bag to the sidewalk and sighed. "Do your parents know you've schlepped with him?" Rodney said.

"Schlepped with him?" Caroline asked.

"Never mind," Rodney said.

"I know I'm dumb because I don't get your jokes."

"*I'm* dumb," Rodney said. "For making them."

A taxi pulled up. Its trunk opened wide and said "Ahh." It had halitosis, despite the black breath mint of a spare tire on its tongue. Rodney fed it Keith's luggage, then Keith's crutches.

"I'm gonna miss having him around," he told Caroline.

"I'm gonna miss being around," Keith said.

"It was like having a pet," Rodney said. "I'd come home, he was always there."

"Waiting to be fed," Keith said.

"At least I've found him a good home," Rodney told Caroline. "He's house-trained, by the way. Give him a flea bath once a week. And don't let him hump the mailman's leg."

"Too late," Keith said.

"Are you guys finished, because the meter's running," Caroline said. And then, to Keith: "You two are the ones who should be getting married." She got in on the sidewalk side and slid over. Rodney helped Keith into the cab.

"Make sure he wears one of those lampshades on his head, like Edith," Rodney said. "So he doesn't lick himself."

"Who's Edith?" Caroline said. "And why is she licking herself?" She gave the cabbie Mairead's address and said to Rodney, "We'll see you tonight."

Rodney stood on the sidewalk to see them off.

As the cab pulled away, Keith stuck his head out the window and bayed like a hound.

12

He wore the Gazelles to dinner. God they were gorgeous. Rodney never cared much about brands, was impervious to commercial come-ons. Sneakers were his weakness. He'd seen an orange juice spot the other day. Valencia oranges bouncing and dripping, bouncing and dripping, like a wet T-shirt contest for citric fruit. A seductive female voice said the oranges were "hand-squeezed" and Rodney thought: *They were asking for it, those oranges*.

The ad was for some premium OJ that came in a tall, thin bottle better suited to high-end vodka. "I drink it out of a cardboard can," Rodney told Mairead. "From concentrate. Mixed with water and decanted from a plastic pitcher. It all tastes the same."

"It doesn't all taste the same," Mairead said. "Everyone cares about brands, whether or not they know it."

"You have to say that," Rodney said. "It's your job. Elevating one deodorant over another. Creating diseases for cures, instead of the other way around."

Rodney was drinking a Sapporo, Mairead was drinking sake in some Japanese shabu-shabu joint that Caroline had booked near Union Square. But Keith and Caroline weren't coming. "Keith isn't feeling well," Mairead had said, to which Rodney just laughed and said: "I don't doubt that."

"What are you talking about?" Mairead said now. "'Creating diseases for cures'?"

"Restless leg syndrome," Rodney said. "No one had it until there was a cure for it. Now it's an epidemic. RLS. It's in the crosswords every other day, RLS. The clue was always 'Literary monogram.' Now it's 'Neur. disorder.'"

"Well," Mairead said. "Robert Louis Stevenson wrote, 'Everyone lives by selling something.' So there."

"I'm impressed."

"Don't be," she said. "My boss has that quote on a poster in her office. 'Everyone Lives by Selling Something.' But that's why we have brands, to distinguish one thing from another."

Stevenson made Rodney think of Jim Hawkins, from *Treasure Island*, more or less growing up in a pub: the Admiral Benbow.

They had removed their shoes at the door. Rodney had protested. "I just want to eat," he told the kimonoed hostess, while trying not to think of Curt Mayhew's repeated references to open kimonos. "I don't want to bowl." And now Mairead said to Rodney, "If you don't care about brands, why don't you take *any* pair of shoes when we leave here?"

Rodney didn't say anything. But every time a party got up to leave, Rodney's eyes followed them to the door, making sure no one made off with the Gazelles.

"It's because you love Adidas," Mairead said. "You care about labels."

Rodney smiled. "I practically cried the last time I moved, when I thought I might get a 646 area code. I knew my friends would be too lazy to call if they had to dial three extra numbers."

"And you like the 212," Mairead said. "It's a designer label."

"You're thinking of my *brother*," Rodney said.

"I've never met your brother," Mairead said.

"But that's him," Rodney said. "To a tee. I remember at dinner once, when I was a kid, my parents giving him shit about only wearing Levi's. They said he only wore them for the tag in the back pocket. But Jimmy said Levi's fit best, that he couldn't care less about the tag. So I saw his blue Levi's cords on the clothesline. They had that orange tag in the right back pocket. I got a needle-nosed pliers off my dad's workbench. And I ripped the tag out."

"What a jerk," Mairead said.

"I know," Rodney said. "It was like pulling a healthy molar. It took forever and left a jagged hole in the pants. I came in the house, dropped the tag on the kitchen table, and waited for my parents' applause. But my mom was *livid*. She said, *I paid twenty-seven dollars for those pants!* I thought she was gonna tear *me* a jagged new hole with a needle-nosed pliers. It was like I'd ripped the hood ornament off her Rolls-Royce."

Mairead said, "What did Jimmy do?"

"He beat me for two weeks," Rodney said. "He'd just pin me to the ground like a butterfly in a book and pound on my chest with his fist."

"Nice."

"It's called a Ninety-nine Bump," Rodney said. "All the while he was doing it he'd let a big loogie fall out of his mouth, then try to suck it back in at the last second."

"What's that called?"

"That's called a Bungee Jumper. Except that he was usually unable to suck it back in. In which case it's called a Kamikaze Bungee Jumper."

"Do we have to talk about this during dinner?" Mairead

asked. "And could we try not to say *kamikaze* again in a Japanese restaurant?"

"My bad," Rodney said.

"The Levi's were as much a status symbol for your mom as they were for your brother," Mairead said. "She liked her son wearing Levi's."

"Then explain why she always bought me Thom McAn when I wanted Adidas," Rodney said. "She claimed four stripes were better than three, like I was being promoted from commander to captain."

"Thank you," Mairead said. "You've made my point. You care about brands. You acknowledge their differences. Or you'd just drink Robitussin when you ran out of Guinness."

"I've done that," Rodney said.

Mairead was always slagging off her work, but tonight she defended it, in the way that Rodney could ridicule his own family but would fight anybody else who did. That, to him, was love.

And anyway, he loved all this arguing, this give and take with Mairead. He could see in it the kernels of future arguments, bigger and more serious ones, and he loved the thought of those, too: domestic disputes.

Domestic: *Of or relating to family or household.*

He'd looked it up, in the big red dictionary, among all those books that filled his apartment with people, none of whom really existed.

Rodney remembered something else Robert Louis Stevenson said: "Books are good enough in their own way, but they're a mighty bloodless substitute for life."

After dinner they ordered mochi, a golf ball of green-tea ice cream covered in pulverized sticky rice. The waitress jammed a lit candle in the center of one of the balls, so that it looked like a mini version of a cartoon bomb—a bowling ball with a burning fuse. Mairead didn't sing "Happy Birthday," but Rodney didn't mind. And afterward, when they retrieved their shoes, he said, "I'm gonna give Keith a call. He wouldn't want to miss Armen's memorial piss-up." They were going to Boyle's to honor Armen and—though Rodney couldn't say it out loud—to spend what might be everyone's last night at the place.

"Keith's not there," Mairead said.

Rodney looked up from his phone and she said: "He left. For Chicago. Three hours ago."

Rodney squinted at Mairead: "You said he was sick."

"I didn't want to spoil your birthday," she said.

"So you lied."

"Not exactly," Mairead said. "He looked pretty sick to me."

"He didn't sleep well last night," Rodney said. He hadn't told Mairead that he and Keith had spent the night in an open trailer in Harlem, human tag sale items that nobody wanted. So he left it at that.

"Looks like it's just you and I," Mairead said, taking Rodney's hand.

"Yep," Rodney said, powerless to stop his tongue. "Just you and me."

Mairead removed her hand from Rodney's. "Nothing turns me on like a grammar lesson," she said.

They stepped outside. New York's garbage bags were ripe and ready for harvest. "Shall we walk off our shabu-shabu?" Rodney said.

"We shall," Mairead said.

"The best meal I ever had was shabu-shabu," Rodney said. "In Bora Bora. Or was it mahi-mahi in Walla Walla?"

"Washed down with Coca-Cola?" Mairead said.

Rodney opened his mouth. "That doesn't . . ."

"Shut up," Mairead said. "I know it doesn't make sense." She took his hand. "I've had too much sake. I don't even like sake."

"Me either," Rodney said. "Rice wine, rice ice cream. Why did Caroline make *us* eat at a Japanese restaurant when *she* wasn't even going to be there?"

"Because she's a controlling control freak who likes to control people," Mairead said.

Rodney laughed. "Put *that* in your wedding toast," he said. "That'll liven up the reception."

They were walking hand in hand on Broadway, looking up a lazy river of red taillights, when Mairead said: "There won't be any wedding toast."

Rodney stopped. Without looking at him Mairead said, "I told Caroline about Keith."

For an instant, Rodney felt his heart stop—*heard* his heart go from vital to dead, like the sound of a vacuum cleaner when the plug is pulled.

"Told her *what* about Keith?" he said. Rodney's right hand still held Mairead's left, but they were facing each other now. Rodney wondered if she could feel his palm beginning to sweat.

"Told her what she has every right to know," Mairead said. "That the man she planned to marry was cheating on her."

Rodney felt his stomach acids churn volcanically. It wasn't the mochi. Or not only the mochi. "Why did you do that?" he said. His mouth was dry from beer and anxiety.

"I'd want to know," Mairead said. "If it were me."

"He'll never talk to me again," Rodney said. "He'll think I told you."

"He already thinks that. He thought that last night, at Cliffs."

A pedicab tinkled its bell in solicitation. Rodney needed air. But he also needed to sit. He looked at the pedicabbie and judged him to be an NYU student. "Let's get in," he said. Mairead didn't argue.

The rickshaw pedaled into traffic. A slow barge steaming up Broadway. Rodney leaned back and looked up and thought of Huck Finn. *It's lovely to live on a raft. We had the sky up there, all speckled with stars, and we used to lay on our backs and look up at them, and discuss about whether they was made or only just happened.*

Rodney looked up, squinted, tried to see the stars. And wondered which one of them was Armen.

It took forever to get to Boyle's. The kid was pedaling like Lance Armstrong but it didn't make a difference. Mairead was wearing some kind of dressed-up flip-flops. She was talking about what happened that afternoon, after Keith and Caroline arrived at her place from Rodney's. Rodney admired Mairead's toes as she talked. The nails were a metallic burgundy, like a car finish. He was thinking of the words *pedicab* and *pedicure*.

When Keith and Caroline showed up at her apartment, Mairead said, Keith immediately took a nap. Caroline dragged Mairead out shopping, to some boutique on Madison Avenue with a Frenchy name and a door buzzer. "I know there's not going to be anything there for a six-foot chick," Mairead said. "I might as well be going to Baby Gap. But she didn't care."

When they met, Mairead said—on their first jobs, at an ad agency in Chicago—Caroline brought Mairead a CTA map and a Zagat's book and told her which coworkers were nice and whom to suck up to and which creeps were most likely to harass her. She taught Mairead how to arrive late without being noticed and how to stay late while *being* noticed. Caroline brought her to the Wiener Circle for lunch and the house she grew up in for her mother's chicken Florentine and generally took care—and possession—of Mairead as she would a house pet.

Rodney wished the kid would pedal a little faster, enough to generate a breeze.

"The first time she tried to set me up with you I said no," Mairead said. "Just on principle. I didn't want her running my love life, too."

He knew it was just an expression, but when she said *love*, Rodney felt his chest constrict. He wondered if this was what Armen felt before the heart attack, this thin line between love and a myocardial infarction.

Rodney was impatient for the story. "So you went shopping . . ."

"No, we didn't," Mairead said. "We never made it to the store. Walking through the park I told her."

"Told her how?"

"I said, 'There's something I need to tell you, and I'm so sorry, but I couldn't live with myself if I didn't say this: I think Keith is cheating on you.'"

"What did she say?"

"Nothing."

"Nothing?"

"At first. And then she was indignant."

"Understandably."

"Not understandably," Mairead said. "She's mad at *me*."

"For telling her?"

"I guess."

"What did she say?"

"She said: 'You don't think I know that? I know he was

unfaithful in the past. You don't think he and I have *talked* about that'?"

"They haven't," Rodney said. "Talked about it. She didn't know until you told her."

"Then she asked me how this was any of my goddamn business," Mairead said. "She said she hoped *I* felt good for telling her, she hoped that *I* could live with myself now."

"Christ. Did you?"

"Did I what?"

"Feel good," Rodney said. "Telling her."

"How can you ask me that?"

Rodney thought she *did* enjoy telling Caroline, that she savored the shift in power. It was only a guess. But Rodney found the trait unbecoming, a word his mother always used when describing the clothes of various anchorwomen in Minneapolis.

"So the wedding's off?" Rodney said.

"The wedding *toast* is off," Mairead said. "The wedding's still on. I just won't be invited. I don't *want* to be invited. Standing next to her at the altar, knowing what I know about the two of them?"

A taxi drifted into their lane and the pedicabbie tinkled his bell impotently. The bell, the bike—they reminded Rodney of the Chinese food delivery guys, the spawning salmon of the city, always cycling the wrong way up Columbus.

"How are they still getting married?" Rodney said.

"She said she loves him," Mairead said. "She said there are all different kinds of marriages. It makes me wonder if her dad cheated on her mom."

"Maybe she's right," Rodney said. "Maybe there are."

"Or maybe she wants to avoid the embarrassment of calling off her wedding," Mairead said. "I can't really say, because two minutes after I told her, she said she wanted to walk back to my apartment. Didn't say a word the whole way. Walked five feet in front of me. But she needed me there to let her in. Then she woke Keith, grabbed their stuff, and left."

Rodney looked at Mairead's flip-flops. They weren't all that dressy, on closer inspection. He remembered that she hated to buy shoes, could never find a woman's size twelve, except in places that catered to cross-dressers.

A troubling thought occurred to Rodney, and it had nothing to do with Keith's marriage: Between him and Mairead, Rodney was the one with the shoe fetish.

They walked in and a bell tinkled. Darts Night. The twelfth Saturday. Rodney laughed: They hadn't postponed it. Five-Oh must've stepped aside to let the door swing in, because Rodney found him standing next to the door frame, like the boulder rolled away from Christ's tomb.

"I'm not surrendering my shoes in this place," Mairead said.

"You'll only have to surrender your dignity," said Rodney.

He was called Five-Oh not because he was a cop. Or not *only* because he was a cop. Nor was Five-Oh the Richter-scale measurement when he walked into Boyle's. It was much higher than that. Five-Oh was 275 pounds of Famous Ray's and Foster's Lager and what used to be called bonhomie.

They called him Five-Oh because he lived in a perpetual five o'clock, embodied in the phrase "It's five o'clock somewhere." His face was forever five o'clock shadowed. His left hand—his non-darting hand—always held an alcoholic beverage.

"Five-Oh," Rodney said, extending his left hand and wincing preemptively.

Five-Oh put down his beer and pumped Rodney's hand like a man drawing water from a deep well. Jesus he was strong.

He gave Rodney a Knuckle Floater, squeezing Rodney's hand until the knuckles were undulating. They were worry beads in Five-Oh's grip. And Five-Oh wasn't even left-handed.

"Tragedy, huh?" Rodney said.

"Yeah," said Five-Oh. "It's a fuckin' tragedy."

Darts were all that ever touched his magnificent right hand. "Arrows," he called them.

"He even wanks left-handed," Armen once said in admiration when Five-Oh wasn't in. Five-Oh once told Rodney he was reluctant to raise his right hand when testifying in court, for fear he'd strain his darting wrist. And yet he often had it raised in the crush of humanity at Boyle's, holding both hands chest-high, like a surgeon getting scrubbed.

Such precautions were unnecessary, as everyone at Boyle's had a rooting interest in protecting Five-Oh's fingers from harm. More than any other, *he* was responsible for the six consecutive league championships won by Boyle's team, the Tossers. It's why they didn't suspend Darts Night for Armen's memorial. The two events were one and the same, a celebration of Boyle's.

Five-Oh was like any virtuoso whose delicate hands were insured by Lloyd's, protected by oven mitts, fetishized by fans. When Chopin died, a plaster cast was made of his left hand. It was tiny. When Rodney saw it—online, under glass, in some museum in Milan—he thought: *It belongs on the end of a backscratcher.* It reminded him of Marisa's shoes, something to hang from a charm bracelet.

Chopin—there was a guy who left a mark: the sonatas, waltzes, nocturnes, and études. The grave at Père Lachaise in Paris. The single hand, housed in a box like Thing on *The Addams Family.*

The other night Rodney noticed, for the first time on the back bar, a bottle of something called Chopin—"Luxury

Potato Vodka"—with a portrait of the piano virtuoso just below the bottleneck.

Now *that*, thought Rodney, was immortality: having a drink named after you. Not a mixed drink, like a Harvey Wallbanger or Tom Collins or Shirley Temple. But something people could drink straight from a bottle, a bottle emblazoned with your name and perhaps even your portrait, like Sam Adams or Dom Perignon.

Rodney believed in transubstantiation: that wine was changed into the blood of Christ, which he drank every Sunday at Mass after receiving communion.

Communion, he thought, seated at the bar. *That's what this place offers: spiritual fellowship*.

Mairead put a hand on Rodney's knee and said, "Happy Birthday." And in the doorway an unshaven Cupid threw his arrows.

Dom Perignon was a Benedictine monk who didn't actually invent champagne. Nor did he utter the line that was often attributed to him, a line that had echoes of Alexander Graham Bell: "Come quickly, I am drinking the stars!"

But Rodney was doing just that, sitting next to Mairead, listening to "Ladies and Gentlemen We Are Floating in Space," by Spiritualized, in the half-light of Boyle's.

Drinking the stars.

Out of respect, Wanamaker was wearing a short-sleeved dress shirt. It gaped at the neck. His tie was the width of a baby's bib and every bit as stained. Still, Rodney admired the gesture.

There were two bartenders. A young guy, maybe twenty-three, whose Invisalign braces made him look even younger. And a lady, fifteen years older, with short black hair and an asymmetrical half-smile that reminded Rodney of a check mark. He thought of her face as a box on a questionnaire.

Rodney ordered two pints from the woman. When she brought them, he introduced himself. "I'm Flora," she said. "Gary's little sister." Rodney and Mairead offered their sympathies and Flora thanked them. "We've had the rug pulled from under us," she said. "But we're coping."

Rodney recalled for her the time Armen snatched the toupee off a belligerent drunk in an effort to sober him up and then—when he had the guy's attention—slapped him across the face with his own hairdo. "Like Patton slapping the GI on Sicily," Rodney said. "We always said that guy had the rug pulled out from *over* him."

Flora laughed. Rodney felt strange calling Armen "Gary." He said, "Gary was one of my best friends. But half the people here could say that."

"He was the best man at about fifty different weddings," Flora said. "It's one of the reasons he never got married. He said he was bound to offend forty-nine other people when he had to choose his best man. Are you two . . ."

"Married?" Rodney said. "No." He laughed. "We're . . ."

"What?" Mairead said. "We're what?" He could see that she was enjoying this, deliberately making him uncomfortable.

"Friends," Rodney said.

"We're friends," said Mairead.

"The kid with the braces, what's his name?" Rodney asked Flora. He wanted her to say, "Fauna."

"His name's Tom," she said. "Gary's friend Cliff recommended him. But the darts team, they're all calling him S.O.B. I don't know why. He's nice enough."

Rodney called him over. "S.O.B.," he said. "Why's everyone calling you that?"

"School of Bartending," S.O.B. said. "They think I just graduated. First night here, I'm a little nervous and all that."

"Don't be," Rodney said. "I'm about to start a new job myself."

"You are?" Mairead said.

"I might," Rodney said.

S.O.B. excused himself to pull a pint and Mairead said, "The bank job?"

"When you say it like that," Rodney said, "it sounds like I'm planning a heist."

"So you're going to take it?"

"It's either the bank job or the job bank," Rodney said.

"What about it is most appealing to you?"

"Spain," Rodney said. "I like the idea of sipping martinis in the bar of the Palace Hotel in Madrid, like Jake and Brett."

"Jake and Brett who?" Mairead said.

"In *The Sun Also Rises*," Rodney said. "Brett says to Jake, 'Isn't it a nice bar?' And Jake says, 'They're all nice bars.'"

But they weren't all nice bars, Rodney knew. He would never find another place like this.

"I want to drink three bottles of rioja and eat a whole suckling pig upstairs at Botín's," Rodney said. "Like Hemingway."

"I have no idea what you're talking about," Mairead said.

"Madrid," said Rodney.

"I thought the job was in New York," she said.

"It is."

Mairead sighed. "Let me ask you something," she said.

"Fire away."

"What's your beehag, as my boss would say?"

"What's my what?" Rodney said.

"Your beehag."

"What's my *beehag*?" Rodney said.

"Your BHAG," Mairead repeated. "Big, Hairy, Audacious Goal. B-H-A-G."

"Your boss sounds like a D-bag," Rodney said. "D-B-A-G."

"You don't have a beehag?" Mairead said. "Everybody has a beehag."

"I have Small, Hairless, Achievable Goals," Rodney said. "I have . . . SHAGs."

"I don't believe you."

He couldn't say if it was Mairead or the mochi or getting ferried uptown by bicycle rickshaw—a human order of moo shoo pork. But Rodney's stomach was beginning to bother him.

Flora banged a pint glass with a soup spoon, as if proposing a toast. "Can I have everyone's attention?" she shouted, and then, when the din receded: "May we observe a moment of silence for your friend and my brother, Gary, God rest his soul."

On an easel behind the bar was a poster of Armen—the same picture that was used on the flyer on the door. On the poster, professionally printed, was the phrase "We Love You Gary." Beneath that were the year of his birth and the year of his death, connected by a dash. Rodney looked at that dash, at that typographical life span, blown up to 192-point type and still ridiculously abbreviated. A hammock strung between oblivions.

The bar was silent save for the hum of the Smoke-Eater and the choleric cough of a Tosser.

And then an Irish bagpipe skirled softly, and Rodney looked up to see, to his eternal wonderment, Wanamaker seated on his stool, playing a note-perfect version of "She Moved Through the Fair."

Rodney recognized it as an uilleann pipe. An off-duty cop, a member of the NYPD's Emerald Society pipe band, once explained to him that a traditional highland bagpipe blew at 116 decibels, the equivalent of a chainsaw. But an uilleann pipe could be played indoors, at the bar, while seated, as Wanamaker was now proving.

The bagpipes breathed in and out like a sleeping child and Rodney thought of the twelve-year-old daughter Armen never got to see, and of the girl's mother who made certain of that, and of the words to this Irish folk song: *The people were saying no two were e'er wed / But one has a sorrow that never was said . . .*

It began as so many jokes do, with "A guy walks into a bar . . ." That's what happened, more or less: A guy walked into a bar.

A guy walked into a bar and a bell rang. (That's how fights start, too, Rodney thought later. With the ringing of a bell.) At the time, no one thought anything of it. Ask not for whom the bell tolls. Mairead was the only one who even acknowledged it, reciting the line from *It's a Wonderful Life*: "Every time a bell rings an angel gets his wings."

"Not in here," Wanamaker said.

"A guy *named* Angel *ordered* wings in here once," Rodney said, rising from his stool. "Does that count?"

Rodney excused himself. He headed to the Gents. Even before he got to the door he stopped breathing through his nose.

The bell rang again. *It tolls for thee*. He couldn't think of a worse place to vomit than Boyle's. Its lone bowl, stained brown, reminded Rodney of a rotten molar. Just looking into its cavity was a powerful emetic, more reliable than ipecac.

He prostrated himself before the bowl, and a thought arrived involuntarily: *Ipecac* is an anagram of *ice cap*.

Ice cap made him think of *Ice Capades*.

He closed his eyes and thought: *Lord have mercy*. An air bubble rose inside him and popped in the back of his throat. Rodney wanted to gag. *Christ have mercy*.

His lips tingled. Rodney wished himself anywhere else. His forehead was cool and beaded, like a lemonade glass. He noticed the floor for the first time. For the first time ever. It was done in subway tiles. He was kneeling on them. He should probably throw these pants away when he got home.

The door to the Gents opened and closed on its air hinge. Privacy would be too much to ask on a Saturday night.

He would *definitely* throw these pants away when he got home.

His chest rose and fell. And again. Like Wanamaker's bagpipe. He braced himself—here we go—and something hot and bilious shot up through the center of his being. Rodney pictured the cartoon cross-section of a man in a medicine commercial, some over-the-counter elixir going in the mouth, down the throat, and finally painting the stomach in Pepto-Bismol pink.

This was that, only in reverse.

But before it hit the back of his throat, the bile fell, unable to ring the bell in this carnival midway game.

The one-ply toilet paper hanging to Rodney's left was translucent. Thin as onion skin. And about as effective, Rodney knew from experience. He counted nine squares hanging nearly to the floor. They swayed in some invisible, industrial breeze.

He braced for the bile's return. Rodney imagined himself a thermometer, mercury rising in a red line at his core . . .

Through the space beneath the stall wall, Rodney saw a pair of boots walk by. Then a pair of sneakers. It was the second time today he found himself regarding footwear from ground level. Either two guys just walked in or there was a horse at the urinal wearing Timberlands and Reeboks.

"Where is he?" It was a voice Rodney didn't recognize.

"Check the stall." Another voice.

"It's occupied," Rodney called.

But the guy must not have heard, or didn't care, because Rodney heard the stall door burst open and then felt something slide under his left armpit. It was another man's arm. Rodney's first thought was *Jesus, this guy must really have to take a dump.*

Then Rodney realized where the man's *right* hand was: on the back of Rodney's head, trying to force it face first into the toilet.

"There you are, motherfucker."

For a moment, Rodney was back in junior high, about to get a Sudsy or a Swirly or some other lavatorial torture whose name Keith would surely know: Gargling Toilet Water, perhaps.

Gargling Toilet Water. It made Rodney think, at once, of Listerine and listeria, and how both were named for the English surgeon Joseph Lister, the Edison of antisepsis.

At the same time, Rodney was reflexively resisting—his left hand was on the rim of the toilet bowl and his right on the handicapped grab-bar bolted to the wall. Rodney had used that bar before, as one half of a gymnast's parallel bars, the better to lever himself off the toilet seat and hover just above it when forced, by fickle nature, to use the stall at Boyle's for its intended purpose.

His assailant must have clocked on that he would never force Rodney's face into the toilet, that Rodney would not go bobbing for cholera. So the guy hooked his right arm under Rodney's other armpit and began pulling him to his feet.

Rodney wondered when some full-bladdered fucker would come in here and break it up.

Through the wall, in the bar, he heard "Jump Around" on the stereo and thought: House of Pain. I'll say. His fucking neck was being broken.

All manner of things came to mind while he was getting jumped in the john. But mostly Rodney remembered the J. P. Donleavy line: "When I die, I want to decompose in a barrel of porter and have it served in all the pubs in Dublin."

Rodney's feet were finally on the ground. But the man's arms were still hooked under Rodney's armpits, and were attempting to forklift him into the air. Except he couldn't, because Rodney was taller.

So Rodney bent over, lifting this prick's feet off the ground: Rodney now wore his attacker like a backpack. He remembered a pro wrestling move called the Airplane Spin, but there wasn't sufficient clearance in the stall, and it would only exacerbate his motion sickness.

He'd come in here to barf and found himself in a bar fight. *Barf* and *bar fight*. Like *ice cap* and *Ice Capades*.

Rodney backed the guy out of the stall and clocked his face in the funhouse mirror: Longneck, his head as red as an angry pimple.

He smelled some cheap fragrance on Longneck, not a deodorant but its opposite: some kind of odorant.

In the mirror he also saw De Niro, holding the door closed with his back. Longneck yelled, "Help me here!" And De Niro bum-rushed Rodney, whose hands were occupied with the troll on his back. De Niro started pulling on Rodney's belt buckle. Only then did it occur to Rodney what they wanted: not just his blood but his pants.

The air hinge sighed. But instead of the cavalry it was a college kid, who said, "Sorry" and stepped back out, as if what he'd just witnessed—one guy on Rodney's back, another trying to de-pants him—was consensual.

Rodney kneed De Niro in the chest, but not before the guy had unbuckled his belt and began pulling Rodney's pants off at the waist. Rodney's gymnophobia was now in full flower.

He caught De Niro in the face with his right knee, drawing blood that transferred to the knee of Rodney's khakis. Or maybe it was Rodney's blood. He had struck something sharp with his kneecap, and now Rodney saw what: De Niro's front tooth. The right one was no longer there.

Rodney tried to flip Longneck off his back, but managed only to pull his T-shirt up over his head, as in a hockey fight, loosing all manner of odors that had been trapped in the Dutch oven of Longneck's black undershirt.

"What, did you die in here?" It was Wanamaker's voice, just outside the Gents. Then the door swung open and he said, "Because it smells like *something* did . . ."

The human brain is not capable of processing all that came at Wanamaker in the nanosecond that followed. Rodney would realize that later. And Wanamaker's brain was less capable than most. A shirtless man in a black executioner's hood rode Rodney, whose blood-stained pants were falling down, thanks to the guy with the jack-o-lanterned mouth, who rose from the floor at Rodney's feet and flew at Wanamaker, who may or may not have recognized him as the friend of the man who'd been frog-marched out of Boyle's the previous weekend.

No, Wanamaker was simply reacting when he swung his bagpipe, the chanter and drones windmilling toward De Niro's face. They looked to Rodney like Celtic nunchucks. "Irish warpipes," the British called them, banning them in Scotland as an "instrument of war." Something that looked like a billy club—the bagpipe's bass regulator, with its metal keys—strafed De Niro across the left temple, buying Wanamaker an extra second. He used it wisely, pulling a can of Lysol off the paper-towel dispenser and macing De Niro in the eyes with it, an act of violence that called to Rodney's mind the overzealous greeters at Macy's perfume counter.

From the bar, over by the dartboard, Rodney heard a cry of "Bull's-eye!"

De Niro crumpled to the floor, convulsing.

Armen played "Bullseye," by Lakeside, after every Tossers victory. But Flora wouldn't know that.

"Wanamaker, how 'bout a hand?" Rodney said. He was panting. But Wanamaker was already gone, the fucker, and Longneck was trying with both hands and renewed vigor to separate Rodney's head from his neck, screwing it this way and unscrewing it that way, as if trying to recall that mnemonic: Lefty loosey, righty tighty?

Rodney thought of the guy in Chicago who made the papers after custom-ordering a coffin for himself: a giant Pabst Blue Ribbon can.

Maybe that was the white light you saw when you died— the pop top opening on a can of Pabst, with you submersed inside it. Rodney felt himself falling: into a beer or a barrel of porter. And then the hand of God raising him up in celebration.

> *I'd like to give a lake of beer to God*
> *I'd love the Heavenly*
> *Host to be tippling there*
> *For all eternity.*

Only it wasn't the hand of God raising him up. It only felt like that. Rodney was in the divine right hand of Five-Oh, whose left hand held Longneck, his face still hidden in his T-shirt. Wanamaker had retrieved Five-Oh and S.O.B., who was now trying to get De Niro off the bathroom floor.

S.O.B. dragged De Niro, blinded, out of the bathroom and through the bar and along the filthy linoleum. "Talk about mopping the floor with a guy," said one of the Tossers, a guy who called himself Two-Minute Tommy, for the time it took him to finish off opponents in darts. Everyone else at Boyle's called him Too-Many Tommy.

Five-Oh perp-walked the other one through the bar, Longneck's face still shrouded in his own T-shirt, just as in the perp walks on TV.

Then Five-Oh pushed him face-first through the swinging front door of Boyle's, causing the overhead bell to jingle.

Rodney followed them onto the sidewalk, where Five-Oh peeled the T-shirt from Longneck's face, as if revealing the true identity of a villain on *Scooby-Doo*, and placed him prone on the sidewalk.

"You know this mook?" Five-Oh said, taking a knee on Longneck's back.

"Not really," Rodney said. And then, because he couldn't resist, and he'd seen too many movies: "But his face just rang a bell."

"My *God*," Mairead said, for Rodney had gone to the bathroom and returned bloodied and bathed in sweat, with red streaks on his neck that resembled grill lines on a pork tenderloin.

"They thought I was monopolizing the stall," Rodney said. "They must have really had to go."

Mairead said, "They left a mark. Lots of them."

But Rodney excused himself: The two cops who'd been

chatting on the sidewalk with S.O.B. and Five-Oh summoned him for his statement.

Rodney knew the drill. Two weeks after 9/11, a homeless man tried to mug Rodney in Central Park. He was walking back from a jog just after dark, around 7:30, when a crazy guy with a white skunk stripe down the middle of his salt-and-pepper 'fro stepped in front of Rodney, removed a rubber hose from his backpack, and began whaling on his shoulders, as if violently knighting him.

Rodney wasn't hurt, but he didn't want to feel responsible for any other attacks. So he ran to Tavern, where the door-man called the cops, who arrived in two minutes and were profoundly . . . *apologetic*. A friendly cop with an Irish sur-name and a soft face said, "This kind of thing doesn't usually happen here." But after 9/11 the city shut down Manhattan below 14th Street, causing a diaspora of crazy people, many of whom settled in Central Park. The cop said, "Statistically, the park's safe, one of the safest places in New York. You'd be surprised."

There was none of that from the cops outside Boyle's. On the contrary: This type of thing—a bathroom beatdown—was *precisely* what happened in bars like Boyle's on Saturday nights. Or so Rodney was given to understand.

They drove Longneck and De Niro away in a squad car, a slight disappointment to Rodney, who was hoping for a paddy-wagon, that New York invention whose name ranked first in his affections among enduring cultural stereotypes, above even the Fighting Irish mascot or the Lucky Charms leprechaun.

Boyle's was closed—perhaps forever. Mairead and Rodney were still inside. S.O.B. was cleaning glasses. Vance, the cook, leashed Edith and headed for the door. Thank God—at least

Edith wasn't orphaned. "Not much of a watchdog," Mairead said. "He didn't exactly come to your rescue."

"S.O.B.," Rodney said. "They teach you how to fight at the School of Bartending?"

"No sir," S.O.B. said.

"Well I appreciate you risking all that orthodontia on me," Rodney said. "For future reference, those guys are barred."

Flora came out of the kitchen with a hamburger bun on a plate. She put it on the bar, struck a match, and solemnly planted it in the cake, as if she were planting a flag at Iwo Jima. "I'm told it's your birthday," Flora said. "This is the best we can do on short notice."

It was quiet, just the slosh of the dishwasher and thrum of the Smoke-Eater. Armen always kept the Smoke-Eater running, even after the smoking ban. The Smoke-Eater still ate. Feasted, in fact. But it now subsisted on farts and halitosis and cologne decanted from coin-op machines.

"Is there anything better than this?" Rodney said, and instantly regretted it: They were mourning Armen, after all. The match self-extinguished before Rodney could make a wish.

"Yes," Mairead said. "Almost anything."

But Flora didn't appear to take offense.

"Not the cake," said Rodney. "Not the circumstances. I mean *this*. The quiet after a crowd."

Rodney asked S.O.B. to put on "Hymns to the Silence."

"My brother had no use for the quiet," Flora said. "He loved the crowd. The work. He was a glass-half-full kind of guy."

"Trust me," Rodney said. "He was a your-glass-is-empty-can-I-get-you-another-one kind of guy. An emtpy glass was a joy to him. An excuse to talk to a stranger."

Flora smiled weakly. The truth was Armen wasn't crazy

about strangers, presuming every unfamiliar face to be a health inspector or process server. He'd seen too many patrons served with papers while sedated on their stools. But Rodney admired the human reflex to praise the dead, to endow them with virtues they never possessed in life.

Rodney already missed him, and felt his presence in the bar, the way an amputee feels his phantom leg.

"Well he loved this place," Flora said. "When Dad died, Mom had no interest. And Gary just took it over."

"Will you keep it open?" Rodney said. Mairead kicked him under the bar and Rodney tried not to wince in front of Flora.

"We'll try," she said. "But I don't know. I'm a schoolteacher, not a bartender. I've got an eight-year-old and a six-year-old. And the rent is going through the roof."

Years ago, Rodney was on a flight in turbulence so severe the oxygen masks fell. He remembered thinking he was going to die and was surprised to discover that the prospect wasn't terrifying. That same serenity, strange and unexpected, stole over him now, at the prospect of losing Boyle's.

Flora was cleaning the glass globe of the orange-handled Bunn coffeemaker. "The funeral is Monday morning," she said. "Ten o'clock. If you can make it."

"Of course," Rodney said. He had a sudden desire to give Armen the St. Brigid's prayer card, from off his fridge. He wanted to slip it into Armen's jacket pocket. "Excuse me," Rodney told Mairead. "I'll be right back." The keys were in the door lock. Rodney turned them and let himself out onto the sidewalk, into the hair dryer that passed for a breeze.

"Curt," Rodney said, when Mayhew's voice mail picked up. "Rodney Poole, calling at"—he looked at his watch—"2:13 a.m. I'm glad you're not at your desk. Listen, I can't make our interview on Monday. I'm afraid I have to attend a funeral."

He looked in through Boyle's front windows and saw, in

the golden light of the back bar, a Hopper painting: Flora, S.O.B., and Mairead. Rodney continued: "I'd ask to reschedule. But the truth is, I don't think I'm right for the job. If I'm being completely open-kimono with you."

Standing in a sirocco on Columbus Avenue, Rodney had opened his kimono. And it felt good.

S.O.B. was stacking sodden singles on the back bar when Rodney returned. Tip money. "Reminds me of my days as a Chippendale dancer," Rodney said.

"That's the second time you've used that line," Mairead said. "You might want to start fronting your jokes, the way I front my underwear."

"What was the first time?" Rodney said.

"On our first date. At Rococo. You came out of the men's room and said the attendant had a wicker basket full of singles. And that you put a dollar in it, but he refused to strip for you."

"It must have been memorable."

"It was," Mairead said. "The first time."

"Don't think of it as a repeat," said Rodney. "Think of it as an 'encore presentation.' Like what *Saturday Night Live* calls its reruns."

"That was the night some freak ogled me on the street on my way into the restaurant," Mairead said. "Then I get inside and see it was you. You're blushing."

He was. Rodney had forgotten about that. He didn't know what to say, so he said, "In England, there's an Earl of Ogle."

"You were the Earl of Ogle that night," she said. And then: "Who is this? I like it."

"George Ivan Morrison," Rodney said. "'Hymns to the Silence.'"

The song was nine minutes long. They sat in silence for the final third of it. When "Hymns" faded out and the next track started, Rodney said: "This is what I heard in my head, walking home from our first date."

It was "On Hyndford Street," and as Van Morrison spoke of St. Donard's Church and the cregagh glens and the Castlereagh hills, Mairead said: "Did you walk home through Ireland?"

"Belfast, actually. And yes, I did."

They listened for a moment and Mairead said, "Riding a bus to get ice cream? That's what you thought of walking home from our date?"

"Listen," Rodney said.

And they did. And Van Morrison of 125 Hyndford Street reminisced—about ice cream, and apples on the train tracks, and moths in lamplight, and listening to the radio on summer nights. And the silences that supervene in life.

"I did that," Rodney said. "I'd lay awake at night, listening to faraway baseball games on my clock radio. WLW from Cincinnati, WGN from Chicago, WJR from Detroit. The fifty-thousand-watt flagship stations. Every once in a while, the announcers would stop talking and you'd hear the distant cry of a vendor. And I'd lie in bed and think, *I just heard a guy selling popcorn in Anaheim, California.*"

"I did the same thing," Mairead said. "But I'd listen to music. Try to stay awake to hear my favorite song and imagine what the deejay looked like."

Rodney said, "And the numbers on the clock cast everything around it in a green glow."

"What was around it?"

"A plastic longhorn steer from my uncle in Houston.

An astronaut I got at Cape Canaveral. Two ceramic sailors that were always just there, from before I can remember—these salty sea captains who looked green and seasick in the clock light."

"My numbers were blue," Mairead said. "That's what *I* thought of on our first date, when everything was blue lit at the restaurant."

"Mine were green and glowing," Rodney said. "The same green glow that comes from under the escalator." There was a momentary silence and Rodney said, "I don't see my childhood through rose-colored glasses. I see it through night-vision goggles. Everything is cast in the green light of that radio."

"My parents left the hall light on," Mairead said. "So I could see a beam of light under the bedroom door."

"I'd listen to my parents talking in front of the TV downstairs," Rodney said. "It was better than a nightlight. I couldn't always make out what they were saying. But just the rhythm of it was comforting. And my dad's laugh at Carson's monologue. That was the best sound you could hear from bed. Besides bacon sizzling."

"Me too," Mairead said. "Until my dad died. Then I just heard the TV. *Cheers* reruns after the ten o'clock news. Like you said, it was impossible to make out the voices—they all sounded like Charlie Brown's teacher. But I could hear the laugh track."

She shifted on her stool and said, "That's what we had after my dad died—a laugh track instead of laughter."

Van Morrison sang of "silence at half past eleven on long summer nights," and of listening to Debussy on the radio. Debussy said music is the silence between the notes. It certainly was tonight.

They left the place of communion, passed the Benedictine monk and the Dominican friar, the church pews and the priestly pints. And when they pushed open the punched red nose of the front door, the bells of St. Boyle's tolled.

Just inside the door of 4K, Mairead shed her shoes. Rodney looked at them and said, "I hope you're not expecting, you know . . ."

"I *don't* know," Mairead said, putting her arms around Rodney. "You hope I'm not expecting *what*?"

"Japanese food," Rodney said. "Because I'm all out of shabu-shabu."

Mairead kissed him.

They were ten feet inside the door. Rodney was standing against the back of the couch. Mairead pushed him, and he pulled her, and they both flopped over the back and onto the cushions. Rodney went over backwards, Mairead went over forward, and Rodney briefly thought of them as high jumpers: Rodney doing the Fosberry Flop, Mairead performing the Western Roll.

It was appropriate. He had high-jumped in high school and the names for various techniques—Western Roll, Eastern Cut-Off, Scissors and Straddle—seemed lifted from the Kama Sutra.

Mairead shrieked when they fell. They landed on the cushions. She said, "Is this what they mean by falling head over heels?"

"What *do* they mean by that?" Rodney said. "Your head is always over your heels—except when you fall. Then you're heels-over-head."

She was on top of him, still breathing hard. "Which are you?" she said.

The AeroBed was still set up for Keith. From the couch, Rodney and Mairead rolled onto it, landing like high jumpers.

They kissed. Something was digging into his back. She was beautiful. It was the remote. He shifted his weight. They were still kissing. He shifted again. The TV came on. Mairead withdrew and started giggling.

They had turned on the Weather Channel.

And then—to Rodney's everlasting astonishment—the Weather Channel returned the favor.

A female meteorologist gave the national forecast. And as she did there was convergence and friction layers and rising heat and ball lightning and moisture and dewpoints and rocky elevations, until localized pockets of warmth gave way to growing areas of low pressure and—*yes I said yes I will Yes*—two fronts collided.

Afterward, Mairead walked to the kitchen and Rodney beheld her naked form. Not an hourglass figure, exactly. A pint glass, the kind that was narrow at the base, with that pleasing bulge at the top, called a sleeve. The sleeve prevented the glasses from sticking together when stacked. And it kept the lip from chipping when tipped over. Armen had told him that.

Mairead returned to the AeroBed with a bottle of water. Rodney watched her, gymnophobically secure beneath the blankets. Mairead would definitely not chip if tipped over.

She slipped beneath the blankets and they listened to the rain fall outside.

And on TV, the Doppler radar map shone the iridescent green of Rodney's clock radio.

The AeroBed was set up just under the air conditioner. Rodney couldn't fathom how Keith had done it. "I feel like a hobo," Mairead said, "sleeping in a refrigerated boxcar."

And so she cocooned herself in the blankets, from which

she emerged, two hours later, a butterfly from the bedclothes. Rodney watched her shed the chrysalis of the comforter and wrap herself in a sheet. A corner trailed behind her. He said, "Where are you going?"

"I didn't know you were awake," she whispered. "Do you have a real bed we can sleep in?"

"It doesn't fold out of the wall," Rodney said. "If that's what you mean by real."

Rodney wrapped himself in a blanket, as if he'd just run a marathon.

"You scared me," he said, getting off the AeroBed. "I thought you were a ghost. Or a bride. Or one of those ghost brides who haunt the guys who stood 'em up at the altar."

"You could never stand me up at the altar," Mairead said. Whether this was because Mairead considered marriage to Rodney out of the question or because she knew he was powerless to resist her she didn't say. And Rodney wasn't about to ask.

He followed her into the bedroom. The numbers on the clock radio glowed—4:58. Mairead went back to sleep. Rodney lay awake and thought of his bedroom back home, of childhood and all its facsimiles of life—and all those that followed adolescence: of plastic livestock, of trees that required assembly, of trying to hatch a naked woman. Hearing the *sound* of language but not the language itself. All the writing he'd done for other people—throwing his voice like that.

Rodney considered the difference between today's roommate and yesterday's, the difference between domesticity with Mairead and its karaoke version with Keith. And he realized: He had never been unhappy. But he had never been this happy. Tonight was laughter, not the laugh track. A real woman in an inflatable bed, not the other way around.

Mairead was sleeping next to him, sheet-wrapped like

Lady Justice. Rodney thought back just a few hours earlier, to when they left Boyle's. They walked up Columbus and into the unknown, and the string of traffic lights stretched out before them looked like an endless emerald ellipsis.

On Sunday morning Rodney dreamt of wind chimes and woke to the clinking of silverware, a table being set. Mairead came into the bedroom. "I wanted you to hear bacon sizzling in a pan," she said. "But I couldn't find any. Bacon, I mean. Or pans."

She was wearing last night's shirt, which just covered her fronted underwear. Like Ziggy, Rodney thought: a shirt and no pants.

She pulled on last night's slacks and said, "I'm going to run out for bacon and eggs. I'll pick up a paper, too."

As a kid, Rodney loved Sunday mornings, as much for the Sunday funnies as the bacon. But the *Times* didn't have comics, and Rodney had stopped reading them in New York, one of the few times he'd succeeded in putting away childish things. He didn't know if *Ziggy* still ran, or if its title character ever revealed what happened to his pants. Perhaps he'd surrendered them to Longneck in a lavatorial tug-of-war.

Rodney reached for his laptop, on the floor in front of the nightstand. The tip of the power cord glowed green: His laptop was fully charged, in every sense of the phrase.

He sat up in bed and turned on the computer. It was almost like having breakfast in bed, the warm tray of his Mac-Book—never repossessed by his former employer—radiating on his lap.

The cursor pulsed in counterpoint to his head. Rodney blinked at the cursor. The cursor blinked back. They'd been having these staring contests for years. Rodney always blinked first.

His neck felt sunburned, where Longneck had tried and failed to remove the childproof cap of his head. Rodney thought of what Mairead said last night, in Boyle's, when she saw what Longneck had done: "They left a mark."

His fingers were in ready position, the left-hand ones on ASDF, the right-hand ones on JKL;. He'd taken typing in high school and he sometimes wondered if it was all that remained of his education, the only vestige.

Rodney reached for the dictionary on the nightstand. *Vestige*, from the Latin *vestigium*: "Footprint; a trace of something left behind."

The cursor winked.

He'd change the names later, maybe even change the voice, to first person. But for now he wrote:

To say that Rodney went there religiously was not just
a figure of speech, for Boyle's resembled a church even
at noon, when no one was yet kneeling in the Gents,
asking God for His mercy.

Acknowledgments

Thank you to Bill Thomas, Esther Newberg, and Melissa Danaczko—first for making this a book, then for making it a better one. Bob Roe encouraged me to write fiction, Jill Rushin agreed to read it, and Greg Auman granted me access to his extraordinary brain. I owe a debt of gratitude to Michael Jaffe and a debt of cash to Merrell Noden, who stood countless rounds at the Emerald Inn, the best bar there ever was or will be.

This book owes its existence to the faith and generosity of Rich O'Brien. I owe *my* existence to the authors of the author: Donald Edward Rushin and Jane Claire Rushin (née Boyle).

Meet with Interesting People
Enjoy Stimulating Conversation
Discover Wonderful Books

VINTAGE BOOKS / ANCHOR BOOKS ⊕
Reading Group Center
THE READING GROUP SOURCE FOR BOOK LOVERS

Visit ReadingGroupCenter.com where you'll find great reading choices—award winners, bestsellers, beloved classics, and many more—and extensive resources for reading groups such as:

Author Chats

Exciting contests offer reading groups the chance to win one-on-one phone conversations with Vintage and Anchor Books authors.

Extensive Discussion Guides

Guides for over 450 titles as well as non–title specific discussion questions by category for fiction, nonfiction, memoir, poetry, and mystery.

Personal Advice and Ideas

Reading groups nationwide share ideas, suggestions, helpful tips, and anecdotal information. Participate in the discussion and share your group's experiences.

Behind the Book Features

Specially designed pages which can include photographs, videos, original essays, notes from the author and editor, and book-related information.

Reading Planner

Plan ahead by browsing upcoming titles, finding author event schedules, and more.

Special for Spanish-language reading groups

www.grupodelectura.com

A dedicated Spanish-language content area complete with recommended titles from Vintage Español.

A selection of some favorite reading group titles from our list

Atonement by Ian McEwan
Balzac and the Little Chinese Seamstress by Dai Sijie
The Blind Assassin by Margaret Atwood
The Devil in the White City by Erik Larson
Empire Falls by Richard Russo
The English Patient by Michael Ondaatje
A Heartbreaking Work of Staggering Genius by Dave Eggers
The House of Sand and Fog by Andre Dubus III
A Lesson Before Dying by Ernest J. Gaines

Lolita by Vladimir Nabokov
Memoirs of a Geisha by Arthur Golden
Midnight in the Garden of Good and Evil by John Berendt
Midwives by Chris Bohjalian
Push by Sapphire
The Reader by Bernhard Schlink
Snow by Orhan Pamuk
An Unquiet Mind by Kay Redfield Jamison
Waiting by Ha Jin
A Year in Provence by Peter Mayle